T0364365

*Karimayi*

THE INDIA LIST

# *Karimayi*

CHANDRASHEKHAR KAMBAR

Translated by Krishna Manavalli

LONDON NEW YORK CALCUTTA

SERIES EDITOR

Arunava Sinha

*For my Guru, Pt Rajeev Taranathji*

Krishna Manavalli

**Seagull Books, 2017**



First published in English translation by Seagull Books, 2017



ISBN 978 0 85742 390 0

**British Library Cataloguing-in-Publication Data**
A catalogue record for this book is available from the British Library.

Typeset by Seagull Books, Calcutta, India
Printed and bound by Maple Press, York, Pennsylvania, USA

CONTENTS

# *Preface*

When I look at my writing through all these years, I realize how much my 'place' has meant to me. As a writer who has embraced the folk mode of writing, I find that this place is at the creative centre of my being. In essence, my writing is linked to the markedly spatial paradigm of myth-making. I identify strongly with my little village in Southern India. This folk community, its stories, people and the structures of life lived in this little region—these are what gave me a nearness to my land. I made a conscious choice of telling the story of my place and its people in my writings. My friend and critic Rajeev Taranath makes a fine case for my way of writing when he says, in his introduction to my play *Jokumaraswami* (1972): 'In this country, with its variety of social and intellectual structures, ranging from the heavily abstracting Sanatana to the non-reducing sensibility of [the indigenous and] the oppressed, it is possible to relate to one's environment with a power and variety that is unthinkable . . . elsewhere,' and therefore, 'a mythical episteme is still valid, natural and real here.' It is this mythical episteme that keeps me connected to my region and language. It gives me my sense of belonging. I see the whole world mirrored in my Shivapura. This is not to say that the microcosmic 'Shivapura' that I create in my writings is cut off from all the changes happening in the world around it. This Shivapura too is aware of, and is affected by, such national and global changes.

So if you ask me how my work is contemporary or relevant in the contexts of an increasingly hybrid, diasporic and globalized world of today, I will say this: yes, writings from countries like ours have often been made to fit into Eurocentric generic models which fail to express our different cultural experiences. No doubt, our colonial past and access to English education and literature during the twentieth century led to new trends in Indian writing. New genres such as the novel and autobiography surfaced at this time. First, Indian literatures from different regions felt the impact of the nineteenth-century Western models of writing. Then there was the powerful influence of the European modernist movement on both Indian writing in English and writings in the regional languages. No doubt, we adapted the 'navya' into our own contexts in very creative ways. But the native traditions did not die out completely. Besides, popular culture nourished these local traditions and literary conventions in a crucial way. For instance, in Southern India, whether they were forms like Yakshagana or Harikatha, or even our cinema, they all remained connected with the earlier modes of orality and myth.

How are we really different from our European and Western counterparts? My answer is: Because we are predominantly storytellers.

Whether it is the epic, or the folklore, we have always had a strong tradition of storytelling, of a literature that addressed, and emerged out of, a 'community' culture. And despite the distinct influence and stamp of Western modernism on both English and regional literatures in India, many writers have continued to link themselves to the older native traditions. Think of a range of literary traditions in Karnataka through the centuries, both written and oral—whether the *vachanas* of the twelfth century, or the later *Dasarapadas*—they all either address God directly, or speak to a shared devotional community. The writers of these songs do not address an 'individual' in the high modernist style of twentieth-century writings that emerged later in Indian languages.

My writing connects strongly with such older folk traditions of Karnataka. Beginning with *Karimayi*, which I wrote in the 1970s, to my recent novel *Shivana Dangura*, the same 'Shivapura' surfaces repeatedly, and in many forms. Not only the material of my novels but also the response, variety and breadth, and the very breath of my imagination, are drawn from it. In *Karimayi*, the tragedy of Shivapura is figured in the loss of the goddess' golden idol. This is not just material loss—it is also the loss of the myth of an entire community, of all beauty and meaning that this myth gave to the lives of those people. In today's corporate and global world, is it possible to build back this Shivapura of my imagination? Or to at least recover the communal and human bonds it fostered?

I have searched for an answer to this question. I am searching for it even now.

I tried to create this fullness and plenitude of Shivapura in the novel *Shikharasoorya* which I wrote a few years ago. At its end, the Shivapura on the Hill of the Mother challenges, and finally triumphs over, the linear, historical, competitive and rapacious modern world which destroys everything, including itself.

This Shivapura will always be at the core of my writing.

## *Introduction*

RAJEEV TARANATH

Many years ago, I tried my hand at translation with Kambar's play *Jokumaraswami*. And the quiddity of that experience is what I am trying to reach back to, and connect with, in Krishna's translation of *Karimayi*. I record now, somewhat haphazardly, bits of that experience, the satisfactions I received, the problems I needed to deal with, and the questions I raised as a close reader of the Kannada matter in front of me. Let me begin with a persistent wish of mine—whenever I look at a translation, I desire a seamless read. That being the given, I begin to perceive the seams, so to say, especially with Kambar's kind of writing. What can I say about Kambar? In my reading of literature, Kambar is a massive presence. Kambar, as I have said elsewhere, is a master at handling the South Indian non-brahmin myth. The myth is the only lens he uses to look at life and arrange his perceptions. In work after work, he projects, extends and polishes his own understanding of the myth. A translator dealing with Kambar's creativity must necessarily deal with the heavily figurated kind of language/perception that is Kambar's main mode.

Next, *Karimayi* is hardly a novel—it is history. And history need not be true. Rather, its truth must be felt by those whose history it is. It is at once a story, a narrative, scattered pieces of experience strung together, an external myth but also an intimate truth to everyone born and living in that experience. So this *Karimayi* is very far from what we have learnt to identify as a novel—it's a piece of North Karnataka village/life/values alongside things such as town/modern/corruption and so on, terms and meanings with which we readers are more familiar. Abstracting a little, you can perceive from a distance the clash of powerful values at, shall we say, a moral level? It would be futile to think of heroes and heroines and the evolution of characters, lessons you learnt once upon a time in literature classes, when you want to steep yourself in the experience of *Karimayi*.

*Karimayi* projects as nothing else can do Kambar's familiarity with a region where myth and reality are indeed one. Or where perhaps time does not exist. The experience itself is so massive that minor human efforts to move time forward are seen to be no more than than the little businesses of little men. Note, for instance, the busy numerousness of characters in *Karimayi*, fulfilling every symptom of little-ness under the unseen, unwavering presence of Karimayi. Every human effort at doing good or evil, clumsy at best, and always little, reveal the pathetic nature of a human endeavour trapped in mighty cosmic mythical forces. The seriousness with which this experience occurs in Kannada, in rural Bijapur Kannada, is not of course easy meat for the translator. The essential problem is that of preserving the balance between the native seriousness in Kannada and its possible dilution when one seeks to transfer it into an alien medium like English without the all-too-familiar linguistic tricks of exoticism and the like. Besides, the rhythms of Kannada are everywhere in Kambar's work (this is not at all surprising, given his mastery of the sounds and the movements of the language). Added to this is the stuff with which he deals. I am tempted to grab at the term 'folksy', but its use in Indian writing in English pushes it towards easy exoticism. So the translator has to fill herself with the rhythms of the folk Kannada of North Karnataka and then try and preserve that rich experience while shutting out glib exoticism.

Language-to-language transfer is the most difficult part of a Kambar translation. The experience is dense and doesn't 'give' easily. Place the task of translating Kambar in the context of Indian writing in English—a Kambar in translation has to sit necessarily among people like Raja Rao, Aurobindo and Narayan and what have you. Now the problem of the translator is not so much the Kambar 'matter'. I have noticed with pardonable subjectiveness, a certain archness among some translations of Kannada works into English. Just the other day, I came across a compound neologism such as 'house-lamp spirit'.

A translation which possibly took off on the Kannada term *jothamma* or some such familiar coinage. Such terms sprinkled here and there in our translations suck out the *wasein* of language in a particular word of a particular author. The power and density evaporate, and what remain are the arch and the exotic.

The main problem and task for the translator shapes itself thus—here is a 'source' language in all its pristine 'paganness', building a world in which myth and actuality are fused together so finely that everything achieves equal vividness and clarity. Gods and men co-exist. Over time, the world of literature narrowed itself and reduced its field of vision towards things such as focus and highlight. But in Kambar's writing, we see a vividness, with its large spread, similar to that in our epics.

At the other end is the target language in which the sense of myth is no more actual or lived—it is only an item of knowledge and information at best. In other words, the translator has to cast herself into two separate modes of being in order to sense and preserve the legitimacy of both these worlds—Kambar's Kannada world, as well as the world of modern English language into which she seeks to draw and re-create that experience. All along, there are constant risks of unmeant linguistic exoticism, or the simplification of the experience of the Kannada work.

I should think the difficulties of a translator choosing a novel like *Karimayi* are self-evident by now. Krishna's achievement in this quite formidable task is one of testing restraint, finding modes of consistency in the midst of almost unmanageable numerousness, and a deep determination to keep her use of English in this context importantly neutral, perhaps with a touch or two of the native Kannada idioms. Krishna has achieved her biggest success, as I perceive it, in preventing her translation from reading like a translation. She is attempting to be contemporary in her choice of language—syntax, vocabulary, movement, intonation—while preserving an essential distance from such contemporaneity of choice and use of language which can push the experience into pointless anonymity.

*Karimayi* is a rich and necessary experience which has to be preserved. Has Krishna succeeded in preserving this experience of *Karimayi*? I believe so. Krishna's whole effort has come together beautifully and made this translation perhaps an important addition to creative writing in India.

*Karimayi*

# A THOUSAND SALUTATIONS TO YOU, MOTHER KARIMAYI!

Shivapura is not a big village. You can't find it on the map of Belagavi District. Only in an old atlas at the elementary school, to the north of Belagavi, about three inches above it, can you spot a village by this name. Once, Gudsikara showed it to the farmers and they felt so proud.

The one who grasped the art of instantly recognizing it on the map was Gudsikara's disciple, Thief Sidrama.

This was indeed an easy art for Sidrama. Since Belagavi is a big city, it is bound to be on every map. And he could recognize the letter B of the English alphabet. What begins with the letter B must be Belagavi. His logical argument was: if you move about three inches north of Belagavi, you must land in Shivapura. As a result, the Shivapura he showed was sometimes Delhi, sometimes a village near Calcutta, sometimes simply any other village in Hindustan. He was so adept at this art that he could identify Shivapura even on the world map. After all, what do we do? This is the story of all villages which must be identified only in relation to the big cities.

The villagers didn't believe Thief Sidrama's talk in the beginning. They too know which villages are in their neighbourhood, and how exactly their village is positioned in the middle of these others. After all, what the Helava mendicants say about the plains on Sri Ramakshetra of the Jambu Island do not really appear on these new maps, do they? Shivapura also surfaces in the songs of Lagumavva. She sings of the world from the very beginning, from its embryonic stages, and Jambu Island figures in these songs too. How can such origins and such signs be false?—they argue. But Thief Sidrama's specialty lies here—he can fuse all these details together and point to Shivapura on the map. So even people who were sceptical at first slowly started believing in his words.

When you see the village from a distance, it is a speck in the middle of an intensely coloured expanse of lake and jungle. At night, it is like a lone flaming torch, and in the day, a dark spot. Because of the highland with its thick forests in the west, the sun sets here before it does in the other villages. And the darkness, when it falls, is more dense. It is always better to reach the village when there is still some light, although it isn't as if you can see it only during the day, or that it goes to sleep the moment it's dark. There are fields and knolls in the east and south. There is a lake in the north. There are hundreds of byways to reach the village, but the main road is to the east. It's just a bullock-cart road. If you have to come and go anywhere at all—even to Belagavi—you must take this road. At the end of it is Karimayi's temple. We begin our description of the village here because those who are leaving, or those who are entering, will always prostrate and salute the goddess before they proceed further.

There are two stone pillars to the left of this road. This is the village entrance:

They brought the stone from Madras
And built the village entrance

Such is the description in Lagumavva's song. From there, straight ahead, you see the temple of Dark Mother Karimayi. Not big, not even beautiful. In the front, there is a stone slab on which the lamp post stands. There is a wall all round. Then the temple at the center. What is special about this temple is the three huge beehives inside. And there is the inner sanctum. The temple has a small door. You must bend to enter.

When you enter, your eyes confront utter darkness and your body feels the cold inside. And suddenly, for a few seconds, you feel like the temple is screeching. This is because of the bats. People who enter for the first time might run for their lives. Or start screeching themselves. But if they are brave enough to stay for a bit, slowly, like a bud blossoming into a flower, the details begin to unfold.

The buffalo lying with its dead eyes and slit tongue, the dagger stuck in its neck, the foot half-visible from behind the folds of the saree, the cascading pleats of that gold-bordered saree, the right and left hands, one holding a sword and the other blessing the world. Another hand clutching a demon's head. Yet another in a dance posture. Sometimes this can be frightening because the hands seem almost human. Then you look up, and you see two large eyes made of silver. Stretching across the face, from ear to ear. A befittingly slender nose. Lips parted to smile perhaps? Forehead, chin and crown—everything, everything fills your eyes about this Mother who gave birth to us, Mother of the Earth, Mother of All Three Worlds, Karimayi Karevva—she looks like she might come alive any moment.

In this village, Karimayi's influence is endless. After all, it isn't as if these people have hundreds of gods, poor folk! The few minor deities there are have to survive by claiming some sort of kinship with her. People here wake up uttering the Mother's name. They fall asleep uttering her name again. It's always 'Mother'—whether they wake or sleep, sit or stand, when they start work and when they rest, when they eat, meet, for all the good and bad that happens here—even the whoring or the thieving—people invoke the Mother for every beginning and every end.

## KARIMAYI'S STORY

Like the village's tory, Karimayi's story is a little unclear. We can deduce the following through available sources such as Lagumavva's songs, Dattappa's *Chintamani* and the prevalent customs and forms of worship.

Once upon a time, sin prevailed on Earth because of the war between the gods and the demons. There was no rain. The crops failed. People suffered, and good sages like Jademuni had to face many hindrances to their penance. Then Mother Earth went to Lord Shiva and Parvati. She begged for alms, she begged to be saved. Shiva wiped the sweat off his brow and threw it on the ground. In a moment, it turned into a marvellous female form. That was Mother Karevva.

It was a scorching summer. Unable to stand the sun, Karevva grew thirsty. As she was searching for water, she heard a voice screaming: 'Ayyo, save me! If you are a man I'll call you Shiva, and if you are a woman I'll call you Parvati! Save me please!' When Karevva went to find out who was calling for help, she found a sage who had fallen into a well. The sage had stumbled on a stone while running away from the demons. How could she save him? Since there was nobody around, she took off her saree and threw it down the well. 'Close your eyes and hold on to the cloth,' she told the sage, 'Don't open your eyes until I tell you. Or I'll kill you.' He held one end of the cloth. She held the other end and pulled.

Once the sage came up . . . what can we say about the distracted mind of this man? He opened his eyes. There in front of him was this nude vision! His mind became distorted with lust. Immediately, Karevva drew seven lines on the ground with her dagger and said, 'If you cross this, you're finished.' Jademuni must have got scared. He stood still for a while. After Karevva put on her saree again, he filled the seven furrows she had drawn with his blood. It is said that they turned into seven rivers. He crossed them all and came to woo Karevva. He named her Karimayi and married her. They spent their life together in the forest near Shivapura, in the Sri Ramakshetra of Jambu Island.

Now their enemies were of two kinds: the demons, who maintained that it was wrong of Karevva from the demon clan to have married Jademuni from the world of gods. The gods on the other hand believed that Jademuni had defiled their caste by marrying a low-caste woman. 'We will kill them both,' they swore.

By then Karimayi was heavily pregnant.

One day, when Jademuni was performing his penance and Karimayi was fetching water from the river, the gods descended and killed Jademuni. It was a full-moon day. Since Karimayi became a widow that day, it came to be known as Randi's Full Moon, or Widow's Full Moon. But the gods were still not satisfied—they wanted to destroy Jademuni's child. So they aimed at Karimayi's womb next. Karimayi, who couldn't fight the gods, bore her womb to the forest. But the clairvoyant gods did not take long to find out where she was. They made it impossible for her to get food and water. So Mother cooked stones and ate them. She boiled thorns and ate them.

Running from the gods, she came into a mango grove and hid there. Her mouth began to water at the sight of a bunch of unripe mangoes hanging from a branch. She began to crave them. But they were not within reach. She struggled to pile stone upon stone, then climbed onto them and was about to reach for the fruit when she heard voices: 'Don't pluck the unripe fruit, you whore.' When she looked around, she saw on one side the gods aiming arrows at her womb. On the other, the seven-headed and many-armed demons with their maces. Before she could exclaim, a thousand and one arrows and a thousand and one maces hit her womb.

Karimayi screamed.

Then she folded the torn womb in her saree and secured it at her waist. Hearing her screams, Shiva shuddered in Kailasa and sent his bull, Nandi. Parvati sent her tiger. Karimayi sat on the tiger and chased the gods and the demons, hunting them down wherever they scattered. She crossed yards and yards of land to fight the villains. Oblivious of dark nights and pouring rain, she chased them, killed them, screaming 'Get those thieves and bastards.'

The gods were frightened. They ran away to heaven. The demons, on the other hand, are sorcerers. If one drop of their blood falls to the ground, a thousand demons rise. Karimayi didn't know what to do. In the end, she stretched her tongue on the ground. Before drops of their blood could fall to the ground, she licked them up. By the Mother's grace, the blood turned into honey!

Finally, she beheaded all the demons and then went to Shiva. 'Will you give back the lives of my husband and children, or shall I devour you too?' she asked. Shiva got scared. He put life back into the twenty-one embryos. They became twenty-one children. Jademuni also got his life back. That day, Karimayi became a wife again and put vermilion on her forehead. So it is called Muttaide or Wife's Full Moon.

Karimayi, her husband and children all came back to Earth. But she remained afraid of the gods. So she would let her children play until sunset and then turn them into cowrie shells. Then string the shells into a chain and wear it round her neck. Which is why, even today, there's a string of shells around the neck of the Karimayi idol.

Later, there is a story about how she threw up the demons she had gobbled. They became bees, and her minions. Which is why, even today, there are three beehives in her temple.

Here, Hara Hara, here Shiva Shiva
Here ends our story.

So ends Lagumavva's song. The rest of the story can be found in the story of the Gowda's genealogy which the Helava narrates.

Here, in Shivapura, which is in Sri Ramakshetra, Adigowda ruled the land from his fort, with his ministers and generals. He had a thousand and one milch cows. The safe was full. The treasury overflowed with riches. Yes-man for a minister and submissive subjects. What's the use though? He was not blessed with children. The king and queen sorrowed over this fate.

Meanwhile, the thousand and one cows always gave a hundred and one cans of milk. One day, they gave only a hundred. People asked why this was so, and discovered that one of the cows hadn't given any milk that day. The king, who had been observing the cow, followed her into the forest and saw her shedding her milk over an anthill. He ordered the anthill to be dug up. And there lay the wooden idols of Karimayi and Jademuni!

That same night, Karimayi appeared in the king's dream and said, 'Give me a place to live, and I will turn everything you touch into gold.' That's when this temple was built. After he built the temple, everything the king touched turned to gold and rubies. The crops prospered. Within a year, the queen gave birth to a male child. It was then that the king had a golden face made for Mother's idol. It's still there. On Shige Full Moon, the idol wears the golden face and the villagers have a feast.[1]

There have been a hundred Gowdas in their line. Although you see only a few names in the songs of Helavas. The last one is Paragowda. The hundred and first.

Karimayi was called the Golden-Faced One only because Adigowda had the face made for her. We don't know the name or place of the man who made it. There are no records, no documents. After they distilled a hundred barrels of waste and gold dust, they were left with a barrel of sterling gold. The face was made out of that. According to some, it was not made—it manifested itself. People adore it. The golden face is indeed very beautiful.

# THE GOLDEN-FACED ONE

Beautiful-Bodied One, Golden-Faced One
Vowing with the right hand and keeping faith
with the left
Mother, you protect us always

With these words, saluting Karimayi a thousand and one times, let us say:

Beyond the three worlds
Is Karimayi's mystery.
How can we divine it? Never forget this fact.

When we look at the golden face, we can well believe what Lagumavva says in her song. Whether in fear or in anger, the open eyes stretch from ear to ear, the slender nose looks like it's breathing and the lips like they have stopped laughing to their heart's content only a moment ago. Or they look as though they are about to curve into a smile now. Angular chin, curls stuck to the brow with drops of perspiration. Above, the crown studded with eighteen gems—one look at it, and it fills your eyes. Fills your heart! The villagers are so in awe of it that they are afraid to stare—as though their gaze will break the idol. Therefore, except during Shige Full Moon, Widow's

Full Moon and Wife's Full Moon, they always keep the golden face in the Gowda's house.

If Mother's golden face appears in the dreams of pregnant women, they are sure to give birth to male children. In some cases, her golden face has spoken to them in their dreams. Mother is a symbol of luck for all those who bow before her, she gives them whatever they ask for. She has given everything to this village—pride, learning, intellect, respect and devotion. Mother is not a mean goddess.

She has made the other goddesses of her class like Chanchali Mayavva upset. Dyamavva of Lokapura and Savadatti Ellavva are rather envious of her. To her obedient flock, she has given the boon of children in rocking cradles, children who drink from silver cups. She gave a large stomach to all eighty-four species of life, from the ants to the elephants. She gave them hunger too. She also gave them life enough to satisfy their hunger. She has made the fence green, given water to sand, made the sun hot and given the moon its light.

She has turned blind those who stared at her audaciously. She has made barren land fertile and given children to barren wombs. She gave these children a will and a purpose to their will. Then she multiplied the possibilities of their purpose. She gave a trim waist to the young. Then filled their firm waists with youth. She gave their youthfulness a swagger. To this swagger she added unbridled desire. She has given wisdom to the aged. She has made the wise content. And she has crowned that contentment with death.

And in her zeal to give, not caring what she gives and to whom, this mother who gave us all prosperity has also given to some a thieving mind!

This Golden One is the mother of all beginnings, the one whose end none knows, the Idimayi. It is she who gave Chandrashekhara the wits to write—Chandrashekhara, the son of Kambara Basappa, disciple of Sangayya of Bhoosunoorumatha and devotee of Savalagi Siddhalingeswara Swami.

May she grant the boon of children, with rocking cradles and silver cups, to our readers too.

# DESCRIPTION OF THE VILLAGE

There is probably a lot of exaggeration in the ancient descriptions of Shivapura. In those songs:

Breadth of six leagues
Length of seven leagues
If you go around
It's twelve leagues

Such is its description. Not only this, but also:

Fort of engraved stone, on its door
a festoon of pearls.
And how shall I describe the vastness
of those battlements?

There is this description of the fort and battlements of Adigowda. In addition, they say that there were banana plants in the middle of the village and flower gardens with a hundred beautiful rows of *rasabale* banana! If we look at the current state and breadth of the village, this description might seem exaggerated. Those forts and battlements are nowhere to be found now. There is no trace of any of these things.

As it stands now, the village is small. It's only two years since the village panchayat came up here.[2] In the village songs, there is the following description of Karimayi: 'In the village of three houses, you became a goddess and made this place be strewn with the remains of sacrificed bulls and sheep.' So we can conclude that this village, which once had only three houses, has now grown, and in the hands of Paragowda has grown big enough to have a panchayat of its own.

The temple faces east, and the village has grown along Karimayi's back. It looks like the village is sheltered by Karimayi's back. At the back of the temple, there runs the only main street of the village. It ends in the village square. There are a few narrow streets winding in and out of this main street.

The high-caste street,
The Lingavanta's[3] street
And a hundred streets of the
wandering jangamas[4]

True, there is this description of the village in the annals. But with the exception of the outcaste neighbourhood, people of all castes have built their houses wherever they want. On the narrow street, which runs left of the village square, is the Gowda's house. A big house, old of course. Needless to say, there is also an attic. On the street that runs right of the square is the house of Dattappa. This house is exclusive. The only brahmin house in the village. If you walk about twenty steps, you will see the house of Gudsikara (our protagonist!). This is the only house which is somewhat modern and wealthy-looking—obviously, a house built by someone prosperous.

Let's stop describing the village for now, and start our story with Lagumavva's verse:

Until this time, the tale had the fragrance of jasmine
Sweet to those who know
I'll tell the rest of the story, and of all its beauty
Bless us with your boons, Mother Karimayi!

# MEMORIES

Shivapura's Paragowda is now sixty or sixty-five. Not much really. If you look at him, this is what you see—his eyes are red as if he is intoxicated, but they're always laughing, the straight line of his sharp nose, the etched lips that end in deep dimples, the bushy moustache, the face with full and rounded cheeks. He hardly shaves his beard. Sometimes he wears a turban, at other times it just sits next to him. Gold earrings. On the right hand, four rings on four fingers. A perfect-bodied, six-foot man. It's impossible to forget him, or his name, if you have but seen him once. Despite his age, there is not a single wrinkle on his face, not an inch of sagging skin.

It's a real pleasure to see him laugh. In that fair face, his teeth look like a row of pomegranate seeds. So lovely. If spades and axes are other people's weapons, Gowda just uses his charming smile. With this smile, he has tamed his fiercest enemies. Kolavi Mudukappa came to fight with him, but was so charmed by this smile that he listened to the Gowda and simply went back. When the villagers asked him why he came away without fighting, he said 'What could I do? He smiled.'

Women can't help stealing glances at him. One night it seems Basetti's wife was talking in her sleep. Basetti was awake. He sat up, and listened to what she was mumbling. Then he told himself, 'Even we men feel a bit disturbed when we see that Gowda. So what can we say about these women?' And just went back to sleep.

In keeping with his looks, Gowda was also a man with a glad eye. But he never crossed the limits in anything, except perhaps drinking Not once, not twice—he was married four times. The first three died during childbirth. Their names slip through the memory of the villagers, and our story. The fourth was Nijagunavva, Kolavi Mudukappa Gowda's sister. She too died in the following manner. True, she gave birth to a male child after a few years of marriage, but the child died and the mother survived. Gowda suddenly realized that you should enjoy life to the hilt before you die. So he started living according to this philosophy. There are about a hundred stories of his escapades from that time. Lagumavva herself has sung about a couple of these adventures. After all, Gowda is a man. He can live like an unbridled horse. But Nijagunavva? She thought she had brought darkness into the house. She withered away feeling the lack of children. What if they couldn't find a solution to the problem? Will accountant Dattappa's *Chintamani* remain mute on this matter?

Dattappa came to Nijagunavva. Called her 'Mother!' Made some small talk. Gave examples and cited epics. Then, slowly, he brought up the issue of adoption. Even went on to daringly suggest that 'There is Gowda's son born to the hunter-caste Shivi—why not adopt him?'

It was no secret that Shivi's son Shivaninga was born to the Gowda. Shivi had chosen to remain at her maternal home even after her marriage only because of the Gowda. It was Nijagunnavva who had thrown tantrums and barricaded Shivi from going into Gowda's fields. Nijagunnavva didn't agree to Dattappa's words at first. But Dattappa wouldn't let go either. After a day or two, he even made the priest say the same thing to her. (It's difficult to say when the Goddess possesses this priest. He is unaware of what he says when he is possessed, for it is the Goddess who speaks through him.) 'Fine, such is Karimayi's will,' thought Gowda's wife. The adoption took place.

Shivaninga was a fit son for the Gowda. He never behaved in a manner that diminished the honour of the Gowda's house. He took care of the Gowda's wife as if she were more than his mother. They made arrangements for Shivi to live in the hut in the Gowda's fields. The Gowda's wife put her head on Shivaninga's lap and died, saying, 'Take care of the Gowda, son!' People appreciated this.

The Gowda had done the right thing. He set the misadventures of his youth right with this act by accepting Shivaninga as his son. Shivaninga was lower in caste than the Gowda's family on his maternal side.

So? He was the Gowda's son, after all! It was a great act even on the part of the Gowda's wife. She had a long line of relations. She could have adopted anyone from among them if she had wanted. Brother's son, uncle's sons, sister's son—despite this long line of people in her family, she chose to adopt Shivaninga, right? People admired her for it.

After Nijagunavva's death, Gowda began to be scared of his memories. He stopped sleeping in the house in the village. He started living in the hut in the fields with Shivi, now called Shivasani. Shivaninga lived in the house in the village. Nijagunavva's mother lived there too.

## *DATTATREYANAMA*,
## OR THE SAGA OF DATTATREYA

The Gowda's history would be incomplete without mention of Dattappa. Not because they were boss and accountant. Their relationship was deeper than that of brothers. Like the 'king's son and minister's son' of Lagumavva's stories, they did everything together—learnt to write, played, grew up and enjoyed the adventures of youth. Then, later in life, took responsibility for governing the village.

There are many stories about Dattappa's ancestors. One of them says that his forefathers came here to become the priests at Karimayi's temple. Another says—it's a song in fact—that unable to cope with the strict rules of Dattappa's grandfather, Karimayi gave the priesthood of her temple back to the lower-caste shudras: 'Mother, deciding that brahmin worship doesn't suit you, you gave the priesthood back to the shudras.' But Dattappa doesn't agree with this version. Even shudra gods want brahmin priests—how can Karimayi ask for shudra priests?

'No, it is not so. My ancestors came here to be accountants. That is what the *Chintamani* says,' maintains Dattappa. Apart from accountancy, over the generations his family has also engaged in astrology and medicine.

The only book that is a repository of all this family knowledge, its learning, intellect and medical excellence is still in that house. This is the '. . . *Chintamani*'. Even Dattappa doesn't know what kind of a treatise it is. Because the word before *Chintamani* was torn off. Therefore, and thereafter, the village came to know it as *Chintamani*.

Sometimes, faced with a problem, the Gowda would ask Dattappa, 'So what does your *Chintamani* say about this?' Dattappa would go back and read it closely. Dattappa has a unique reading style—as unique as the *Chintamani*. He places the spectacles on the tip of his nose, settles respectfully into the lotus position, salutes the book and then opens it to read a line. At the end of each line, whether or not there is punctuation, or even if the word runs on to the next line, he stops reading, shuts his eyes and ponders on the meaning of the line he has just read. And only then does he move on to the next.

It was a strange book, indeed. No matter what the question, it always had an answer. Dattappa could tease out a meaning right for every occasion. When he held the book, his hands shook. It looked as if the book itself was shaking.

That he wore glasses to read the book didn't mean he had bad eyesight. His father read the book with his glasses on. So Dattappa did the same. The glasses seemed like some magical medium to

Dattappa. Because only when he wore those glasses could he read meanings that were not even present in that book.

This doesn't mean that Dattappa's learning was inferior. In the throes of self-affirmation, he had even tried writing poetry. He had read in his Class Four book that Babar, a king who ruled Delhi once, wrote his autobiography and called it *Babarnama*, or the Saga of Babar. He thought, Why shouldn't I write my autobiography too? Poor man, he sat up days and nights for three whole months and finished writing the *Dattatreyanama* in the complex Sanskrit metre of *bhaminishatpadi*! Then he realized that he had to read it to someone. So he took it to the Gowda's court. The court poet Lagumavva and the Question & Answer Master were already seated there.

Thus begins the story of *Dattatreyanama*:

'The wicked Age of Kali came to Shivapura—people lost their faith and sin prevailed on Earth. Karimayi ran to Lord Shiva and begged, "Please, take a new avatar and save my village from sin." Immediately, Shiva called one of his minions. "Go," he commanded, "and be born in Shivapura. Bring back faith among its people." Such was the origin of Dattappa!'

The Gowda burst into laughter. Lagumavva too was convulsed with laughter. Dattappa felt very insulted. 'Yeh Gowda,' he sneered, 'how can a dumb-head like you understand this kind of poetry?' Then he turned to Lagumavva. 'Just look at how she laughs! Hey, crazy bitch, write at least one *bhaminishatpadi*—

then we'll see! Show me another man in this universe who's written 2,000 *shatpadi*s!'

'And you,' he said, turning back to the Gowda, 'you think that my *Dattatreyanama* is inferior to this crazy bitch's songs?' He took his book and left in a huff.

The Q&A Master had in fact liked the poem. He knew how difficult it was to compose even one cycle of the *bhaminishtapadi*. Just think—Dattappa had composed 2,000 *shatpadis*! But before he could venture an opinion on the matter, Dattappa had stormed off.

For the next eight days, Dattappa didn't see the Gowda's face. Everybody forgot about the *Dattatreyanama*. Later, when Lagumavva asked him about it, he said it was lost. Lagumavva has this story about how it got lost:

Even the day after the recitation, it seems, Dattappa kept after the Gowda about his book. 'Show me a flaw in it,' he insisted. 'Dattu,' Gowda said, 'stop being childish now.' But Dattappa persisted, 'You're not the one to appreciate my poem, it's Karimayi, Karimayi herself. Come, I'll show you something.' And he dragged the Gowda to the lake. Like a man possessed, he held the book above his head and proclaimed, 'Karimayi, if there's any worth in this book, make it float. If not, let it sink,' and he flung it into the water. Ah, isn't this the power of Karimayi now? The book promptly sank!

Well, this is what Lagumavva says. Who knows how much of this is true and how much false! From this day on, whenever Lagumavva's song affirms something, the *Chintamani* is sure to negate it. This doesn't mean there's any enmity between Lagumavva and Dattappa. In truth, the two share a subtle bond. If they make a new kind of pickle in Dattappa's house, he'll call the crazy bitch and give her a jarful. If there's good food being cooked for a feast, the crazy bitch is sure to be invited. Lagumavva is the same. On the day of Holi, she chases him around and throws colour on him. Tries to dispel the evil eye by touching the brahmin tuft of hair on his head. Who doesn't know all this? Be that as it may, do we really need to teach people how to understand the intricacies of the situation when she starts calling him 'my brahmin!'

These are the village elders. Gowda, Dattappa, Lagumavva, the priest Basetti and Balu. Gowda and Dattappa are the two most prominent ones. Because of their affection for the Gowda and Dattappa, the others, notwithstanding their claim to eldership, always assent to the words of these two. Gowda knew his business. He knew how to interact with people. He was also a trusting sort of man. Dattappa, on the other hand, was a little short-tempered. And a talker. A poet, he also knew how to be sarcastic. A smart fellow with a sense of humour . . . when he couldn't laugh aloud, he would laugh inwardly.

The people were not all young, nor were they old and bent. Firm-waisted men with gleaming dark skin.

Their eyes, alert yet trusting. Under Gowda's and Dattappa's rule, none complained of injustice. They never said, 'Times have changed. The Evil Age of Kali has begun.' That's how they were. One measure of prosperity lead to many more measures of it. Where there was one thing in the beginning, it multiplied hundredfold. Thousandfold.

The village prospered so much, one day they got a letter from the government. 'The population has increased here,' it said, 'your village needs a panchayat.'

# THE AGE OF KALI BEGINS

The government letter arrived, right? Gudsikara had finished his LLB in Belagavi just then and returned to the village. How does a lawyer begin in a place like Shivapura? He should have gone to Belagavi. But those were the times of the freedom struggle. At a time when government offices and courts are being burnt, who cares about this lawyer? Since Gudsikara's father had died that very year, he had to come back to his village to take care of the house and lands. Which he did.

That Gudsikara stayed back in the village seemed like a good thing to the Gowda. 'Your village needs a panchayat,' the letter said. It would be good to have an Ingreji-educated man to take care of such things. 'After all, what can people like me do,' thought Gowda. Gudsikara was the right man for this job, and he said so to the Elders, the Panchas. 'What's this you're saying, Gowda? He's just a baby out of his mother's womb—the flesh on his head is still raw! Can people like him bear such a big burden?' they'd asked. Even Dattappa was surprised. But Gowda reassured them all. 'In a few days, these young men will learn. Everything, including the administration of the village, will have to go to them soon, right?'

The people consented.

And so it was done. According to the Gowda's wishes, without elections, Gudsikara was appointed chairman. Four lads—who had studied until Class One or Two in the Kannada-medium Boys School—were appointed members of the panchayat. The vacant drum room behind Karimayi's temple became the panchayat office.

To be sure, all this led to a few changes in the village:

(a) Gudsikara's nickname was Gudsyagola. So recorded even in accountant Dattappa's ledger. People had shortened it further, to Gudsya. Gudsya's father in his time had given loans to people at such high rates of interest that many had ended up losing their homes—he had swept up all their earnings. So people called his son Gudasu, 'to sweep'. Now that he was sarpanch, or chairman of the panchayat, it was changed to the more 'proper' Gudsikar. Those who called him by the old name were abused roundly. We too shall henceforth call him Gudsikara.

(b) In front of Gudsikara's house was put up a board on which was written in English: 'G. H. Gudsikara, BA LLB Village Panchayat Sarpanch, Belgaum District.' Except Gudsikara, nobody even glanced at it—they couldn't read English.

When he put it up, everybody stood in front of his house for an hour or half, staring at it. For the first fortnight, night and day, a herd of children stood looking at it. There was news in the outcaste neighbourhood that Gudsikara was going to announce a prize of 500 rupees for anyone who could read that board.

(c) Anyway, there was no work to do in the panchayat office. If there was any, its members had no clue about how to do it. So whenever they met, they played cards. Thus playing cards came to be called a 'meeting'. And obviously, some of these meetings went on until midnight.

(d) There were some other things which made Gudsikara happy. Whether or not these people wrote anything, at least the government wrote to them, right? The letters were in English. And Gudsikara would read them aloud, in front of everybody. As he read, I mean, as he made those 'tisspiss' noises in English, people would listen to him open-mouthed.

Even stranger was his reading of the newspaper. Gudsikara visited Belagavi once in three or six months. Whenever he went, he came back with the English newspaper. Until his next visit to Belagavi, until he could buy another paper, this one was all he had. After lunch in the afternoon, he would sit on the terrace alone and read it aloud, loud enough to be heard within shouting distance. Then old women and children from the neighbourhood would come running and stand in a huddle, listening to the 'tisspiss' sounds of English. And knowing they were listening, Gudsikara would read with great style.

Because of this, among the women, some new myths began to circulate:

(1) After hearing Gudsikara's English, some white-skinned memsahib had waylaid him in the middle of the street and asked him to marry her! If he married her, he would have to leave his parents behind and travel across the seas. Gudsikara thought about this and refused her offer.

(2) One day, the daughter of the owner of Gokak Falls —he too an Englishman—went to Gudsikara's college in her car and took him to her house. That bungalow was as big as Shivapura. It seems, they were holding hands and dancing. Meanwhile, her father came and told him in English, 'Son Gudsikara, marry my daughter. I will write the Falls in your name and cover you in green notes all over.' You can always get money and wealth, but once you lose your caste, can you get it back? Gudsikara thought about this and replied in English, 'Impossible!'

(3) There is another version of this story which takes place in the street down the house. The moment Gudsikara refused to marry her, the girl wept profusely, presented him with a watch and began to caress him. The watch that Gudsikara wears now—that's the one she gave him. Strangely enough, when these stories fell on Gudsikara's

ears, he didn't deny them. He laughed and said nothing.

This doesn't mean that Gudsikara is a bad person. Wanting to do good to the village, or, in his own words, 'bring progress to the village' is his true ambition. He made this clear to the members who came to him and emphasized it in the little speeches he delivered at the Kannada Boys School. People didn't have any reason to form a bad opinion of him. True, there was a bit of gossip about a couple of English-mems in Belagavi dying for his love, and his frequent visits to Belagavi because of them. What of gossip? It has no substance. It circulates for a bit, then dies. In the village, he had never done anything to point a finger at. Above all, he wanted to improve the village. What does it mean, 'improve the village'? Does it mean that the village is backward? He was the only person who discovered that it was so. Gowda, Basetti, Dattappa—didn't they know Belagavi? But none of them worried that their village was not like Belagavi.

His only little fault, only Dattappa called it a fault—but what of Dattappa? If Dattappa has an attack of bile, he will call anything a fault. But do people ever listen to reason? Whether or not anyone else talked about it, isn't it true that at least one person saw a fault in Gudsikara? Well, if you also agree that it's a fault, then this is it: he believes that no activity should start without a speech or end without one.

## THE FIRST MEETING

This is probably true, because only after a couple of months of the forming of the panchayat, Gudsikara hit upon the great idea of realizing his dream—of making his village another Belagavi. How? By keeping the village clean. To discuss this, a meeting was called at Karimayi Temple.

When the villagers arrived, what did they see? The school table has been brought out. Behind it, the chair on which the school master sits. That was the only chair in the village. Behind it, the stand on which they keep the sack of grain in the Gowda's house. Next to it, the sack-stand from Gudsikara's house. Some came for the heck of it, others because they were genuinely interested. Including Dattappa, the priest Basetti, Balu, Ningu and Barber Laguma, about sixty people were present. Gudsikara and the members, waiting in the drum room or panchayat office until then, came out. Gudsikara sat on the chair in the front and the members sat one-to-two on the sack-stands at the back.

Some felt dissatisfied already. Poor thing, it's the Master's chair. Even the Gowda had never sat on it. Dattappa thought this was wrong and was quite upset. By then Gudsikara had got up and begun to speak: 'Now we will have the prayer from the Shivapura Kannada Boys School.' He sat down. Four or five innocent infants came, stood in a line facing the crowd, folded their hands in a salute and screeched—

Victory Gudsikara *rige*[5]
Gudasikara *rige*, Leader of the People
Victory to him!

—in a frightened chorus that was also out of tune. Then there was a welcome speech by the Q&A Master. Then the Q&A Master brought a huge garland of flowers and put it around Gudsikara's neck. Then he got a few smaller garlands and put them around the necks of the members. Since Gudsikara had attended gatherings in Belagavi, and knew what to do next, he took the garland off and put it on the table. The members, though, sat in a row with the garlands still round their necks.

People were confused. What are we seeing? Where are we?—some of them just forgot. Dattappa found it all very funny and struggled to hold back his laughter. And Ningu was offended when the Master, after garlanding everybody, sat on the floor: 'Master, you garlanded everybody—how can you not have a garland too? Shouldn't you wear one and sit on that sack-stand?'

'No, no,' laughed Dattappa, 'how's that possible? They are the panchayat members.'

Ningu wasn't convinced: 'So what? Isn't the chair from Master's school?'

Thinking that this shouldn't be allowed to go on, Gudsikara got up to speak. He spoke relentlessly for an hour and a half—without stopping. If Barber Laguma hadn't stopped him in the middle, who knows how long he would have gone on!

This is more or less what he said:

'India is a country of villages. There are seven lakh villages here. Whereas you can count the towns and cities on your fingers. The British are ruling our country and ruining it. They are villains and foreigners. We must kick them out. Every village should become a city. It is only then that the country can progress. What should we do to make every village a city? We must keep the village clean. Look at Belagavi. Even if you drop ghee on its streets, you can scoop it up and eat it. It's that clean . . . '

It's at this point that Barber Laguma interrupted. He was already surprised that everyone else was so quiet. Unable to bear it any more, he got up. 'Look Gudsikara,' he began, 'Belagavi people may have a lot of ghee, so much that they can spill it on the streets and then lick it up again. But we don't have ghee—not even to eat. Why should we be spilling it on the streets?'

What do we say to such rank ignorance!

'No, look,' Gudsikara tried to explain, 'I was only trying to tell you how clean Belagavi roads are.'

'Fine, yes, they keep spilling the ghee and licking it up—that's why the roads are so clean. But why should we?'

'Yeh Laguma,' snapped Gudsikara, 'shut up and sit.' And then he spoke some more. Only God knows what he said. Dattappa was laughing to himself. But the others agreed with Laguma. What does it mean to spill ghee on the street and lick it up? Maybe people of a specific caste do that kind of a thing. Or is it a vow they've made to some god? A clan custom perhaps? We don't have this in our clan. Then why should we do it?

This line of thought stopped only when Gudsikara advanced a 'polite suggestion' in the end: 'We must keep this village clean like Belagavi. So we will appoint sweepers to sweep the village every day. And we will collect a rupee as tax from every house for this.'

The moment the talk of tax came up, everyone got up, one after the other, dusting off their behinds. Gudsikara tried to call out the names of a few to make them stay. But they said, 'Wait, we're just coming,' and vanished. Dattappa had to get up to make some of them stay. 'Look Gudsikara, instead of a rupee per house, how about asking them to clean their own front yards?' he suggested. All those still present liked this idea and assented quickly.

But Gudsikara felt insulted.

'No, no. After all a panchayat office needs a guard. There are at least two meetings every week.

We need a clerk to do the accounts. How do we raise the money for these expenses?'

Did he think the people were mad or something? Many of them thought, 'Oh, these members have their "meetings" every day, right? And now they need a clerk to do their accounts and a guard to make tea for them, oh, oh, oh!'

And they left.

The only people left were the children who'd sung the opening prayer. Poor things, they'd been sitting there for two hours, with folded hands and staring eyes, because they were scared that Master would beat them if they didn't. And the Q&A Master—he too remained. Gudsikara must have felt insulted. But Thief Sidrama, sitting at the back with a garland round his neck, was very disappointed. Because he was the one who was to deliver the speech at the end. He had it written by the Master and then spent the last fifteen days trying to learn it by heart. It was about ten pages long.

On the sixth page was the following line: 'Thanks to all for giving their support to the leader of the people, our Gudsikara-saheb.'

## SECOND MEETING

It was six months since the first panchayat meeting. More or less. Something else happened around this time. Gudsikara got upset with the Gowda.

An inspector came to the Kannada Boys School to start night classes. He stayed at Gudsikara's place. Gudsikara was very happy, thinking that because of this something good was going to happen to the idiots in the village. A meeting was called that night. Gowda also came.

This time, the meeting was at the Kannada Boys school. Behind the table there was only one chair—that only chair in the village—and a sack-stand. Gowda, Dattappa and the Elders sat on a thick cloth spread on the floor. After everyone had gathered, Gudsikara and the inspector arrived. Gudsikara came up and sat on the chair. He left the grain sack-stand for the inspector. The inspector must have panicked at this new kind of seat with its three unstable legs. He abandoned it and sat with the people on the floor. Gowda couldn't bear this. He told Gudsikara, 'Son, he is after all our guest. Let him sit on the chair. You sit on the stand if you want.' Hearing this, Gudsikara was about to erupt like popcorn. What an insult in front of a stranger! I am such an educated man! How educated is this inspector? How can these fools know all this? If we are all from the same village, they should raise my stature in front of others. Should they insult and put me down like this? Whatever they want to tell me, or teach me, should they try to do it in front of this visitor? The more he thought about it, the more angry he got. But he couldn't sit there getting angry at a time like this. So he told the inspector, 'Come up, please come up.' As if he respected the Gowda's words.

People agreed with the Gowda. One must respect a guest. Gudsikara can sit on the chair the next day. Will the chair run away? Or does a man who sits on a chair also take that chair with him when he leaves? Moreover, the visitor is old enough to be Gudsikara's father. He should at least respect the man's age.

Meanwhile, Dattappa got up, went to the inspector, took him by the shoulder, said, 'Come sahebara, why do you sit here? After all, Gudsikara is our lad, come,' and led him to the table.

Gudsikara got up and sat on the sack-stand.

As usual, Q&A Master—we will narrate the story of how he came to be called Q&A Master when the time comes—gave the welcome speech. Then, upon Chairman Gudsikara's orders, the inspector spoke about the government programme for teaching illiterate farmers at the evening school. He said they should all come forward to learn. A village that has a leader like Gudsikara should not lag behind other villages, he felt. 'From today, right here, I will start registering your names. In fact, you, old man,' he asked the Gowda, 'what's your name?'

Forget the people who were sitting there, even Gudsikara was a little embarrassed at this. Some disturbance might erupt if he sat quiet now. But without any ado, Gowda answered, 'Paragowda.' The inspector was now inspired. He questioned Dattappa, 'Yeh grandpa, tell me your name.' Dattappa told him. Both could read and write. What does he mean by asking them their names? Gudsikara had to intervene, 'They can read, Inspector.' The inspector had already suspected something like that. Immediately, he put the pen in Gudsikara's hand and said, 'You write the names, please.' Gudsikara wrote the names of many who had gathered there and then got up for the chairman's address.

It started with, 'India is a country of villages,' and moved onto the theme of Belagavi. But this time, the ghee example was absent. Overall, Gowda was not at all unhappy with the proceedings of the meeting. But it all became crystallized in Gudsikara's mind. The valedictory speech was made by the Q&A Master. Invoking a verse from the Bhagavadgita—'Whenever there is sin on the Earth'—he announced that Gudsikara was indeed God's avatar come to uplift the village.

The dissatisfaction resulting from these meetings exploded in the form of Ningu's case.

# NINGU'S STORY

Ningu is the village eunuch. Not a man. Not a woman. An unfortunate being who was neither this nor that. Not that he grieved about it. Come to think of it, he was the only one in the village who could make fun of, and laugh at, people irrespective of their age, status or gender. No mother. Father Gattivalappa brought him up, being both mother and father. But as the boy grew up, it became obvious that his facial characteristics and behaviour were those of a woman. His peers made fun of him. The Elders scolded him. But he was not to be mended. This is how Ningya, who couldn't be the female Ningi, ended up being Ningu.

People advised Gattivalappa that everything would be fine if he got his son married. Gattivalappa too was tired of eating the same indifferently cooked 'male' rotti and the thick dhal after his wife's death. Maybe he thought if a daughter-in-law came, he could get some nicely cooked food. Or perhaps he hoped his son would improve after marriage. Whatever he thought, he found a bride among his relations and got her married to Ningu.

Getting his son married was within his power. He did that. After that? The daughter-in-law, her name was Gowri, came home. Ningu slept in the house for a couple of days. The day after that, he started sleeping on the porch. Gowri, who went to her parents' house for the festival, refused to return, complaining that she had no nightly pleasure to expect in her husband's house. Gattivalappa had to bring her back with a bunch of lies.

The same joy again. But after this the daughter-in-law didn't remember her parents' home any more. Ningu didn't come home at night. There were rumours in the village that Gattivalappa 'kept' his daughter-in-law. Friends openly showed their disgust and even scolded Ningu. Whatever . . . Ningu slept peacefully outside the house. Not that he wasn't thinking of all this. You can see the lines on somebody's face, but can you see the sorrow that etched those lines? After all, poor thing, is it Gowri's fault? The fault is the father's. Being a father, he sleeps with his daughter-in-law. Has he no shame? Already one foot in the grave. Overall, it was my mistake to agree to this marriage. Or did I agree to the marriage? Wasn't it my father who forced me to accept? Now I know why he forced me to do so. This shame would not have befallen me if I hadn't married. Now I get the bad name, and my father gets to have the fun.

Ningu grew angry when he thought like this. But inwardly, the realization that he too was responsible for everything troubled him. As if all this wasn't enough, Gowri became pregnant. Now Ningu was truly traumatized. People's talk began to hurt him terribly.

One day—that is, Kari Hunt is tomorrow and it is this afternoon—Ningu was tired and fell asleep in the hut in the fields with a woollen blanket over him.[6] What work had he done to feel tired? Somebody taunted, 'The baby to be born—is it your son or brother?' Unable to bear the shame, and unable to answer the question, he slept silently, wrapping himself in the blanket. Wife-in-name-only was in the fields. Father was there too. After a while, the wife came back to the house. The old man, angry that she kept working at this time, came in and shouted at her to rest. Through a hole in the blanket, Ningu could see all this. Pregnant Gowri lay down on the katte outside, very tired.[7] Old man needlessly went to her and started massaging her legs. Asking, 'Why are you tired?' and running his hand over her legs, he became like the dust under her feet, and then a worm in that dust. Drooling over her, he started getting up to his tricks. Ningu was disgusted. He wanted to get up and spit on his father's old face.

'He is sleeping here, move away,' said Gowri.

'So what, what can he do? Wait, I'll be back,' Gattivalappa remembered something and left, closing the door after him. Gowri closed her eyes, tired. God knows what devil got into Ningu—before you could say 'yeh', something like an electric shock ran through his body. He took the stone used for sharpening the sickle that lay near him and rammed it into Gowri's stomach. Before she could draw another breath, she clutched her stomach and writhed in pain and died.

Gattivalappa heard Gowri's dying throes and rushed back. Before he could ask what had happened, Ningu took the sharp axe stuck in the rafters above and brought it down across the old man's throat. The severed head jumped and tumbled towards the daughter-in-law's feet. But the torso kept bounding towards her bed. Whether it was out of fear, or because something had possessed him, Ningu cried out, raised his hands and kept jumping up and down, as if in competition with the hopping torso. God knows what would have happened if the torso had kept up that hopping for another moment. When it hit the katte, it fell face down with a thud like a tree cut off at the base.

In the same possessed state, sharp axe still in hand, Ningu emerged from the house and began to run towards the village. Who knows what would have happened if Thief Sidrama hadn't come along. When the Thief asked, 'What's it Ningu? What happened?' Ningu became human again and collapsed on the ground. His heart began to beat furiously. He started crying and beating his chest in anguish.

Ningu's howling and inarticulate attempts at sign language conveyed to Thief Sidrama that some catastrophe had occurred. He said, 'Run and hold Gowda's feet. Ask him for protection.' Leaving the axe there, Ningu ran towards the village. Thief Sidrama went to the hut to see what had happened. Blood streamed all over the floor. On the katte, Gattivalappa's corpse had fallen on its stomach, its legs splayed. Beyond that lay Gowri's body, its eyes all screwed up. Thief felt his head spin. He bolted.

It was late in the day. On the porch, Gowda was sitting with his son Shivaninga and talking about some business matter. Ningu ran up to the Gowda, clutched his feet and started screaming and banging his head, once on the floor and once on the Gowda's feet. No answer to Gowda's 'Why?' or 'What?' Only the screams, 'Yappa, yappa!' Gowda was patient for a while. Then he couldn't take it any more. He pulled Ningu up by his hair and slapped him a couple of times. Ningu came back to his senses.

After he heard everything, Gowda said, 'You go back to the field. We will go with you.' Then he went to Dattappa's house. Stood at the door and called, 'Dattu, there's some business. Come out.' Guessing that some calamity had occurred, Dattappa followed Gowda right away, asking no questions.

Gudsikara, who had slept after the meal, was not up yet. Thief Sidrama woke him up and described the whole incident—perhaps because he was terrified himself—in horrible detail. Gudsikara too got scared. But when the Thief said, 'I asked him to run and seek Gowda's protection,' Gudsikara felt as if someone had thrown cold water over his face.

'Yeh, in a case like this, what can the Gowda do? Who's the lawyer? Me or that Gowda?'

'Wait, where else can they go?' asked the Thief. 'They have to come to you, in the end. You will be called in a minute,' he said. True enough. Doesn't the Gowda know that I have passed my law exams? They have to come and ask me what to do. I can go then—Gudsikara thought and sat still, bursting with curiosity.

Looking at Gowri and Gattivalappa's corpses, not only Dattappa but also Gowda got scared. They shut the door immediately and sat there, thinking of what to do next. True, Ningu had done wrong, but Gowri and Gattivalappa had also done wrong. How could they get so blindly randy when the son was sleeping right there? Is there no limit to human endurance? Moreover, when had Ningu been in the way of their desires? Old man had become blind with lust. Ningu had become blind with anger. Both had gone blind. The dead are dead. What about the living?

Dattappa knew how Gowda's thoughts ran in cases like these. Hadn't they jointly taken care of the village administration all these years and managed it quite well? Gudsikara's name didn't even cross their minds. On other days, it would have been different. But tomorrow is the Feast of the Kari Hunt. The nayaka boys will go hunting today. It's almost time.

According to custom, before leaving, they will come to take the Gowda's blessings, bearing the auspicious coconut. Suppose they went to Gowda's house? And found that the Gowda wasn't there? All kinds of suspicion would result. Who knows how many people in the village know all this already? Dattappa and Gowda were anxious to give this business some closure before the word of it got out. They both sat thinking and watching over the dead.

Ningu hadn't returned.

Finally, Ningu came back with Gudsikara and Thief Sidrama. Dattappa was furious. When they are trying to save this fool, he goes and brings with him Gudsikara of all people! He exclaimed in disgust. Gowda understood. But his faith in human nature was strong. 'Come lad, you came too? Good,' he said. Ignoring Gowda, Gudsikara opened the door of the hut, peeped in and then stepped away, unable to bear the sight. Gowda said, 'Come, sit.' They asked the Thief to shut the door. He did so. Gudsikara was sweating with fear after seeing the corpses. Nobody spoke for the next ten minutes. Everybody sat still, like stones. Only Ningu was looking from face to face, shedding tears and worrying about what would happen to him.

Finally, it was Gowda who spoke. 'Dattu, how about burning the hut?'

'Right,' said Dattappa.

If Dattappa says 'right,' then it's fine. Gowda is convinced that it is the right decision. 'Ningya, don't move the bodies. Set fire to the house tonight. You don't need to say anything to anybody. In the morning, tell everybody that both died in the fire.'

This struck Gudsikara like a thunderbolt. This is without doubt a murder case! Who else but I can give legal advice? Instead, these two old village idiots are acting as if they know the law and deciding to close the case! Is there no limit to their foolishness? Doesn't the Gowda have any sense? The oldies don't even seem to have noticed my presence. When I sat waiting at home for them to call me, they didn't call. Okay, at least the Thief brought Ningu to me. I came here. Now that I am here, how can they ignore me like this? While I'm planning to win this case in court and save these people, these old hawks seem to think of me as less than nothing. It's murder! Not a small matter! There's the court, there's the law. Look at this old man's guts! He's trying to throw dust in the eyes of the law, in broad daylight too! Did he at least stop to consult me? No, he consulted Dattu.

Gudsikara decided to teach them a lesson. 'Why do you want to set fire to the hut and bring the wrath of the law upon yourself? Just call the police officer, the foujudara, and get the inquest done,' he told them.

'Look, son,' said Dattappa, 'we too know the law and rules—'

'Law and rules are not trivial matters,' interrupted the Gowda. 'This is the bad English government. If the case goes to Belagavi court, Ningu won't survive. We will all decide together. Before anyone comes to know of this, let's finish the business.'

'Why won't Ningu survive?'

'He committed a crime, so . . . '

'Right, if he committed a crime, let him be punished.'

'What do you mean? Do you want send Ningu to jail?'

'Why should he go to jail? I'll fight his case,' said Gudsikara without even realizing the contradiction in his speech.

Dattappa was at a loss to understand on whose side this young man was.

'See, Son Gudsikara, you say that you will be his lawyer, okay? What will you do? Instead of saving him by arguing in court, why don't you save him right here? Can we say what turn the case will take if it goes to court? This is beyond your power. You will argue there and sit back. Who will decide Ningu's fate? The judge, or you? If they say he committed a murder, and he must be hanged—what will you do then?'

'But how can we break the law?'

'How did we break it? What wrong did we commit now?'

'If you go on saving everybody who commits a murder, how can morality and law remain in the world?'

'What? Do you want Ningu hanged?'

Gudsikara was speechless. He didn't know how to reply to this lawless argument. This was an entirely strange and different kind of argument from that in a court of law. In order to begin to understand this logic, I must first understand what my position is here. If we only talk about law and morals, Ningu will go to jail. Even I don't want that to happen. But if we stop caring about it, these old foxes will take the law into their hands, interpret it the way they want and become bogus politicians in the village!

'Look, whether Ningu survives or not is another question, but law and rules are not like the holy thread of the brahmin to play with,' he told Dattappa. Gowda felt bad that Gudsikara brought up the issue of caste. If I remain silent, it will be impossible to stop Dattappa from speaking.

Ningu was already angry with Gudsikara. What's this? Seems like I picked up some nuisance on the street to take home with me.

Even a panchayat member like the Thief was dissatisfied with the way things were happening.

'Okay, what do we do now?'

'Call the foujudara and have the inquest done.'

Gowda thought he should try one last time to put some sense into the boy's head. 'Son, the laws of your city are different. And the laws of our village are different. As you know, our laws are very simple. If there is a fight here, we will decide the law here. You want to impose Belagavi law on our fight. How's this possible?'

'There are no two different laws for the city and the village.'

'Then we should make them different. How can justice be done otherwise? Know this much, you will take the case from here to Belagavi. There, they will make you swear and make you lie. You believe this witness and argue the case. After hearing your argument, the judge will give the judgement. If there is a lie at the root of it all, how can the man sitting at the other end see the rightness in it? You tell me.'

Gudsikara felt that he was losing the argument.

Dattappa knew how experienced Gowda was in all these matters. In his mind, he said 'bravo' to Gowda's words.

'We have all become old,' the Gowda continued. 'Our time is over. Now you should take care of the village affairs. People in our times were naive. They would listen to things. In our times, we never climbed up the court steps. Just because you have passed the law exams, is it right to drag everybody to court? To err is human. If not man, does God err? Just because a man errs, who are you to decide on killing him just like that? Man was not born only to die, he was also born to live. Look at the Goddess. If you look at all our errors, it doesn't seem like she should keep us alive on Earth. Yet, Karimayi hasn't kept us all alive? Tell me why? Because life is bigger than death.'

Gudsikara was convinced that these people weren't going to listen to any kind of sense. There is no substance in their logic. True, but he didn't know how to counter it either.

'Look, today or tomorrow, the police will get this news. Forget Ningu, both of you are going to be caught up in the case. Going to jail at this age does not befit you. Try to understand.'

It was strange that Dattappa had kept silent until this time. 'All right, son. We are also ready to go to jail. But we are not ready to let Ningu down. Ningu didn't do the murder intentionally. He will not do it again either. It was an accident. Both of us will stand by him. If you want to, you go to the police and report it.'

These words stuck in Gudsikara's heart like a stone stuck in a newly built wall yet to dry. Look at the daring of these oldies!

Gowda became aware that the exchange was taking a harsh turn. So he said, 'Okay, son. You give him the punishment you want. We will make him listen to you. Don't say that his crime has no punishment here. But Belagavi people cannot punish a man from our village. What do you say?'

'I am not a judge.'

'We are doing this. If you want to do so, punish us too. If we don't obey you, let our tongues fall off. I swear upon Karimayi. What more do you want?'

Ningu had been silent until now, hadn't he? But he couldn't take it any more. He opened his mouth: 'Yeh, Gudsya! Now I too know what's on your mind. Even if a hair on the head of these two men is harmed, you won't be able to live in this village. Don't forget that.' It was the first time Ningu had ever talked in this manner. In any other context, they would have disregarded it.

'I know your game. If you survive, it's only because of my kindness, you know?'

'Go to hell and take your kindness with you! Do what you want. But first get out of my field.'

Gudsikara stomped off, back towards the village. Dattappa felt that what Ningu said was right. But Gowda was dissatisfied. He sat quietly, contemplating what was to come. He had been observing Gudsikara ever since the latter became sarpanch. He was certain that the boy didn't have a healthy mind. Dattappa had, in fact, decided what kind of a man Gudsikara was long ago. What could be seen in the boy's eyes was only his self-importance, not any concern for the village. He's the kind who could sacrifice the village for the sake of his ego. But Gowda hadn't lost faith in him. He was hoping the boy would come back to the right path today or tomorrow. But even Gowda was disappointed by today's talk. He felt the boy was getting to be dangerous.

God knows how long he would have gone on with his musings, but Dattappa woke him up.

'Now it's already time for the nayaka boys to start.'

'Dattu, somehow this thing didn't go right.'

Dattappa was also concerned about the danger from Gudsikara.

Gowda told Ningu, 'Ningu, now latch the hut. Stay in Lagumi's house. Don't panic. Karimayi will take care of things. Sidrama, you don't open your mouth about this matter. If you do, not only us, you too will get into trouble and be forced to "swallow the sickle".'

Gowda got up. Gowda had never worried like he did today. Even after he got back home, he was disturbed in his heart. He thought of calling the Panchas immediately. Then he thought, 'Anyway, they will come with the hunter boys,' and sat still. But he was not easy in his mind. Meanwhile, Dattappa came again in a hurry. Why was he here again? The Gowda got scared. But all Dattappa breathlessly asked was, 'What do you say? Should we celebrate the festival or not?'

Yes, however much you try to cover it up, the smell of a corpse will soon hit the villagers' nose. If they knew what happened, nobody would feel light in their hearts. It is the pollution period in any case. Gowda thought it would be good to stop the celebrations. But if he said no to the celebrations, it would mean making people curious. He would have to answer them.

Something flashed across his mind. 'Dattu, what does your *Chintamani* say?'

Dattappa had already looked it up. 'It says ask the Mother herself.'

'Go on, then—ask. I'll make the boys wait here until you return.'

Dattappa ran to the temple.

The hunter boys came with their musical instruments. Basetti and Balu came too, with the procession. Soon everybody realized that Gowda was not his usual lively self. A couple of them asked, 'Aren't you well?' Basetti even suggested ginger-stalk essence, a great medicine for such ailments.

Gowda asked everyone to sit. They sat. Dattappa hadn't come back. You had to talk about something if you had people sitting around you. But Gowda couldn't. The people, who thought that the Gowda didn't look well, began to talk among themselves. Shivaninga was with the nayaka boys. The boys told the Gowda they would take Shivaninga with them. He was still very young. Hunting meant he would have to wander in the forest until daybreak. 'Not this time,' said the Gowda. Dattappa still wasn't back.

Usually, there's never any delay at the Gowda's house. It's just a matter of getting the auspicious coconut and speeding the boys off on the hunt. But Gowda wasn't in any hurry. Shivaninga had already brought the coconut and placed it in front of Gowda. It was getting to be night. There was moonlight.

Finally, Dattappa came back. He was angry. The moment he arrived, he whispered in Gowda's ear, 'It seems Gudsya went to Belagavi at dusk.'

'What did Mother say?'

'She said, Don't stop the feast.'

The moment he heard this, Gowda gave the coconut to the leader of the nayaka boys. Although many people had many suspicions, they left without asking any questions. Gowda called four boys he trusted, told them not to go to the hunt but to come to him after dinner.

He also asked the Panchas to stay back.

## KARIBETE, OR THE KARI HUNT

It was morning. On this day, the villagers should be joyful. Because it is the day of Karibete. Karibete is the festival of the nayakas. Gowda was of the same clan. The young nayakas had gone hunting yesterday, right? Today, when they come back, there will be a hunters' procession. They will offer a share of their hunt to the Gowda and then go back to their houses. Tonight, they'll cook meat in the nayaka houses. After dinner, they'll assemble at the Karimayi temple. Drinking arrack, dancing to the hunting songs of the whores, they'll spend the night in fun. None except the nayakas will dance. But the others too have fun watching it.

The songs are full of hunting adventures. They are conventional songs. All the women's eyes become dreamy as they watch the boys show off their bare black brawny bodies, marked with fresh wounds from the hunt. High on booze, the lads dance, shaking their waists and staring hungrily at every nook and cranny of the lusty young whores' bodies. Which sensible whore would miss the opportunity of being the target of so many hungry eyes? There's also the custom of inviting whores from other villages by offering them the ceremonial coconut. Even those who only watch are also curious about who's been invited, who's going to be there. From a fortnight before the festival, if they happen to meet any nayaka boys, they inquire, 'What, Nayaka? Which village are the whores coming from this year?'

But this year, at least among those who knew, there was no enthusiasm left for the festival. As usual, Gowda got up, bathed in the lake, folded his hands before Karimayi and came back home. After breakfast, he headed towards Ningu's fields. Looking at the work of the boys there, he thought, 'Splendid.' Then he went to his own fields. He called for Lagumavva. He made her get a gourdful of arrack, drank it and then just sat on his cot. He didn't even notice that Shivasani was talking to him.

As time passed, and the day progressed from noon to night, more and more people came to know. Unable to bear the curiosity, some even went to Ningu's fields. Women, who went to the lake to fetch water, whispered among themselves. Whenever people met, they were anxious to ask each other, 'Is this true? How did it happen?' Everybody wanted to talk today.

Then Gowda and Gudsikara had a terrible row, they even came to blows. Gudsikara swore on Karimayi that he would change his name if he didn't get Gowda and Dattappa arrested. So on and so forth. Wild rumours spread, rumours turned into stories, stories became facts. Before the evening, Ningu was the protagonist of the story, the story was woven round him. Hundreds of different versions, with newer and newer details, in newer and newer styles. Spreading from mouth to mouth with newer and newer colour.

Some thought the feast should have been stopped that day. But were not sure if the nayaka boys would have agreed. Because that day Durga was going to dance representing the the village. From the neighbouring village, Pashchapura, Sundari had come. Come to think of it, had the dead ones been righteous or good people? Why should the feast stop because of them? And if it had to stop, then the Gowda would have said so. Karimayi's oracle would have guided us. Even as these thoughts flashed through their minds, they saw the hunter procession arrive.

When it was time to dine and sleep, all had gathered in the temple yard. The old nayakas had absolutely no enthusiasm. Not like the old times, when Lagumavva herself stood up to sing the hunting songs, smoothing the pleats of her saree. As the excitement grew, and she walked, swaying and showing off the curves of her body, even the toothless old men gaped and danced with her. Lagumavva could bring rhythm even into those aged bodies with her singing. Today, the Gowda came, true. But he just sat there, quietly. His sense of fun and laughter had disappeared.

One thing that struck everybody—Dattappa never attended this ceremony. But today he was there. Because of this, the atmosphere had turned grave and stifling.

Durga's singing began. The young men's bodies had begun to feel the intoxicating pleasure of the moonlight. Suddenly, as Gowda and Dattappa were dreading, the headlights of the police jeep fell on the group of people. Stunned, everyone scrambled to their feet. Even before Gowda or Dattappa stood up, the jeep drew near the temple and stopped.

A middle-aged foujudara got off with two policemen. The people watched, alarmed. Gowda and Dattappa came up to the officer and saluted. Then introduced themselves. Cutting them short, the foujudara asked, 'Why have these people gathered here?'

'For the Karibete festival. They are dancing.'

'Festival?'

'Yes'

'There is no need to celebrate today.'

The foujudara said this much and turned around. Quickly, Dattappa turned the lantern light up and walked towards the square. The foujudara and the policemen followed. Gowda called a couple of men, said something to them and then walked away to catch up with the foujudara.

The nayaka boys reacted badly to this interference. Some guessed that it was to do with Gudsikara's machinations. Some said they would take Gowda and Dattappa to jail. The boys challenged: 'Why, are there no men in the village?' There were murmurs in the group. The moment they reached the square, the foujudara asked them to fetch Ningu. He chided them for feasting when there was murder in the village.

Gowda said, 'There is no murder, nothing of the sort—would I remain quiet if something like that happened? About celebrating the festival? It is a fortnight since Gowri and Gattivalappa died. Gowri died because the bull gored her stomach with his horns, and Gattivalappa, who took to bed with fever a couple of days back, never got up from it.'

Dattappa nodded from time to time and said that he had entered this same information into his ledger.

When Ningu came to the square, what of the foujudara,even Gowda and Dattappa were taken aback. He was wearing a saree, and had bangles on his wrists. He too repeated the same story. The foujudara was in a fix. His experience shouted out to him that this eunuch could not have committed the murders. There must have been some misinformation.

Meanwhile, one of the nayaka boys came to ask for permission to continue with their celebrations. The foujudara asked him about the murder too. 'Oh no!' said the boy, 'There would be pollution if there was murder. And it is impossible to celebrate the Karibete feast in the period of pollution. If there was pollution in the village, and the festival offering was given to Karimayi, would the Mother keep quiet, sir? Karimayi is like burning cinders and fire. If something like that happened, both you and we would be dead.'

By this time, the food was ready. When the Gowda invited him to eat, 'I want to see Ningu's hut,' said the foujudara. Gowda kept saying, 'We will go there early tomorrow morning' but the foujudara wanted to go immediately. So they went to the fields. A herd of people followed. 'Where is the hut that was set on fire?' asked the foujudara. 'What fire?' was the Gowda's prompt response. 'This is Ningu's field, this is his hut,' he said. The foujudara grew more and more confused. He came back. They sat to eat at the Gowda's place. There was also the curry from the hunt. And unadulterated arrack. As it seeped into him, the foujudara's head started swimming. Outside, the boys' songs and dancing began. Perhaps out of disappointment, the foujudara lost his head completely. 'Stop this!' he screamed, his mouth full of food.

'Neither you nor I,' said the Gowda slowly, 'have the right to stop this.'

'Yeh Gowda, are you teaching me rules? You being the Gowda in the village yet maintaining two parties, getting murders done—'

'What two parties? What murder? What, Sahebara, what kind of words are these?'

'I know, making this feast a pretext, you have planned to get the chairman's party beaten up by the nayaka boys.'

Listening to all this ambiguous talk, Gowda grew quite alarmed about what Gudsikara might have reported. Moreover, it wasn't possible right now to talk to the man in a logical manner.

'Look Gowda,' the foujudara began again, 'when there is a chance of a fight taking place in the village, don't you know that you shouldn't permit such celebrations? Stop this—'

'Sahebara, if there's a fight or something, I will take the responsibility for it. They will just sing and dance. You sleep peacefully.'

The foujudara's blood boiled in rage. The queen of native liquor inside him began to show her power. He thought, 'Just look at the arrogance of this village Gowda.' Then he washed his hands and, still swaying, went to open the door. The door was latched from outside. He pulled at the door, shook it, kicked at it. Finally, his foot hurt, so he came back and sat on the bed. 'Get the door opened, yeh!' he shouted a few times. The two policemen walked up and down trying to see if there was another way out. They became anxious and wanted to call out to someone passing by on the street. There was no one.

Gowda sat there, watching their struggles.

The sight of the Gowda sitting there so calmly made the foujudara even more restless.

'Yeh Gowda, let's see how these men will celebrate when I am here. I'll take care of you too . . . '

Gowda remained unruffled. 'Sahebara, you do not know the pulse of this village.'

'Yeh, this village is under my authority—'

'No, Sahebara, the village is under my authority. If I go wrong, then it comes under your authority. Now no such wrong has been done. Beyond this, if you still want to show your authority, I warn you. As it is, these boys have just become men. They're full of the swagger and arrogance of youth. They wandered into the forest and proudly brought back the spoils of their hunt. Moreover, they're drunk. Perhaps the situation would have been manageable if we only had the local whores. But there are also whores from other villages. These young men are dancing in front of them. If you go and upset them now, I'll tell you the truth—I won't be responsible for the calamity to come.'

The foujudara was silenced. He fell asleep. The policemen followed his example. Gowda laughed to himself. Then he got up and looked out of the window. Lagumavva's voice, mingled with the wild cries of the boys, wafted across the night air:

Hunter, he hunted
The hunter boy
Hunted in the forest

Standing there, he imagined her wiggling body. Awash with the drunken moonlight, it looked as if the entire village was in a stupor, unable to move its limbs, and unseeing with its half-closed eyes. Still swaying, after its mouth had had enough drink, it now opened its ears to the song. True, the village had been surprised and alarmed when the foujudara came. But after drinking in this moonlight, as it seeped inside them, down to their toes, people were back to their natural form. The joy of life flooded into the village. It wasn't the first time that the police had come. They had come twice or thrice in the past on the pretext of searching for freedom fighters. Whatever, these outsiders had always remained outsiders.

When the foujudara woke up, it was fully morning. The door was open. He asked the policemen, 'Where are the Gowda and accountant?'

'They're waiting in the square for us,' they replied.

Finishing his morning rituals, he went to the square. Gowda was narrating last night's events to Dattappa and laughing loudly. The foujudara immediately took them to Ningu's fields. He wanted to make sure about the hut.

The same hut—it looked the same. After Gudsikara went to Belagavi, Gowda had kept the hut intact. He hadn't had fire set to it. He got the corpses buried, though. Had the hut cleaned and restored to its original state. It looked so natural that, let alone the foujudara, even the villagers couldn't have believed that there had been a murder there.

The foujudara came back and sent for Gudsikara. The moment he heard that Gudsikara wasn't at home, his anger turned towards the man. Gudsikara, it seems, had gone to the police station and, despite being educated in law, foolishly babbled all sorts of things and written a report to the effect that there were two opposing parties in the village, that Ningu of Gowda's party had murdered a man of his—Gudsikara's—party, then he had put the corpse in the hut and burnt it, and that it had all been done with the Gowda's support. What's more, he'd also alleged that, on the day of the feast, there were going to be more murders. The foujudara narrated all this—and with great zest—abused Gudsikara and left. Gowda requested him to have some milk before leaving. After consuming four or five eggs and drinking a whole pot of milk, the foujudara got on his jeep and drove away. Good riddance!

The moment he left, Gowda and Dattappa looked at Ningu in his saree and guffawed.

Moved by Ningu's anguish, it seems, Lagumavva had advised him, 'Go and beg before Karimayi. She'll save you.' According to her suggestion, Ningu had begged: 'Mother who bore me in your womb, save me from this. I'll wear a saree and dance in front of you.' Then, even before Karimayi did anything to save him, he had worn the saree. And what do we say of Karimayi's miracle? This just proved lucky for Ningu.

True, the trouble from outside was gone. But vengeance remained in Gudsikara's heart. That day, he too had come with the foujudara in the jeep. But unable to face the people, he'd got off at a safe distance and taken a quiet route home. The next day, when the foujudara sent for him, he told his sister to say that he wasn't in. The same night, he absconded to Belagavi and only came back to the village eight days later. It was difficult to recognize his face now. It was distorted with shame. After his return, he tried to be brazen about his doings. People said things to him for a while, then they too became quiet.

Gowda had to think about Gudsikara now. The boy looked at everything only from his point of view. When he looked at things that way, everything, including the village, looked divided.

During the next festival of Holi, Gowda became even more convinced of this.

# HOLI

In Shivapura, Holi was the truly 'male' festival. The Holi Full Moon Feast in the village was famous in all the fourteen villages around. This may be because all the men, irrespective of status or age, participated in it. Or was it because of the singing competition between the unmarried loafers of the village and the whores? Perhaps it was because, like each village is famous for something—Gokavi for that sweet *karadantu*, Tukola for tobacco and Nippani for *beedis*—Shivapura was famous for its whores. Shivapura whores are great beauties. What's more, according to a poet—

Nowhere in the world can you see
Girls who are so much fun!
They wiggle their full buttocks and make their arched eyebrows dance
The wrestlers are sweating where they stand
And boys too young to marry
Are sighing and readying their thighs
What shall I say about the Shivapura whores?
And of their thrilling waists

Maybe this was why. Or, who knows, maybe there are other reasons. Whatever—the Holi festival in this village is famous throughout the neighbouring villages.

Shivapura people know this. Therefore, even as the Holi Feast is ten or twelve days away, they begin to prepare for it. The moment they see the third day's moon of the fortnight, all the children assemble in the alley and start howling. After performing this 'howling service' for a couple of hours, once people go to bed, they sneak into their backyards, steal dried cakes of cowdung and firewood, store them in the deserted house in the village and go home to sleep. Until the full moon, every day, this programme is carried out without fail.

Older boys, but those who are not married yet, gather in Karimayi's temple at night. They remember the old Holi songs and start composing new verses. They celebrate this festival for two full days. On the full-moon day, under the leadership of the Gowda, all the elders and the Panchas go to the forest with their musical instruments, collect a tender branch from some tree and erect it in front of Karimayi's temple. The youngsters bring out their stash of firewood and stuff and heap it around this post. That day, they have the special sweet dish of *holige* in their homes. At night, they have games and performances devised by the enterprising ones of the village.

The next day is Dhoolavada. Before daybreak, again under Gowda's leadership, people bring their musical instruments to where the god Kama (Cupid), that is, the tree branch, is standing. You should see the scene—this buzzing crowd standing around Kama. Nobody is properly dressed. They all wear old and torn clothes saved solely for this festival. When hordes of men with tattered clothes around their waists are in a hurry to bring their hands to their mouths, the old men staring at Lagumavva's rumps are busy remembering the old times, and the children who cannot see the action at the centre are anxious to squeeze in wherever they can through a gap in the crowd, Gowda sets fire to the heap around Kama. Immediately, the people begin to howl and beat their hands against their mouths. The noise rises up to the sky. And the musicians begin to play their instruments. You can tell people's age by the way they howl. If the old ones howl a couple of times, the middle-aged ones howl a little more. The unmarried youth some more. And the children just don't stop.

After the fire burns out, Lagumavva takes some of the ash in a salver to the village border, scatters it there and then comes back. This ritual, the village believes, will prevent the entry of diseases and ailments. They also believe that now their village will be full of crops and wealth. By this time, it is evening. Lagumavva, who thus marks the village border, goes to the outcaste neighbourhood, herds all the whores together and proceeds towards the temple. After all the tacky songs, there has to be some messing with colour, right? Usually, the whores are in tattered sarees. The more the tatters, the more the gawking of the connoisseurs.

In this manner, the group starts towards the temple, and the boys follow, howling. On the way, between the men and whores, there are arch words and choice taunts liberally exchanged, and some give-and-take business. For example, if the following words emerge from the boys' group: 'This heifer won't stop without drinking water in seven cities,' then from the other side you hear: 'See the one with a face like a wet crow, how much he talks!' Then if there is a taunt like 'If I squeeze your body, I won't find a drop of juice—look at the blabbering mouth,' and if a very young voice answers, 'She cleans her snot hiding behind a saree, if you bite her chin, she creates an uproar, who is this, boy?' the rest of the group name one of the women and start howling. We can't say how this exchange, which starts civilly enough, might turn out later. Until they reach the temple, these barbs keep flying back and forth.

That day, every whore will have a thorny date-palm switch in her hand for protection.

Because when they're messing with colours, and after all they being Shivapura boys who can't understand human language until the poison in their waists subsides, we can't say what might or might not happen. On this day, whatever one does, nobody, not even God himself, can question. For the old whores, this is a nice chance—for they can take revenge on punters who betrayed them. They push into the crowd and beat those men up with their date-palm switches until the men bleed. The punters fight back if they have the guts. If not, they hide behind the boys and run away. This is all a matter of love and pride, arrogance and repartee. The more they are beaten up, the more they take pride in it—I mean, some men do.

When they come to the temple katte, the two singing groups stand facing each other. In the middle the tabor players, and around them the half-naked and open-mouthed male mob—all of them gather. On the katte in the square, Gowda sits and around him sit the privileged ones (the Panchas and the accountant). The moment the Gowda gives them permission, the leaders of the two groups salute him and start singing their taunting verses. This is accompanied by the cheering of the connoisseurs and, at the end of each song, by the howling of the boys. This goes on for a couple of hours, or if it gets more colourful, for yet another couple of hours. At the end, Gowda gives the gift of a rupee each to the two groups, thus indicating his pleasure. The Panchas do the same. With this, the Elders' part in the revels is over. Now it is all young people's fun. Smearing colour on the whores' bodies and getting beaten by their date-palm switches, they keep playing.

This is a custom that has gone on for generations.

But this time, it was different. Except the Gowda, everybody was there. The privileged ones sat on the temple katte waiting for Gowda. The singers were trying out verses they were planning to sing later, discussing the new details to be added, imagining the effect their songs would have on the crowd. In short, they were enjoying themselves hugely. Nayalya, the Dog Man, had warmed the tabor and tuned it nicely. This year, the presence of Durgi in the batch of whores was a special attraction. Some kept saying roguish things, drawing Durgi's attention to themselves and then feeling elated for having done so. The ones without wit laughed loudly, hoping to attract her attention with this noise.

Because of the delay, a couple of infants began to howl and were scolded by their disgusted elders. 'Chi, thoo. Shut up.'

They grew quiet.

By then Gudsikara strode in. Thief Sidrama came along, shoving people to make way. Gudsikara, and behind him the members. Everyone settled down again after they realized who had arrived. Walking past the Thief, Gudsikara went straight to the katte. The katte was already full with the privileged set. A cushion had been placed on the carpet for the Gowda. There was place only for one or two people there. Gudsikara climbed on the katte, walked past the Elders and sat down in the Gowda's place.

For a moment, all those sitting and standing were stunned—they just kept staring at him. Slowly, they began to whisper. They hadn't expected this. The Elders anxiously wrung their hands. Nayalya stopped tuning the tabor and gaped at the sarpanch sitting in Gowda's place, his feet up. The merriment on Dattappa's face disappeared.

The sarpanch felt everybody's eyes piercing him and realized he was the subject of the whispers. But he sat there as if he hadn't noticed anything. He couldn't go on like this. He asked Ningu, who stood by the katte, 'Have you brought your pouch of betel leaves and arecanuts?' Although he tried to ask this naturally, his voice was loud enough for everybody to hear, like that of scared boys who speak in high voices. He wished somebody would reply. He mustn't sit there, mustn't get up. If he sat on, he must bear the staring. It would be insulting to get up now. He desperately hoped that Ningu would say something. But unable to say a word, Ningu just grinned and looked at the crowd.

Dattappa's anxiety was evident. But he couldn't say anything either. Gowda will come any moment. Where will he sit? The dissatisfaction of the people, sitting and standing around them, was now obvious. The members looked like they were guilty of some untold crime but didn't want to show it. So they began to pretend as if they were searching for something in the pockets of their torn shirts or had remembered just then something they'd forgotten earlier.

Finally, Thief Sidrama, realizing that he wasn't acting well, asked Balu, 'Yeh, Balu, have you brought the bag of betel leaves and arecanuts?' Hoping that Balu would at least say no. Balu, chewing the betel leaves and nuts, held the bag out in his left hand and, pressing his lips with the right, spat loudly for everybody to hear. Then he gestured a 'no' with that same hand. The Thief scowled and looked about him as if Balu had spat right on him in front of everyone.

Lagumavva could not bear the silence. Asking, 'Are there no men here?' she stood up as if to say something. Meanwhile, the chairman, acting like he was an Elder and everybody was only waiting for his permission, ordered: 'Yes, Lagumavva, now start.'

Ningu gathered some courage and said, 'This is the place where Gowda sits—it's time for him to arrive. Will you get up?'

Even as he was saying this, 'Sure, let him come. We'll make some place for him here. Why are you so worried about it?'—Gudsikara asked, feigning a nonchalance he did not feel, and added, 'Yes, Lagumavva, now start.'

Lagumavva only turned her back to him and sat still.

Ramesa, one of the members, broke the gravity of the atmosphere. 'Start, Lagumavva,' he said, in a desperate attempt to save the chairman's face, 'Don't you value the village chairman's words? Yeh, Nayalya, start playing the tabor.' Nayalya, not knowing what else to do, was about to stand up when Lagumavva said, 'We're in no hurry. Let the Gowda come, we'll begin at leisure.'

At these words, Nayalya sat back. The sarpanch's face shrank with shame. He had not expected this rudeness. And he fretted and fumed because he didn't know how to counter it. The vexation on his face was as obvious as his nose. He felt all the eyes boring into him. He saw himself in their minds—as someone fallen into, and struggling in, slush. Unable to face them, he put his hands into his pocket, took out a cigarette and started puffing away. Had the circumstances been different, the people would have enjoyed it all—the cigarette, the smoke and the smell.

What was surprising was Dattappa's silence. Whether it was because he thought that whatever reaction he wished to show was already being shown by the people, or because he'd decided, 'Let the Gowda return and then we'll take care of it'—he remained silent. A young boy howled loudly. Immediately, everybody else began to howl. Gudsikara knew that all this was about him. Meanwhile, someone sitting at the back announced, 'Gowda came, Gowda came.' Everybody turned in that direction. The Gowda was approaching in a hurry. Nobody felt that today's singing would go smoothly. Some even imagined that there would be a fight between the Gowda and the sarpanch. There was a keen look of curiosity in everyone's eyes.

People stood up and made way for the Gowda. Some saluted him. Gowda proceeded, saluting back. Then he saw the sarpanch leaning on the cushion meant for him, sitting and smoking in the place meant for him and not deigning to look at him. He looked at Dattappa's face as the latter stood up. He grasped the situation instantly. Naming someone or other, and asking them to 'sit,' he went straight to the katte. He greeted the sarpanch. Then he made some space for himself beside Dattappa and sitting down, said, 'Well, Lagumavva, let's see what verses you've composed this year—start!' As if nothing at all had happened.

Hearing the Gowda's words, Dattappa felt the burden on his head grow lighter. There was still some unrest in the crowd. Their talk was not audible, but by the tightness round their mouths and the movement of their hands, it was evident that they were about to raise some objection. Gowda said loudly, 'See Dattu, our Lagumavva always brings some new composition every year.' Then he looked at the Panchas and drew their attention to Durgi. Lagumavva introduced her, 'Ayya, this is Abai's daughter,' and instructed Durgi, standing respectfully, her head bent, to 'go and touch Gowda's feet.' Durgi became the object of everybody's gaze. A lovely little calf, happy and drunk with praise. Shy and joyful at the same time, she pulled the loose end of her saree, the serugu, over her head, and went to the Gowda. She touched his feet respectfully. She also touched the feet of the Elders beside him. In her embarrassment, she touched the feet of anyone at all before running back like a frightened heifer.

The singing began. Lagumavva stood up and started:

The Age of Kali has begun, righteousness
Hasn't survived a bit
In the Age of the Educated Ones, things of this world
Have turned totally sinful

With this, she also brought out the brazenness of the 'educated monkeys'. This was not a challenge posed to the opposite party. But people enjoyed it so much that even the old men joined in for the customary howling at the end of the song. Is it necessary to teach them who the song is all about? Gudsikara's face became almost obscene. It was evident from his flaming eyes that he was boiling with rage inside. If Gowda smiled and kept quiet, Dattappa laughed aloud. People whistled and laughed. Some laughed till their turbans leapt off. It wasn't possible even for the Gowda to control all these varieties of laughter.

All the Panchayat members looked withered. People's jeers became the hay that fed the fire inside Gudsikara. He got up suddenly, stepped off the katte, threw the cigarette he had lit just then to the ground, stamped on it, squashed it and then flew like an arrow away from the crowd.

The Panchayat members tailed him, one after the other, in single file.

# HE STRUCK A LITTLE BOY

Unaware of what he was doing, Gudsikara beat Balu's son when the the little boy tried to throw colour on him on the day of Holi. It happened thus:

After listening to Lagumavva's song, unable to sit there any more, Gudsikara came away, right? He went straight home. He entered and clambered upstairs. Then began to pace up and down. Lit a cigarette. Sat with a thud on the bed. Unable to sit, he stood up. Unable to stand, he walked up and down. Smoked the cigarette. Threw it away. Sat down again.

The Panchayat members tiptoed up the steps. Without opening their lips, they shrank into themselves and sat huddled on the carpet, like statues. Gudsikara kept pacing up and down for a long time as if he hadn't noticed them. When he sat down to light a cigarette, he suddenly remembered Durgi who had also touched his feet. He took out two five-rupee notes from his pocket, gave them to Thief Sidrama and ordered, 'Go, give it to Durgi. Tell her the chairman gave it to her.' Thief ran up to Gudsikara, took the ten rupees and left.

He had hardly gone about ten steps when Andurama alias Rumps Ramesa got up. 'As it is, he is a thief. I will go and see if he gives her the money or not.'

Jiggly Satira got up next. 'As it is, he is a drunk. I'll go see what he does.'

Lastly, Ayimere Minda, without saying anything, because he couldn't think of anything to say, got up and slipped away.

Gudsikara didn't really need them. He was struggling to think of how to take revenge. He thought: If only I was a sorcerer and knew how to scorch the tongues of all those who howled! If only I'd had the authority to send Gowda and Dattappa and Lagumi to jail! Suddenly, something flashed across his mind, 'Arre . . . re, if I had given the money to Durgi in the middle of the crowd, my ten rupees would have outshone the paltry four annas and eight annas those people usually give. Lagumavva, Gowda, Dattu and all the beggars who howled would have known my value.'

But it was too late now.

Meanwhile, sister Girijavva called him for his meal.

It was late in the day. Children were throwing colour at one another in the alley, laughing and shouting. This woke Gudsikara who had fallen asleep after eating. The noise drew nearer and nearer until he realized the commotion was right in front of his house. He strode downstairs.

Girijavva was standing at the door watching the children play and laughing loudly. 'Don't you have any shame? Standing and watching boys? Get inside,' he scolded her, and then stood in her place. The boys chased one another, throwing colour. When they caught one running away, they would howl and smear colour on him. One boy, Balu's little son—he saw Gudsikara. 'Look, we found the sarpanch,' he shouted, then howled and threw colour on him. The others threw colour too. Gudsikara was burning with rage. Without thinking for a moment , he ran out, caught the little boy and began to beat him senseless. He didn't let go even when the boy began to scream. If the boy ran and tried to hide behind the others, Gudsikara would chase him, catch him and beat him. When his hands tired of beating, he started kicking. When his feet tired of kicking, he beat the boy with his hands again. 'I'm dead!' the boy shrieked. The other boys, alarmed and unable to free him, unable to run or shout, tried to hide behind one another. At a distance, a group of women who had come out of their houses, not having the courage to free the boy, now began to wail.

Luckily, Ningu came along and freed the boy.

'You are beating a little boy, Appa? Where's your sense?'

Perhaps realizing that he had made a mistake, Gudsikara silently went into his house. But Ningu wouldn't keep quiet. 'Look in the mirror, Appa,' he said.

True, in his anger, Gudsikara looked awful with his hair dishevelled.

At Ningu's words, he stopped: 'Yeh, what?'

'Why don't you raise your hand against me like you did to the boy? I'll show you then!' This was enough for Gudsikara. He wanted to do something and had ended up doing something else. He had taken out his anger on someone else. Ningu had understood this. As had Gudasikara himself. Feeling petty, he walked in without replying.

When he saw the stripes on the boy's back, Balu began to rage. Dattappa was actually perspiring by the time he calmed Balu down and talked some sense into him.

After hearing everything, when Gowda said, 'This man is digging his own grave,' Balu retorted in anger, 'No, he is digging the grave of the village.'

# THE QUARTET

The incident of the ten-rupee note resulted in the decision to open a liquor shop.

Gudsikara's followers, that is, the other Panchayat members—Thief Sidrama, Rumps Ramayya, Jiggly Satira and Ayimere Minda, all Gudsikara's peers—had studied together. Then Gudsikara went to Belagavi for higher education. The rest of them didn't. That's it. Once Dattappa nicknamed them the 'Evil Quartet'. Perhaps he was reminded of the Evil Quartet of the Mahabharata. Even now he calls them so. We too shall call them so in our story.

However, there is absolutely no connection between that Evil Quartet and these people. First, they are not evil. Then they aren't very different from the rest of the village. They're a bit conceited about having a little education. Why shouldn't they be? Unless somebody pushes them, they will not step forth. When they do step forth, they are not the kind to worry about consequences. Whether it's a pit or a mound, they close their eyes and walk on. Although they were collectively called the Evil Quartet, we cannot deny that each of them has his own distinct personality.

Among them, Thief Sidrama is a hulk. Once in his childhood, he was caught stealing and thereafter was stuck with Thief before his name. But that is not his distinction. He is an actor from top to toe. He can narrate any incident so colourfully and dramatically that the whole thing will seem like it happened in front of your eyes. Once Gudsikara read the newspaper and told him, 'Look Thief, it seems Jinnah came and met Gandhiji. He asked for a separate country for the Muslims—he wants Pakistan.' This news, which was only about ten words long, was re-narrated by the Thief to Ayimere Minda in the following manner:

'Do you know what things are happening in this country? The day before yesterday, Tuesday, it seems Gandhi was sitting in his hut eating peanuts. Meanwhile, Jinnah came. He saluted Gandhi.

'Gandhi said, "Come, Jinnah-saab, come and sit here. Is everybody fine? How are the rains? How're the crops doing?"

' "Everything's fine! But our boys are making a lot of trouble. Although you live together for a hundred years, you can't stop brothers from going their separate ways at some point. So they want a share of the country."

' "Your father's—! What happiness will you get out of this partition? If we are together, our neighbours and others will fear us, no? Even the tiger makes way for brothers who are together. But if we go separate ways, even a mouse, just a mouse, will not fear us. The neighbours will gobble you up and wash you down with water. Beware, tell them not to ask for a share! If you can't do that, bring them here—we will advise them properly."'

It seems Gandhiji said all this! Do we need a more revealing instance than this to call Thief Sidrama a terrific actor?

During open-air folk performances like the Bayalata, he loved playing the villain, that too the demon. He had heard that, in earlier times, when men who played these roles had come up on stage and roared, pregnant women had miscarried. His wish was to have the same effect, to see at least some pregnant woman miscarry at the sight of him. So whenever he was alone, he practised that famous roar. May Karimayi, who blesses us with infants wearing anklets on their feet, never fulfil his wish!

The second was Rumps Ramayya, alias Ramesa. His original name is Ramayya. Because his rumps were oversized, the Rumps got stuck to his name. Like Gudsyagola became Gudsikara after becoming the panchayat chairman, so too panchayat member Rumps Ramayya became Ramesa. He would sign off as Ramesa. Gudsikara was feared by the people. But even after this one changed his name, people continued calling him Rumps Ramayya.

He didn't know English. Still, very often, he would say 'Yes-yes.' He was even prepared to change his opinions, just for the opportunity to say, 'Yes-yes.'

The third one is Ayimere Minda. This was his distinction: his left eye was smaller and kept tearing from time to time, so he looked as if he was crying with one eye and laughing with the other.

The last one is Jiggly Satira. Whenever his mother walked, her boobs jiggled up and down. So people called her Jiggly. The son inherited the name, and came to be known as Jiggly Satira. Among the four, only he had the fame of being a lech. It happened thus:

He would prowl about and discover the clandestine affairs of the young. Whcn hc caught them in the act, he would take the girl aside and threaten to tell her parents. And he would get the benefits from the girl, with interest.

What's common to all these people is that, like everybody else in the village, none of them is well off. If they ever saw some money, they grew excited with dreams of Belagavi. That's why they went fully crazy when Gudsikara handed over those ten rupees.

Thief Sidrama had hardly gone ten steps after taking the ten rupees. Rumps Ramayya, alias Ramesa, came and joined him. He suggested that they give five rupees to Durgi and spend the other five on drink. the Thief threatened, 'You say this? Wait I'll tell the sarpanch.' Ramesa subsided with a 'Yes-yes.'

Then Jiggly Satira came along. 'Neither of you is trustworthy! One's a thief. And the other a drunk. Give it to me—I'll give it to Durgi.' Were the others 'idiots born in the seventh month' to listen to all this?

'I'll give it to her,' said the Thief. 'Yes-yes, I'll be witness,' said Ramesa.

By this time, Aayi Mereminda had also arrived. 'Yeh, looks like the sarpanch doesn't trust you. He asked me to take it from you and give it to Durgi. Thief, give it to me.'

'Oh, here comes the trustworthy man! Look, if he had such trust in you, why would he put the money in my hands and not yours? Bugger off.'

Nobody wanted to leave Thief Sidrama alone. They were sure he would never give all the money to Durgi. Because don't they know his true nature? They were plotting to get a drink with the bit of money that the Thief was going to keep for himself. Whatever happens, the sarpanch won't go to Durgi and check how much she actually got. Even if he did, they could always say she was lying, or that she'd forgotten how much they gave her. Can't they, who farted so much, also tell a lie?

But the Thief's logic was different. His plan was to fend off these foxes, go to Durgi alone, give her five rupees and with the other five go to Belagavi and have some fun. But there were no signs of them leaving. They, who used to call him 'Thief' every day, lovingly called him 'Sidrama' now. They heaped on him sterling qualities that he didn't possess. Remembering many events of the past, when Thief Sidrama had actually played the fool, they added colour to them and now made him out to be the hero instead. Jiggly Satira assured him that he would take him to Belagavi and spend his own money to show him a film. He described the twin braids of the Belagavi girls and the ribbons at the ends of those braids. Although, in truth, he hadn't seen Belagavi even once.

But the Thief remained as inflexible as an impossible knot. He has the money, though. The three were planning to include themselves in the spending of it. These are people who see each other's face when they get up every morning. Don't they know every line on the other's face? Nobody believed a word of what they said. The Thief was in fact a thief—why would he believe them?

To escape, he said, 'Let's go, let's go. I have to give this to Durgi,' and started walking away with long strides. They followed him.

In the end, they came up to Sidrama's house. But wasn't Thief Sidrama an actor? Acting as if he'd changed his mind, he said, 'God, I'm so hungry. I'll eat first and then give the money to Durgi' and went into the house.

Rumps Ramayya got angry. 'Yeh Thief,' he shouted, 'will you give the money to Durgi right now or shall I go tell the sarpanch?'

'Go tell him,' the Thief shouted back, convinced that Rumps Ramesa wouldn't. Ningu, who was passing by, heard Ramesa's words, but walked on. All three sat in protest in front of Sidrama's house. Sidrama didn't come out. These people didn't get up either.

'Yeh, you go, eat quickly,' suggested Aayi Mereminda 'and come back. Then you sit here, and I'll go. Let's see what this fellow is going to do.'

The other two thought it a fine idea. Saying that they'd eat and be back in five minutes, they left.

The moment they disappeared, Aayi Mereminda rushed into Sidrama's house. He sat in front of Sidrama, who really was eating. 'Yeh,' he said, 'both of them have gone home. Come, let the two of us go and give it to Durgi.'

But Sidrama didn't budge. Who gives away a fortune in their hands? Meanwhile, Thief Sidrama's mother came in and asked, 'What is it?'

'I'll wait outside,' said Aayi Mereminda to the Thief , 'You come.'

After a while, Rumps Ramesa and Jiggly Satira came back. 'Now you go and eat,' they told Aayi Mereminda. But he sat there, saying he wasn't hungry. So they sat there too. Even though the rest of the village was busy throwing colour and celebrating. Thief Sidrama refused to come out. These people refused to get up. They sat on until it felt as though their bums were glued to their seats.

Even at the late hour when Ningu returned after admonishing Gudsikara, the trinity was sitting there. Ningu went straight into the house. The Thief was sleeping on the porch. Ningu yanked the blanket off his head, shook him and shouted. He didn't get up. You can wake up a man who is sleeping. How can you wake up someone only pretending to sleep? But Ningu was clever. He asked, 'Why Gudsikara? Why did you come here?' Immediately, Thief Sidrama shot up. When he got up and saw Ningu clapping his hands and laughing, he realized the prank that had been played on him. He laughed too. Seeming to know what was going on, Ningu asked, 'How much money did the sarpanch give you for Durgi?'

The Thief was alarmed. 'Who told you?'

'I know everything. Tell me.'

Thief Sidrama and Ningu were 'intimate' buddies. Of late, after Ningu wore the saree, their friendship had deepened. Therefore, although the Thief lied a hundred per cent to people in the village, he would be at least three per cent truthful with Ningu. At some vulnerable moments, the Thief had promised to give a few things to Ningu. Ningu didn't believe him. Still, when they saw each other, the way their hearts beat together was simply beyond words.

Thief Sidrama now told Ningu the story of the money. But instead of ten rupees, he said five. Ningu knew how to draw the truth out of him. Soon, he made the Thief confess to the five rupees. When Ningu didn't believe him even then, the Thief pulled out the two fivers, showed them to him and then pushed them back into his pocket immediately.

Ningu's mouth began to water.

'Yeh Thief, buy me a brassiere,' he begged, moving closer to the Thief in his usual familiar way.

The Thief got scared. 'Yeh, take off your hand,' he said and tried to push Ningu away. Ningu moved away but threatened, 'If you get me the bra, that's fine. If not, I'll tell Gudsikara. I'll also tell Durgi.'

The Thief had to give in now.

So the Thief asked what a 'bra' was. The matter of getting a bra was not something new to Ningu. Earlier, Rumps Ramesa had described this item for a good half hour and said that Belagavi girls were really into this fashion. 'You too should be like that, Ningu,' he'd advised. Ningu had given a rupee to Rumps Ramesa when he went to Belagavi, and asked him to 'get that'. But instead of getting a bra, Ramesa got a picture of it, printed on a bit of paper. Ningu had folded it up seven or eight times and stuck it into his bosom. Now when Thief Sidrama asked him what a bra was, Ningu promptly took out the picture.

The Thief couldn't stop laughing.

Ningu felt insulted.

'Why, you don't like me wearing this?' he asked. Thief Sidrama swore on Karimayi that he would get the bra and then sent Ningu away. He was now certain that it wasn't in his luck to claim the money alone. He got up, put on his shirt and came out. The trinity was waiting. He went over and joined them.

While the rest of the village was throwing colour and having fun, this quartet sat on the bank of the lake, their arms round their knees. Conducting a 'meeting' on how best to spend the ten rupees. Because of the morning's incident, the sarpanch wasn't participating in the festivities. The members weren't either, because of the ten-rupee business. They were afraid that if they participated, the Thief would escape.

So they sat there until sunset. The first decision was to spend five rupees on drink and give the other five to Durgi. But how do you give it to Durgi? If Lagumavva comes to know, she's not the kind of a woman who'll let them live. There was a 'sub-decision' that the money should be given to Durgi when Lagumavva was out. There was also a second main-decision—that Thief Sidrama should hand over the money to Durgi but only in the presence of the other three. And they all agreed that the Thief should be given an opportunity to say a couple of words extra to Durgi.

Although Jiggly Satira agreed to this, a thought was burrowing into his head like a worm. Five rupees is not a small matter. Okay, we are giving the money. If we give, there's no doubt that Durgi will agree to anything. Why shouldn't we put her acceptance to proper use? So 'Look,' he said, 'if it's true that we are giving the money, why should we give it in Lagumavva's house? How about taking Durgi to the back of Karimayi's temple and the four of us giving it to her there?'

The sour smell of Jiggly Satira's words hit everybody's nose, the thrill made the hair on their arms stand up and they agreed unanimously. But Rumps Ramesa made a small amendment. Instead of Thief Sidrama alone giving the five rupees, they could change the note. And while the three of them gave a rupee each to Durgi, the Thief could give her two. After another amendment—that the Thief should, if possible, grab Durgi first—they got up.

Night had fallen. People still sat here and there on the katte, laughing and talking about the fun they had all day. Some talked about Gudsikara beating Balu's son. The quartet got the two five-rupee notes changed into ten one-rupee notes at Basetti's shop. Thief Sidrama put all the ten in his pocket. Then they strode towards Lagumavva's house.

Ningu was already at Lagumavva's house-cum-bar, waiting for them. He was the one to welcome them: 'Why are you so late? Come, come.' The Thief felt guilty, though he went in without showing it. All four sat on the bamboo mat, their eyes restlessly searching for Durgi.

Lagumavva asked 'What?'

'Give us four gourds of arrack,' the Thief answered bravely.

'Give the money first.'

'Are we going to run away?'

'Sarpanch has given you money. Spit it out,' Ningu intervened.

The Thief grew more alarmed, the others positively frightened. He gave five rupees to serve four people and got five gourds in all. They gave one to Ningu, who sat right next to the Thief and began to drink. Jiggly Satira pulled out a cigarette packet from his pocket, lit a stub and offered another to the Thief. Usually, Jiggly Satira collected all the stubs after Gudsikara smoked his cigarettes. By then Durgi arrived. Everybody grew animated. Even Rumps Ramesa and Aayi Mereminda begged Jiggly Satira for a stub, got one each and then lit up.

As the gourds began to empty, they began to lose control over their heads and tongues. Meanwhile, the Thief had gone up to Durgi under all kinds of pretexts and shown her the money. Jiggly Satira motioned to the Thief to give him the money, so that he could go and show it to her too. Thief Sidrama gestured back his refusal. A couple of customers sat outside. Durgi, who was moving in and out of the house, looked different to each of them.

When the gourds were completely empty, there was some talk in hushed tones about what to do next. The three suggested that Thief Sidrama ask Durgi to come to the back of the temple. Of course, the Thief thought this a good idea. But he was afraid to be so bold. Besides, they had also given Ningu a drink. So he shifted the responsibility onto Ningu's shoulders.

Ningu asked them all to wait at the back entrance of the temple and promised to send Durgi there.

They all got up.

Although the moonlight was thick outside, it was dark in the yard because of the surrounding trees. Durgi will be here now. She will be here soon. That thought led to a tightness in their thighs and a warmth in their bodies. Rumps Ramesa ran out to piss four or five times. The Thief hadn't given the one-rupee notes to the others yet. He was delaying the handover, telling them that he'd do so as soon as Durgi arrived.

Durgi arrived.

The Thief quickly gave them the one-rupee notes. He held one out, just like them, and put the last one in his pocket. The moment she came close, he said, 'Take it, Durgi,' and stretched out his hand. The thought of what he was going to do next made his mouth go dry. Rumps Ramesa came up too and told Durgi, 'That isn't what Gudsikara gave—it's mine,' and leered. His teeth shone even in the dark. Jiggly Satira and Aayi Mereminda also stretched out their hands. Durgi took all the money and stood still. Nobody had the courage to make a move. Then she turned back silently. Fearing that she would leave, Jiggly Satira pounced on her from the back and held her. Immediately, Thief Sidrama and Rumps Ramesa jumped up too, keen to satisfy their special appetites.

Suddenly they heard Lagumavva's voice. 'Thoo, randy pimps! When Gudsya gave ten rupees and asked you to give them to Durgi, you drank all that and pissed, didn't you?'

Saying this, she spat. Ningu clapped and laughed and ran to Lagumavva. The four now knew that the one who had come to them was not Durgi, but Ningu. When Lagumavva rushed towards them saying, 'Wait I will tell Gudsya,' they ran for their lives.

In all, Ningu got four rupees. He gave three to Lagumavva and kept one for himself. Later, when he saw Durgi, God knows what he felt—after all, he had a woman's heart—he gave his rupee to her without Lagumavva's knowledge. She hid it inside her bosom.

When the quartet came running to the panchayat office, Gudsikara was sitting there alone, drinking. All the four sat down, huddled like wet crows. Nobody spoke. Since Gudsikara didn't speak either, the Thief began to suspect that Ningu had told him everything. Jiggly Satira was lost in smoking a stub that Gudsikara had thrown away.

After a long while, Gudsikara spoke. 'Thief, did you give the money to Durgi?'

'I gave it. But Lagumavva's arrogance has crossed all limits,' he answered, trying to cover up his elaborate plot.

'Che che, a very cheap woman!' Aayi Mereminda interrupted, 'What did I say that I shouldn't have said? When I said that it was wrong to make such verses about the sarpanch, she reacted like she was possessed by the devil and started gesturing and talking badly!'

This was enough for Rumps Ramesa. 'Yes-yes. Poor fellow! When Sidrama gave the money, saying that the sarpanch gave it, she started shouting, "Isn't it only five rupees? I know your sarpanch's level."'

Jiggly Satira became aware that he hadn't spoken. 'She said, "Gowda gave twenty. Your sarpanch only gave five, right?"'

Afraid that Gudsikara would go off and fight with Lagumavva, the Thief added: 'You know what she said? "Let your sarpanch come to me—I'll teach him a nice lesson."'

They all talked without a break, as if they would rather be doomed than let Gudsikara open his mouth. In the end, believing everything they told him, he asked, 'Yeh, when I asked you to give it to Durgi—why did you give it to Lagumi?'

Thief Sidrama came up with another lie. 'We went to give it to her. When we tried to call her and give it, the old devil came and stretched out her hand for it.'

They still weren't certain if Gudsikara believed them. So they abused Lagumavva roundly again. Then they brought up the names of Gowda and Dattappa. The others kept praising the Thief's civil behaviour from time to time. The Thief praised them in turn. Whether it was the effect of the native stuff they had drunk, or the fear that the sarpanch hadn't believed them yet, or perhaps the apprehension of his coming to know of the matter later—whatever the reason, they talked on and on. Finally, they stopped.

And Gudsikara said, 'We should bring Lagumavva's level down . . . '

Suddenly, all four relaxed. Now they were certain that Gudsikara believed them. One said they should beat her up. Another suggested kidnapping Durgi. A third thought of stealing her arrack. Even as more suggestions were pouring in, Gudsikara cut them short: 'How about we too open a liquor shop?'

'Oh, yes. I'll sit in the shop if you want,' said Aayi Mereminda.

Rumps Ramesa was so thrilled, the hair on his arms stood up.

'Yes-yes, if Lagumi sells home-brewed arrack, we'll sell foreign brandy, what?'

But Jiggly Satira wasn't convinced.

'Who will have a gulp of brandy here? Tell me about something more accessible.'

The moment he said this, Thief Sidrama came up with the answer, 'Why do you worry? We'll mix water with brandy and sell it.'

'Yes-yes, even if we sell water calling it foreign brandy people will buy it. We can easily earn five or six hundred rupees from one bottle,' said Rumps Ramesa, eager to show off his business acumen.

The Thief looked at Gudsikara and asked expectantly, 'Who did you say should sit in the shop?' Gudsikara replied, slowly smoking his cigarette, 'Let's bring a tart, a chimana, from Belagavi. We can put her in the shop.'

The moment Gudsikara mentioned Belagavi, Rumps Ramesa got so excited that he stood up. 'Sahebara, sahebara, anyway they'll bring a chimana on Kara Full Moon Day, won't they? We can start then.'

The heaviness in Gudsikara's head increased. 'Why will they get the chimana?'

'They have fun and games that day, right?'

Gudsikara smoked on. And letting the foreign god seep into his native mortal body, he slowly poured himself another drink and finished the bottle. Now everything was nicely falling into place, he was able to gather all the stray thoughts flying hither and thither. He wiped his mouth. The quartet kept watching his face. He nodded, as if approving of his own thoughts. Then, opening his tight lips, he said, 'Let them have their play. We'll put up a play too. Let the chimana come to us. They'll have the play in the open. We'll have an indoor theatre with lights and a loudspeaker. After the play, let the chimana stay with us. Not a liquor shop—we'll start a tea shop. What do you say?'

He felt that this plan would help in paying back, with interest, and compound interest, all the defeats and insults he had suffered! If instead of going to the Bayalata performance the people came to their play, wouldn't it break the Gowda's horn of pride? By getting the chimana here and opening the tea shop, I'm breaking Lagumi's pride too, right? Besides, won't this be the first step in making the village another Belagavi?

He went home with his head full these thoughts, feeling thrilled and proud.

While he was eating, his mother kept talking: 'Yeh brother, we have to find a bridegroom for Girijavva. She has grown up. All the girls her age are now married, some even have children. If the elder of this house was here, he would have done something. It seems there's a suitable boy in Gokak . . . ' and so on.

There was no room in his head at that moment for any thoughts of his sister's marriage. He murmured a 'yes' to whatever his mother said and then went upstairs to sleep.

# DURGI'S DREAM

If thoughts of Kara Full Moon, alongside those of the tea shop, were eating away at Gudsikara's mind like a worm, the thought of the one-rupee note he'd given her was piercing Durgi's tender young heart.

Of the ten Gudsikara had given, she, at last, had got one rupee and that too thanks to Ningu's pity. When she secured it in her bosom, rather than the burden of her youthful desires, it was the weight of the note that oppressed her heart. Mad girl. She walked in and out without any reason like a puffed-up young calf. Like a butterfly that has just sprouted wings flits here and there—leaf to leaf—flower to flower—flying up and down—she glided, her feet not touching the ground. In the dark, hiding from Lagumavva's eyes, she put her hand to her bosom again and again and touched the note. God! Her body grew hot, the poison rose from foot to head, her thighs sweated and the blouse on her bosom felt tighter. She was in the grip of such a thrilling sensation.

When Lagumavva called her to dinner, she just pretended to eat and then went to bed. As if to loosen every nerve that had become taut, she stretched her body, filled the bed with her long arms and legs and yawned. A young thing who doesn't know how to swim, washed away in the flood of a hot stream, caught in the eddying swirl of its waters, she struggled. Then she turned on her stomach and thrust her bosom into the pillow four or five times to lighten that pressing feeling in her chest. Finally, she felt better and fell asleep. And in her sleep, she had a dream:

The magic of moonlight spread. The whole village went to sleep with dazed eyes, but she alone was awake. Laughing, she left her footprints on the sand, and her anklets jingled on the rocks on the river bank. Gudsikara came, lifted her up and flung her like a doll into the sky—

Oh, when she thinks she is falling, there's the grass rick below—

With a thud, she falls face up, her bosom swells and her blouse is torn

*Khok, khok, khok* . . . like the Bayalata's villain, Ravana—laughing and smoking a cigarette

When the white smoke mingles with the rick, it thickens a hundredfold

The rick is full of smoke

It fills the village

Someone is treading on her with sibilant noises

And playing with a ball—Mother, I'm dead!

Screaming thus . . .

—she got up. Clutched at her heart and sat up. Wiped the sweat on her cheeks, neck, forehead and nose. Drank some water. And heard the god himself sobbing in the next hut.

# Q&A MASTER

Gowda, like every other day, got up, had his bath in the river and came back home. In the yard, Nayalya was getting the farming tools ready for work and yoking the bullocks. Gowda was telling him that since the ground in the lower field was still hard, he must loosen the earth first before making the furrows. Q&A Master, who had just then got up and was going out, saw the Gowda, folded his hands, water pot still in hand, and asked, 'You already up, Gowda?' Gowda heard him and saluted back. Meanwhile, they saw Gudsikara walking towards them from the lake. Although he had seen Gudsikara, Q&A Master acted as if he hadn't. And to avoid him, instead of taking the open street, he disappeared into an alley. Gudsikara too went back home as if he hadn't noticed anything amiss.

Ever since the Kannada Boys School started in the village, Q&A Master had been the only teacher. He was old. He came to this village many years ago, left his family in his own village. Here, he lived in an old house. He did one session of classes on Saturday and left, reappearing only on Tuesday. The boys would sing about him on the sly: 'The one who comes only three days a week and leaves.' Since Monday was the day of the village fair, without taking any permission from the government, he had declared it a holiday. Although it was many days since he had come to the village, he hadn't put down roots here at all. Always one foot here and the other in his village. He kept to himself and his school. Now he was about to retire. Deciding he should stay nice, like sweet jaggery, with everybody in this place, he never poked his nose into village affairs. Wasn't he an outsider, after all? He never found out the truth about anyone in the village until the end. He didn't try to either. Therefore, whomever he met, he greeted them with an obsequious salute. Anxious for them to be certain of his politeness, he would smile, address them again and again with respect and ask after their well-being. Then, perhaps feeling that his concern may appear like a preamble to a loan or something, or perhaps unwilling to trouble them with answering his questions, he would answer them himself. Let's say he met a good man of the village. Immediately, he'd ask, 'How're you? Are you well?' And then answer himself, 'Yes, you should be fine. A look at your face shows that.'

'Are the crops doing fine?'—'Indeed, why shouldn't they be fine? It has rained like crazy.'

Many times, he would go on with this question-and-answer routine even with people who had no land, no crops. Moreover, his thinking processes were unclear. In order to get some clarity, he talked to himself as he thought. Will people, who gossip without any reason, stay quiet when they have so much to talk about in the Master? It was thus that the Master became the Q&A Master.

That morning, without seeming to notice, Gudsikara had observed the Q&A Master salute Gowda. That night, Q&A Master was summoned to the panchayat office. Has some inspector come? Who knows? Has some government order arrived? Who knows? He kept the question-and-answer sequence running through his mind all the way to the office.

Gudsikara, and at a distance the quartet, sat drinking and conducting 'a meeting'. After all, come to think of it, it was the Master who had taught a few things to these people at one time. Thief Sidrama still hadn't forgotten the text, the 'Beggar's Dream'. So the quartet felt a little embarrassed at conducting their 'meeting' in front of him. But they didn't want to anger Gudsikara, so they just carried on.

By then one or two gulps of foreign bhirandi was inside each of them. After all, weren't they members of the panchayat now? Those who opposed the Gowda himself? Why should they take the Master into account? In fact, according to Lagumavva's song, the Age of Kali had stepped into the village through these very people.

By the time Q&A Master came in, he had shrunk into a little ball. 'I salute you, Sarpanch-sahebara,' he said. Gudsikara didn't bother to look up. Nor did the others ask him to come in. Before Q&A Master arrived, Gudsikara had briefed the others about what had happened that morning. When he saw them sitting quietly, Q&A Master felt his legs grow weak. And restless. It became evident from his gestures that he was questioning and answering by himself. Perhaps they hadn't summoned him? Thinking that somebody had played a prank, he asked, 'Then shall I leave?' He gave himself permission to do so and got up to go.

Thief Sidrama's reverence for the man finally broke through. 'Sit, Master.'

Q&A Master flopped down. Everybody was busy looking at their cards.

Rumps Ramesa asked, 'What, master? What's this great familiarity you have with the Gowda?'

'My familiarity? There's none!'

'If there's none, why were you saluting him early in the morning?'

'Saluting? Yes, when you get up in the morning, is it wrong to ask someone if they are up too? No, not wrong.'

When Q&A Master denied having done something wrong, it roused Jiggly Satira's old thirst for revenge. Because in his childhood, whatever he'd written and showed to the Q&A Master, the latter had always said that it was wrong.

'What do you mean it's not wrong? Instead of teaching boys well at school, do you go asking everybody who gets up in the morning, "Did you get up?" and "Did you get up?" If you ask any boy what's six times seventeen, nobody knows the answer. Is this the way you teach at school? You are here three days a week. Four days, you're in your village. Today, if Gudsikara-saheb writes about this to the higher officials, what will be your fate?'

Q&A Master was struggling as if a huge boulder had been dropped on his chest. He folded his hands and said, 'No, no.'

Even Jiggly Satira hadn't thought that his words would have such an effect on the Master. Aayi Mereminda was the dumbest of the lot. So his heart melted quickly. After all, wasn't he the Master who taught them to read and write? Why this roundabout way of questioning? You could ask him directly.

'Look, look, Master. From tomorrow, go to Gudsikara-saheb's house and ask him if he is up. If you meet any panchayat member, also ask him, "Are you up?" That Gowda and that Dattu—don't you talk to them from now on? Understand?'

Gudsikara didn't approve of such direct instructions. 'Not every morning. See, the school is under the panchayat authority. If we write about you to the higher-ups, then Gowda can't save you. Even Dattu can't save you. I didn't say all this to make you salute me, all right? Just understand this.'

Q&A Master began to behave like a madman. He would try to get up and say something. He would sit back not knowing what to say. There was no limit to the fluttering of his hands. Those who were looking at him could only see his hands and body move but not hear a word of what he was saying.

Aayi Mereminda felt bad at his plight. Even the Thief.

'Now go, Master.' He gave the permission on Gudsikara's behalf. At the very next instant, Q&A Master leapt out of the office and ran for his life. Once he got back home, he kept questioning and answering —'Are these disciples?' 'They're outcastes!' 'If they have a public meeting next, should I give the chair?' 'Impossible,' he said to himself. But how could he not? Finally he decided to break one of the legs of the chair and then consoled himself with that thought.

The moment Q&A Master left, Gudsikara began to laugh. The others laughed twice as hard. To tell the truth, they had goose pimples all over. Nobody had been so scared of them since they became panchayat members. Just think, Q&A Master, who had scared them so much in their childhood, how scared he'd been of them! Each bragged about what he said to the Master and laughed. Gudsikara gave a drop of bhirandi to each of them, poured the rest from the bottle for himself and emptied it. Joyful at the extra drop, they laughed again.

Meanwhile, Gowda's servant Nayalya arrived, smiling servilely.

## THE EPISODE OF NAYALYA, THE DOG MAN, THAT IS, ANGIYALYA, THE SHIRT MAN

Nayalya was a chap full of fun. He had many feats to his credit. He was the only one in the entire village to have twin names—Nayalya (Dog Man) and Angiyalya (Shirt Man). Only two men, Ningu and Nayalya, had become living legends in the village: 'Nayalya hasn't the luck of a shirt and Ningu hasn't the luck of a wife.' People use this proverb whenever they want to say that one needs luck for everything.

There's nobody like Nayalya for drinking.

His original name is Muniyalya. From his childhood, he's been a servant at the Gowda's house. He owns a hut, even land, one acre. It was three acres earlier. But afraid that, with his drinking, he'll lose even the remaining one acre, Gowda cultivates it himself. And employing Nayalya as a servant, he takes care of the basic needs of his family. No question of exploitation here.

Except for a couple of dogs that the nayaka boys had trained to hunt, Shivapura doesn't know of keeping dogs as pets. But there is no dearth of dogs on the streets. There are packs and packs of them in every alley. These dogs go and wag their tails in front of everybody's house. Good people throw them a bit or two of rotti. So they are known as 'charity dogs'. Their main occupation is to bark at night or whine. If one dog on one street barks for some reason, all the other dogs in the village join in. There's no rule that they should bark only for a reason. They were born to bark. The villagers know this. They often ask, 'Why do you bark like a dog?' Or about someone who talks too much, they say, 'Well, he's like the charity dog.'

Among these nameless dogs was a black dog. God knows whether it was because of some likeness in colour, or likeness in nature, or because of some cosmic connection, whatever, the dog felt a great sense of loyalty towards Muniyalya. He only had to see Muniyalya coming from a distance. He would jump up, run to Muniyalya, wag his tail and lick his feet. He would follow him back home, whining with delight. Once or twice, after his meal, Muniyalya had thrown a bone or two to the dog, right? With that he'd bound himself to the animal's life.

In any case, he believed that the dog had been his brother in an earlier birth. He said this to people when he was drunk. Sometimes even when he wasn't drunk. Nayalya felt proud whenever the dog wagged his tail at him. A kind of arrogance that went straight to his head made him talk to the dog in the same way in which the Gowda talked to him. He would call it 'Muniyalya'. 'Yes, son . . . right, son,' he'd say, mimicking the Gowda and showing his importance. God knows what he got out of it, but he seemed to truly enjoy it. If his wife wanted a share when he brought home arrack and meat, he would lose his temper. But he might give some to the dog—or not. In his view, loyalty should be unconditional like that of this dog. Therefore, from time to time, it became his practice to give the example of the dog to his wife Rangi.

One afternoon, Yalya was getting the sugarcane watered. Suddenly, there came a scream from the neighbouring woods. A shepherd was shouting for help: 'Ayyo, come, come, my sheep my sheep are being mangled.' Muniyalya immediately threw down his pickaxe and turned his feet in the direction. Six or seven people from the field next to Gowda's also joined him. When they got there, they saw that same dog pouncing on the sheep and tearing them to bits. Two sheep thrashed about on one side, half-dead, while the dog had pounced on another—as if he was a born hunter dog. If someone tried to hit him, he pounced back like a tiger. What a dog! Look at what he has become! Until then that dog had never hunted, never barked at thieves. Since he had a tail he wagged it, and since he had a mouth he barked—that's all! Until that day, he had never even shaken a fly off his tail. What does it mean if such a dog becomes such a bloodthirsty animal?

Thinking that there must be some secret behind it all, Muniyalya pounced on him like a dog and caught him. The dog kept rushing at people, his mouth hanging open. Eventually, everybody examined the dog. Muniyalya smelt his mouth—the smell of arrack hummed and hit him hard. He's Muniyalya's dog, right? He had drunk his fill from the liquor in the woods which Lagumavva brewed from old jaggery. When Muniyalya told them this, everybody burst out laughing. They said if this dog could become so crazy after drinking it, was it such a big thing that Muniyalaya too goes crazy when he drinks?

The rest of the village came to know of this and from then on, the dog was nicknamed Muniyalya and Muniyalya was called 'Nayalya'. Because he too was an expert at stealing arrack. The dog seemed to be perfectly happy with his new name. Whenever he heard someone shout 'Muniyalya, Muniyalya,' he would wag his tail.

Muniyalya, that is Nayalya, too was overjoyed. Because the shepherds gave him the thigh piece of the sheep mangled by the dog.

## HOW NAYALYA BECAME ANGIYALYA

For as long as he knew, Nayalya had always worn Gowda's old shirts. He had not had a new shirt made even once. Even if he was given money for it, he would spend it on drink. Gowda grew weary. A donkey, even a donkey, makes the one-anna-worth rope that he is tied with, snap. Is it right that Nayalya hasn't even worn and torn a new shirt? So Gowda had two shirts made to Nayalya's measurements.

Nayalya, in his new shirt, felt on the top of the world. He walked up and down the village for no reason. He asked after the welfare of everybody who passed by. How carefully he would take the shirt off when he worked! If the wife tried to touch him, how angry he grew about her grubby hands. When he wanted to sleep, how he shook the blanket and dusted it before spreading it on the floor! To add to his excitement, the Savalagi Fair came. He was the first to go and roam around. He compared his shirt with everybody else's shirt at the fair.

On the day after the fair, he came back to his hut. Wearing only his loincloth.

When Rangi asked him what had happened, this was what he said:

At night, he went quite early and sat with the lower-caste shudra community to watch the Bayalata. Suddenly, he thought of his shirt. The sweetened rice or huggi he'd got from the Guru's matha—the Guru's monastery—was sitting like a lump of concrete in his tummy. He'd also drunk some arrack with the two annas that the Gowda had given him for the fair. And he'd walked quite a bit in the excitement of his new shirt. Soon, his eyelids began to droop. When he sat up and looked around, he saw that not a single shudra was wearing a shirt like his own. He thought, 'Once I fall asleep—is my sleep anything ordinary?—I sleep like a log—what if someone takes away my shirt? Should I sleep? But does sleep ask my permission to come? So if I take off my shirt and keep it under my arm when I'm watching the Bayalata, the cool breeze on my body will prevent me from falling asleep. And even if I fall asleep, when somebody tries to grab the shirt, I'll certainly wake up.'

Thinking thus, he took off his shirt, bunched it up and stuck it firmly under his arm. He sat up for a while. Then sleep came.

You know the rest of the story.

This is how Nayalya lost his first shirt.

Once, at midnight, under the darkness of the new moon, God knows what possessed him, Muniyalya (the dog), howled loudly, rending the silence of the night. The other village dogs, who heard him, suddenly jumped up in their places, faced the outcaste neighbourhood and started howling. Their din just wouldn't stop. The sleeping people all woke up, thinking there were thieves in their houses. But they found none. Wasn't it the new moon day? Karimayi walks on the streets that day to protect the village from evil spirits. People thought that the dogs must have seen Karimayi and went back to sleep.

But Nayalya used this situation nicely to his advantage. When people started shouting—Thieves? Thieves?—he entered the house of Madara Bharama, the basket-maker, thrust his hands into the chicken basket in the porch, noiselessly brought out a chicken, twisted its neck, put it in his hut and then came out as if nothing had happened . Like the others, he pretended to be surprised by the barking dogs and shouted: 'Who? What? When?'

After a while he came back home. Rangi had already boiled the water and dipped the chicken in it. But he had planned to finish the chicken before morning, without the knowledge of his wife.

But isn't Rangi Nayalya's wife, after all?

Curbing his intense disappointment and anger, he sat in front of the stove.

In a little while, even as they sat, Rangi popped a piece of chicken into her mouth to check if it was cooked.

Nayalya lost his temper. 'Yeh, bastard, I was the one who stole it and brought it here, and you start gobbling it up even without showing it to me?'

'Can't you sit quiet? I want to see if it's done or not.'

'Why? Can't I see?'

'Hey pimp! Shut up and sit. Or shall I tell Madara Bharama?'—she said as she put another piece into her mouth. You can't open your mouth, nor can you be silent. If he shouted at her, she would go and tell Bharamya. If he kept quiet, this bitch would, without doubt, finish everything until she was scraping the bottom of the pot. Fine—he too ate a piece. This checking whether or not the chicken was cooked led them to finish half of it. Forget cooking, seasoning and making it delicious—he thought they wouldn't get even as far as boiling the meat properly.

Eager to win the competition, Rangi wasn't even spitting out the bones. As a last resort, he asked, 'Yeh whore! Will you at least leave a little for the kid?'

'It's okay—we can give the child some juice.'

And she ate some more. When it became certain that he wouldn't get even a bone, he stopped her hand and said, 'I swear on Karimayi, if you take another morsel—'

She too swore on Karimayi. Finally they both decided that they shouldn't touch the meat until it was seasoned and made into a curry. Neither believed they would keep their vow, though. In the heat of this vowing match, Nayalya had come nearer to the pot. The moment Rangi realized this, to prevent him from eating, but as if lovingly, she hugged Nayalya tight, like a forest creeper winding round the palm tree, and refused to budge.

Finally the meat was cooked. When they threw out the water and set the meat aside for seasoning, they heard Muniyalya growl. It was clear that someone had come. Nayalya told his wife to see to the door. She asked him to go instead. Even as they kept fighting about it, they heard the Gowda shout, 'Muniyalya!' Thinking that if he went to the door in a hurry this bitch would finish it all, he moved to the door holding her hand.

Outisde, it was already dawn.

Gowda was standing there. How can he keep holding his wife in front of the Gowda? So Nayalya let go of her. Gowda ordered him to de-husk the coconuts and left. By the time Nayalya shot back inside like an arrow, Rangi had already eaten everything and was busy chewing the bones. Nayalya almost wept in anger. Screaming, 'You whore!' he pulled her hair and kicked her. And she grabbed at, of all things, his shirt. In the heat of the battle, he didn't pay any attention and kept hitting her. She tore the shirt. More angry, more disappointed and more in pain, he hit her some more. She also tore the shirt some more—until it was in tatters that couldn't be patched together.

People laughed at this story of how Nayalya was bereft of his second shirt too. From that day on, they generously renamed him Angiyalya. Thereafter, he only had Gowda's shirts to wear. Gowda's big shirts hung loose on his thin body. But he didn't crave new shirts any more. As time passed, wearing Gowda's shirt, the Shirt Man Angiyalya, sometimes, that is, when he was drunk, would even feel a little proud of it.

Then he would lovingly call his wife Rangi 'Rangasani'.

## A VERY HEARTY MAN

Nayalya is a hearty man, in drinking, in playing the tabor, in everything. If he thinks he can get a glass of drink from you, then you should listen to his colourful talk. If necessary, he may even compose a verse for you and sing, he may tell a riddle, he may stand up and dance, he may lie, or he may tell the truth—whatever, he can do anything.

Omkarappa's banni tree is famous in the village for being haunted. People believe that on every new-moon day, at midnight, five shining female figures come to the tree holding the aarti salver with lighted camphor, perform the aarti, go round the tree, perform a bigger aarti before dawn, and then, at the break of day, run towards the lake. Some claim to have seen this strange sight. For the bet of a bottle of drink, Nayalya went to the tree on a new moon day of all days—how brave!

In Shivapura, the news of the village panchayat meetings was getting about a lot, right? The villagers had only begun to hear about it but our Nayalya sniffed it out before them. He thought he should drink that foreign bhirandi at least once in life. So he told the story of the ghost to the quartet. But they couldn't do anything. Because how could they give it? He decided to get hold of Gudsikara himself. But Gudsikara was a short-tempered man. Not inclined to ghost stories. To make it worse, Nayalya's ghosts were all in Gowda's fields. Still, there was one story in Nayalya's ghost-story collection that Gudsikara liked. Gudsikara had heard this story twice or thrice and sent Nayalya back without giving him anything. Even when Nayalya openly asked him for a drop of brandy, Gudsikara evaded him with a promise that he would give it later.

All of them had been laughing after Q&A Master left, right?

Now, without Yalya's knowledge, Gudsikara put some water into an empty bottle and called him in.

Even before Gudsikara had finished calling, Nayalya had come in. 'Nayalya, tell me that story of the Gowda's ghost again,' said Gudsikara, pouring the water from the bottle into his glass and drinking. Nayalya's thirst melted and dribbled down his mouth. Believing that the thirst of many days would be fulfilled today, he opened his eyes wider. His face shone. Remembering Karimayi, he prayed, 'Mother, give Gudsikara a generous heart,' and got ready to tell the story. He saw the faces of the quartet once. Even they were laughing at his excitement. It was not a story they didn't know. But today there was a new and special liveliness to his narration. His face was shining like the face of a bridegroom going to his bride's bed on their first night.

He started telling the story with great gusto:

Once upon a time, in a village, the king, the minister, the general, the army, the people—everyone lived happily. In Shivapura, there was a couple, Nayalya and Rangasani. Nayalya was the father of all drunks—there was nobody to beat him at drinking in all the villages around. One day, he drank to the hilt in the hut of the grand old woman of the village, Lagumavva. After drinking, he remembered his wife. He went home and slept. Suddenly, in the middle of the night, he got up thinking that since there was nobody in his fields, that is, in the Gowda's fields, thieves might come for the peanuts which had been put out to dry. It was a dark new-moon night. He was scared. But he thought of Karimayi and set off.

As he neared the fields, he felt a little braver. Because, before him, the Gowda had already come there and was sitting with his legs stretched, warming himself by the fire close to the threshing floor. Since he was late, he thought Gowda might scold him. Feeling scared, he went up to the Gowda to apologize. But when he came close, he saw that it wasn't the Gowda at all—but Gowda's ghost! Spilling its huge pot-size balls in front of it, the ghost was burning its own legs in order to warm itself. Nayalya ran for his life, brought some water from the hut and sprinkled it on the ghost. And the ghost was gone, vanished into thin air!

Although he saw the Gowda continuously for the next three days after this incident, Nayalya still felt scared. Even now, it seems, he never looks the Gowda in the face at night.

So they are there, and we are all here.

Thus, Nayalya ended his story.

Nayalya can tell a thousand such stories. If he can get some drink. Although he is the hero of all his stories, his stories always begin with, 'Once upon a time, in a village . . . ' But there is a difference between his ghosts and the ghosts of others—all his ghosts are scared of water. In every story he comes out victorious. After all, isn't he still alive! Some female ghosts even steal liquor for him, sleep with him and then leave!

Everybody laughed loudly when they heard the story. Gudsikara became jovial, gave the whole bottle, that is, the bottle filled with water, to him, saying, 'Go, sonny, think of me and drink it.' The moment Gudsikara gave it, Nayalya didn't say a word but put the bottle to his mouth, drank it—bottoms up—stuck it under his arm and then sat still! The quartet guffawed so loudly that it sounded as though eight people were laughing. Then he saluted Gudsikara and left. The village was already asleep.

Earlier, Nayalya had been asking the quartet about the taste of bhirandi. The four had told him four different things. Thief Sidrama had said, 'The tummy feels rummy, the head starts spinning and the feet feel like prancing ponies.' 'As though,' Rumps Ramesa had said, 'one becomes four or eight.' 'Like you're swimming in the lake,' was Jiggly Satira's take on it. And 'Yeh, as though you're in heaven,' Aayi Mereminda described, adding, 'The other day, I saw my grandfather, your grandmother—everybody. My grandfather was chasing your grandmother!' After hearing all this, Nayalya had concluded that, 'God appears to each according to his or her own fancy.'

He had been very excited about what would happen to him, how he would feel, when he drank some. He thought: if ever he drank the bhirandi, he too would get hold of Mereminda's grandmother. Now it seemed as if the four different experiences of the four different men were happening to him simultaneously. The road was too narrow to walk. He felt like he was sitting on a pony. Each thing appeared to be four or eight. It was as though he was swimming in the lake. He saw the heavens, thought he was face to face with Aayi Mereminda's grandmother and immediately tried to hug her, saying, 'Got you girl!'

But the one who came into his embrace was Ningu!

Nayalya realized what was happening to him. It wasn't possible to stand. It wasn't possible to talk. Looking at the bottle stuck in Nayalya's armpit, Ningu recognized it as Gudsikara's. Thinking that if he left to himself, Nayalya would be lost in the street,

Ningu held his arm and led him to his hut. Nayalya lost his balance and hugged Ningu's waist. Even in the darkness, Ningu felt bashful and rebuked him, 'You rascal!' All the way to his street, Nayalya spoke nonsense. He said Ningu looked like a beautiful puppet. 'Chimana is nothing compared to you,' he told Ningu. In any case, since his wife was going to die the next new-moon day, he promised to marry Ningu immediately after. He even swore upon Karimayi. When they finally reached his street, Ningu said, 'Get into your hut, pimp'. And then thinking of all that Nayalya had said, ran away back to his own house.

Nayalya went to his hut and knocked on the door. He heard someone ask 'Who's it?' His anger rose. 'Who's it?' he shouted back, 'It's your husband—open the door, woman!' He kicked the door. Still kicking, he stammered the song from the play *Krishna Parijata*, 'Open the door Rukmini / My pet parrot, Rukmini.' The door opened, he rushed in.

A hullabaloo started inside.

Because it wasn't Nayalya's hut—it was Madara Bharama's.

Bharama wasn't at home.

But Bharama's wife and mother were. Now they screamed, scolded, abused Nayalya's whole genealogy, and snatching at every dish or broom they could find, they began to whack him with utter disregard for which part of his body they hit—his mouth or his limbs. They raised such a hue and cry, their neighbours thought a thief had come. So they rushed in. And then they too began to kick him and beat him.

Nayalya, still confused about where he was and how and why he was getting beaten, saw the neighbours arrive and immediately decided that he would not survive this ordeal. Crying, 'Yappa, I'm dead,' he shot out like a gob of spit.

It's Nayalya!

From the hut in the corner, his wife Rangasani had got out of bed and come to the door when the women from Bharama's house had rushed out crying and shouting for help.

Now, his intoxication vanished, Nayalya began to fall at everybody's feet, explaining, 'I was sloshed, I made a mistake.' The crowd that had gathered spat at him in disgust. Bharama's wife and mother were still shouting. It took a lot of time for the others to console them with 'Let's complain to the Gowda tomorrow,' and send them back to bed. Rangi dragged Nayalya to the hut, kicked him a few times, left him outside and went to sleep.

'Look what happened, Karimayi!' mumbled Nayalya as he slumped outside his door. Beside his dog, Muniyalya.

# LAMB SACRIFICE

Next morning. It was quite late in the day. Nayalya had been sent for from the Gowda's house. He had guessed this would happen, so he got up before anyone in the village did and went to the fields. The watchman came too. Realizing that there was nothing or none to save him, and getting ready to be scolded, Nayalya came to the Gowda.

The Gowda's house was full of people. There were the Elders. And Bharama and his mother What was more surprising, outside, on the katte, sat the sarpanch. The quartet was there too. Thief Sidrama began to laugh when he saw Nayalya.

Nayalya went in, looking pathetic, and stood near the cattle shed.

What's there to inquire? Gowda asked, 'Is it true what Bharama said?'

Nayalya fell to the ground—'Forgive me! All kinds of things happened when I was drunk. I have never done this kind of a thing before. Sarpanch gave me some sort of bhirandi. The new chap made all this mischief!'

Until this point in the quarrel, there had been no mention of Gudsikara. Why should there be? Nayalya's drinking was no secret. It wasn't even news. More like saying—fish drinks water. Although he hadn't crossed the limit like this ever before. He hadn't stepped into the zone which the villagers 'had marked with their spittle' as wrongdoing. Everyone, including Bharama, thought that for a man like Nayalya to have done this, there must have been some special stimulus.

As if speaking all their thoughts aloud, Dattappa opened his mouth—'See, it's true that Nayalya is a drunk. But he has never crossed the limits of decency. Since he starts drooling the moment drink is mentioned, we on our side should be careful too. Our man falls all over the place by merely drinking the stuff from Lagumi's glass. Imagine what must have happened with this foreign bhirandi?'

Balu still nursed a lot rancour against Gudsikara. He hadn't forgotten the beating his son had got on the Holi Full Moon day. He said, 'Yes! Why did we form the village panchayat after all? So that people could learn to drink foreign bhirandi? Or was it to do some good to the village? As it is, people are fools. If they are also taught such addictions, tell mewhat'll happen?'

'If you ask me, the sarpanch himself must give the fine which Nayalya is supposed to give.'

Gowda didn't know what to say to this. Because Nayalya was Gowda's servant. So he looked at Dattappa, as if to say: decide this case somehow so that both are satisfied.

But before Dattappa could say anything, Devaresi gave the verdict: 'It's like insulting the madara clan. If it's the issue of the clan, it's not a small matter. Let them give a lamb as fine.'

What is Angiyalya worth? How can he give a lamb? It is not as if Devaresi doesn't know this. But such is the fine for such cases. After the words were out of Devaresi's mouth, what could anyone else say? But who should give the lamb? That was the question. Devaresi was a naive man. Let's collect a lamb in Nayalya's name—so what? It's been ages since all the clan sat together and had some meat. At least, it will open up our dead taste buds.

The moment the lamb was mentioned, Nayalya collapsed. Couldn't say a word. Just pleaded for mercy with his eyes whenever anyone looked at him.

'So—when will you give the lamb?' Devaresi asked again.

'I made a mistake. Please, just this once, overlook my error, forgive me,' begged Nayalya and prostrated before all the gods.

But would these gods send him a lamb?

Still, how can these people force him to give the lamb? Nayalya went over to a shallow pit in the ground, held his right ear with his left hand, his left ear with his right, and did a couple of sit-ups in a gesture of contrition.

But can sit-ups produce a lamb?

'If you want me to, I'll even drag myself on my bums all the way home.'

Will the lamb come if he drags himself home thus?

But—it came!

Dattappa was about to say, 'See, Yalya—' when Thief Sidrama interrupted: 'Don't worry, Nayalya the sarpanch will give the lamb.'

Nayalya rushed to clutch at Gudsikara's feet.

The Elder Panchas agreed with the idea: 'Yes, let him give.'

The Gowda kept quiet. Dattappa too.

Then everyone left. But the Elder Panchas stayed behind. This didn't look good. Nobody was worried about Angiyalya. They hadn't liked Gudsikara's interference. Only Basetti said okay. But the others didn't feel that it was right on Gudsikara's part to send such a message with Sidrama even before the EldersPanchas had given a verdict on Nayalya's case.

'No, it wasn't right—' said Dattappa. Everyone remained silent. 'Well,' he continued, 'they are educated boys. We thought they would do some good to the village, so we gave them the panchayat. It seems now that we "gave the office to a crow". It seems right to take it back . . . '

'Tell us what we should do,' said Balu.

'Is that right? That we should take back the panchayat and manage it ourselves?' said Basetti.

'Don't be in a hurry. Surely there is a way to get these boys to see sense?' the Gowda insisted.

The others didn't agree. This was their argument—since they had made the panchayat and the sarpanch, when they didn't like it, they should be able to take it back.

But Gowda knows that this isn't an easy thing to do. Dattappa knows too. Finally, with everybody's consent, they took a stand: on behalf of the Elder Panchas, Dattappa should go to Gudsikara. He should ask the latter to resign from the panchayat.

## SWORE ON KARIMAYI AND LIED

That same day, Gowda called Angiyalya and scolded him. He made Angiyalya swear on Karimayi's bhandara that he wouldn't drink bhirandi again. But Angiyalya was also called Nayalya, right? Like the dog's tail, he became crooked again. He turned back on his vow to Karimayi. It happened thus:

Gudsikara gave the lamb to Nayalya, didn't he? Whatever the older people thought, in the eyes of the quartet, he became a big man. They thought, 'What a generous man!' In truth, Gudsikara pitied Nayalya. Anyway, now the fine is paid and they can have the lamb feast. That day he made a heart-felt decision to give Nayalya some real brandy instead of water.

Everyone laughed when they thought of Nayalya. Look how the man acted after drinking just water, they mocked. They recalled, imagined and enacted the whole incident. They spiced up the matter nine-fold. To tell the truth, they laughed till their sides split.

To laugh like that, the quartet had another happy reason. The moment they realized that Q&A Master feared them, there began a new routine in their daily lives. They had pestered the Master the other day, hadn't they? The very next day, Thief Sidrama deliberately met Q&A Master and inquired, 'What, Master?' Poor thing, Q&A Master smiled obsequiously and said, as instructed, 'I salute you, Sahebara.' The Thief felt very happy, thinking that Q&A Master addressed only him and Gudsikara as saheb.

As soon as Aayi Mereminda heard this, he rushed over to the Kannada Boys School. Q&A Master smiled and called him saheb too.

Aayi Mereminda was perhaps a little embarrassed. 'Did you salute the sarpanch?'he asked.

'Salute the sarpanch? Don't I do it every day?'

'Did you meet the Gowda?'

'Meet the Gowda? Yes. But I didn't salute him.'

Aayi Mereminda felt a little sorry for him. And then thought, 'The Master shouldn't think that I came only to be saluted'. So he left with this advice: 'Teach history and geography well to the students.'

Thereafter, whenever he met any of the four, Q&A Master would promptly say, 'I salute you, Sahebara. And no, I didn't salute the Gowda.' On the one hand, the quartet felt proud—because they were so fortunate as to be saluted by the Master who had taught them; because they were disciples who had outdone the Master. On the other hand, they felt bad. After all, they were old students. They thought, 'Poor fellow.'

From that day, Q&A Master's name was changed to Poor Master.

One day, the quartet got together and went to the school. And they had an incredible surprise waiting —not only Poor Master but all the students stood up with folded hands. When they had been at school, they used to stand up like this when some inspector, or the Gowda, or Dattappa, visited. Now the students were standing for them!

They were so happy that from that day on they began laughing for no reason.

Gudsikara gave the lamb—that is, the money to buy the lamb, right? The same day, the madigas—the cobblers—had made arrangements to have the feast.

Where Nayalya was in a festive mood, Gudsikara was perturbed. The boys from the next village were practising a play to perform in front of the Gowda on this Kara Moon day. The thought of it made his mind restless. He sent word for Poor Master to come to the panchayat office. The quartet too was present. When Poor Master arrived, Gudsikara ordered, with dreams brimming over in his eyes: 'Teach us a play to perform on Kara Full Moon Day.'

Poor Master had never acted in a play before. In his whole life, he had seen only about four or five plays. Besides, he was too old to be engaging in such entertainment and fun. 'How's that possible? It's not possible. What do I know of plays? I don't know.'

The quartet worried that if Poor Master refused, they would lose their chance of acting in a play. So they too began to beg and plead. Finally, that ultimate trick: 'Sarpanch-saheb himself is asking you. Don't you value his words? If we write about you to the higher authorities today, what will happen to you?'

Who knows what would have happened?

But Poor Master got scared.

They decided to perform 'The Abduction of Sita' from the Ramayana. They talked about getting lights and decorations and costumes from Belagavi. They also decided to insert a 'dance' sequence in Ravana's court, and to get a chimana from Belagavi for it. They distributed the roles among themselves. Except for Gudsikara. Who can perform Ravana's role except Thief Sidrama? The moment he was sure about playing Ravana's role, Thief Sidrama recommended Ningu for Sita. But Gudsikara didn't agree. So Rumps Ramesa became Sita. Narada and Hanumanta —Aayi Mereminda was to play both. Jiggly Satira was to play Shiva. The rest of the roles like Rama, Lakshmana and so on, they distributed to boys in the village who were on 'their side'.

Someone suggested that Poor Master be given a role too.

But he leapt to his feet and said 'No, no' with folded hands. So they left him alone.

By the time everything about the play had been decided, Nayalya arrived. Because of Gudsikara's benevolence, Nayalya had been able to pay the fine of a lamb, right? The madigas had arranged for the feast on that day. Since it was a clan feast, Gudsikara's presence was not mandatory. But because he was the one who'd given the lamb, that too to Gowda's servant, and because he wanted the people to see him as the image of generosity, he had said he would attend. Nayalya had paid the fine, and he too would get a share of the meat. He was the sort who danced until his feet ached when someone else was performing a feast. Now should we ask how he was feeling? He came to invite them bursting with excitement. He must have come running, because he kept belching. 'Sahebara, everything is ready. Please come!'

The moment they saw him, the quartet felt like laughing again.

Laughing, Jiggly Satira said, 'Nayalya, the other day you drank that foreign bhirandi, right? How did you feel?'

Nayalya didn't want to remember any of it. Embarrassed, he said, 'It was like falling into slush, all right?'

'It seems, you swore on Karimayi that you wouldn't drink bhirandi. Have you?' asked Aayi Mereminda.

'Yes, Gowda made me swear.'

'You won't drink if anyone gives it to you?'

'No—in fact, don't mention that bhirandi in front of me.'

Gudsikara slowly held up the brandy bottle he had kept aside for Nayalya. And saying, 'See, Sonny,' he brandished it in front of Nayalya's face.

God knows how Poor Master could smell it. But he covered his nose with the loose end of his dhotra. Nayalya's mind had melted, become as thin as the brandy in the bottle. But he couldn't open his mouth and say it. Desperately trying to control himself, he closed his eyes and muttered, 'No, no. Impossible! Please take it away.' Gudsikara could have taken it away. But Nayalya had vowed in front of the Gowda, hadn't he? Gudsikara felt as though someone had poured lamp oil into his stomach to make it burn. He felt he was in pain too.

Meanwhile, Poor Master intervened, 'How can he drink? He swore in front of the Gowda. It means he has stopped drinking. Doesn't it? He is poor. Has wife and children. Yes. So don't drink, son!'

'Che,' Thief Sidrama snapped, 'what does a vow like that matter to a fellow like this? When you are giving it to Nayalya,' he said, turning to Gudsikara, 'how can Gowda's vow stop him? Will the Gowda come here to see what's happening? Who knows who gets lucky? Drink, drink, sonny!' Poor Master couldn't bear it: 'What is Nayalya saying? He says no. Why are you forcing him? Leave him alone.'

Suddenly, Gudsikara stood up: 'Master, if Nayalya drinks now—what's the bet?'

Poor Master was stunned: 'What can I bet? Nothing.'

Gudsikara opened the bottle and looked at Poor Master.

'Shall I go now?' said Poor Master, getting to his feet and folding his hands in farewell,'I will go.'

'Stop,' shouted Gudsikara, and went over to Poor Master. Poor Master covered his nose again.

'Bring your hands down,' Gudsikara chided and forced the bottle into them. Poor Master was trembling like a leaf. 'Am I not the master who taught you? No!'

'It's not for you,' scolded Gusikara before Poor Master could finish stammering the words, 'It's for Nayalya. Go and give him a few drops. He will drink.'

'Nayalya, cup your hands and drink. This one day,' he ordered.

As if caught in a moral dilemma—because he was sure of getting it anyway, or because he thought that if he pretended to hesitate he would get more, yet behaving in such a way that his real intention was evident to Gudsikara, Nayalya refused with a smile. 'No, I don't want it.'

It seemed as though Gudsikara was being rather soft with Nayalya. 'Nayalya, Sonny, is your vow bigger than my reputation? Have you forgotten my help of giving you the lamb?' he said, and thumped his chest a few times when he mentioned 'reputation'.

Quickly, Nayalya said, 'Let it be, let it be. Why do you take this to heart so much.' And cupped his hands.

Poor Master could only look from Gudsikara to Nayalya, as though he was seeing a ghost.

'Okay, Master! Pour it out to him,' ordered Ramesa.

Poor Master just kept standing there, cursing his fate, until Gudsikara shouted, 'Didn't you hear him, Master?'

Poor Master ran up to Nayalya and began pouring from the bottle. He was trembling. So the bottle shook in his hands and some drops splashed on Nayalya's shirt. Nayalya promptly licked them up. How tasty! Gudsikara was so happy at the sight of Nayalya licking his shirt that he ran up to Poor Master, snatched the bottle and said, 'Open your mouth!'

Nayalya tilted back his head and opened his mouth. As the quartet watched, drooling, feeling victorious, Gudsikara poured the brandy into Nayalya's mouth, onto his face and his shirt. Nayalya gulped down the stiff brandy even as it burnt his insides. And his shirt grew wet. He licked it all up. A few drops had fallen on the ground. He ran over to the spot, wiped it with his hands and then licked them dry.

'See here,' said Gudsikara, 'some has fallen here too—lick it up!' and stretched his feet out. And

Nayalya licked his feet. The others laughed. The Thief was already practising laughing like Ravana.

Looking at them laughing, each more than the other, as if they'd all gone mad, Poor Master got frightened and ran away. None noticed. Remembering his vow in front of the Gowda, either to forget it or because he too was frightened, Nayalya joined in their laughter.

Suddenly, God knows what got into Aayi Mereminda, but he stood up, and in a fit of valiant passion, shouted, 'Victory to Gudsikara—Jai Hind!' The other three also shouted, 'Jai Hind!'

Nayalya merely said, 'Karimayi!'

'We'll come shortly,' Gudiskara told him, 'You go ahead.'

Nayalya ran off to the lamb feast.

Gowda was lying down, his head propped on his hands, on a blanket thrown over the bullock cart which stood in front of the hut in his field. Shivasani was rubbing his feet. The summer air was warm, as if the Earth was sighing. In the faint starlight, it seemed as if the Earth was tossing from one side to the other, unable to sleep or wake. The trees and plants rustled in the breeze every now and then. Suddenly, Gowda heard the entire village give out a terrible scream. He opened his eyes. Listened again to make sure if he had heard correctly. Yes, Shivasani had heard it too. Yes, someone was screaming.

Gowda got up, threw the blanket on his shoulder and ran. Ran straight to the place where they had the madara festival. Angiyalya's wife was wailing, unconscious of the saree slipping away from her body. Thumping her chest. The children were screaming. Some people were rubbing mud on the body of Angiyalya—unconscious on the ground. Lagumavva was abusing Gudsikara's entire genealogy.

Meanwhile, someone had run to Dattappa. Angiyalya's body was fully burnt, and the skin on the left side had peeled off. The body lay there, fallen, like a mass of roast meat. You could tell he was alive only because he kept opening his mouth from time to time.

In a few moments, Dattappa arrived. He asked them to take the body into the hut. Two boys gently lifted Nayalya and took him in. Gowda followed.

Finally, someone in the crowd told them what had happened.

Nayalya had drunk to the hilt. When the sarpanch and the members arrived at the lamb feast, Nayalya had wanted to play the tabor. He snatched it from the tabor player, although he could hardly stand, and, swaying, began to drum. Then when Gudsikara threw four annas at him, he tried to touch the coin to his forehead with one hand while playing the tabor with the other. He lost his balance and fell into the fire. Some of them pulled him out as fast as they could, but they couldn't douse the fire quickly enough because his shirt was drenched in alcohol.

It's your karma after all. Gowda sat quietly.

After doing what he could, Dattappa came out of the hut, and started walking. He walked on and on without saying a word. Gowda hoped Dattappa would say something. But by the time they came to a turn, Dattappa still hadn't said a word. So Gowda called, 'Dattu.' Dattappa turned and stood. Then he walked over to a boulder and sat. Gowda threw the blanket on the ground and sat as well, his arms round his knees. Dattappa sat there waiting for the Gowda to talk. Gowda sat there thinking about what to talk. For a long time, they both sat in silence. If anyone came out and saw them now, they would surely get a fright thinking they were ghosts. What's more, if someone said, 'Last night Gowda and Dattappa were sitting on this boulder,' nobody would have believed them.

A long time passed before Dattappa opened his mouth. 'Gowda, the devouring goddess, Mari, has entered this village.'

Gowda was silent.

'Tomorrow, early in the morning, I'll go to his house and tell him to resign from the panchayat.'

Gowda was still silent.

'Say something.'

Gowda opened his mouth slowly. 'Think a bit, Dattu. What's the use of taking the panchayat back from his hands? Where is it for us to take back? So we snatch it back. Those five will get together, drink in the house, ruin themselves and also ruin the village. There's no panchayat in the village, Gudsya has money. He is arrogant. First, find some way of getting that boy back to his senses.'

Gowda's words were also true. To tell the truth, where is that panchayat? The villagers had never taken it seriously. People like Nayalya drink and fall into slush. Not having the strength to get out of it, they struggle. One day, they die.

Neither of them could think of a way out. Who knows? If they snatch the panchayat from Gudsikara, his conceit might suffer a blow. He might feel ashamed enough and come back to his senses. In any case, in the absence of any other option, it was the only thing to do. Who knows what might happen after both of us die? A least when we are alive, we can't let the village be ruined. They got up.

And they heard the screams from the outcaste neighbourhood—Nayalya was dead!

Muniyalya, the great soul, drank and ate and scraped every joy he could out of life. Saw Karimayi, saw the ghosts. He made up stories out of what he saw. Until he became a story himself, and for the villagers an aching memory. He named Karimayi, he named his wife, was himself known for his three names. He became an example of what happens if you go back on your vows to Karimayi.

Let us pray to Karimayi to make him one of her minions in the otherworld.

## UDYOGAPARVA[8]

The next day, a little later in the day, Dattappa set off for Gudsikara's house. Gudsikara was sitting upstairs, loudly reading in English. His mother and sister were surprised—Dattappa coming to their house? Girija, his sister, ran upstairs and told Gudsikara about their guest. His old mother went out to greet Dattappa, full of respect and excitement. She spread the carpet and invited him in. Dattappa sat, saying, 'Yes, your daughter has grown up. Shouldn't we be looking for a good bridegroom?' Girija ran inside, feeling shy. Even as the old lady was saying, 'You look for one, please. Get her married soon,' Gudsikara came downstairs. His mother went away, leaving them alone.

Asking, 'What Dattappa, you have come to my house?' Gudsikara sat on the sack-stand. He didn't like the excitement that his mother and sister were displaying about Dattappa's visit. But he couldn't say anything. He guessed that whatever the reason, it must be important enough to make Dattappa come himself. Perhaps it was Nayalya getting burnt and dying. Dattappa must have come here to blame him for everything. The thought frightened him a little.

He prepared all sorts of answers in order to shed the blame.

Meanwhile, Dattappa sat there, wondering how to begin. He realized that this boy wasn't one of them—how long could he just sit like this?

'Brother, I have something to say.'

'What's it? You can say it here.'

'See, Appa. All of us, the Elders, told you to take care of the panchayat when we placed it in your hands. We thought you would do some good to the village. Well, that didn't happen. The people are all asking us to take it back. So you give it back before we ask.'

Gudsikara hadn't expected this. But he realized that if didn't answer this properly, he was going to lose.

'Look, the panchayat is not your family property to give and take whenever you want to. This has to do with village governance. There are laws for forming the panchayat. Rules—and regulations. And everything we have done, we have done according to the rules. Now if you ask for it back, how can I give it? There will be elections in six or eight months. You stand for the elections—we'll stand too.'

'Right,' said Dattappa. 'It's not my family property. But neither is it yours. You talked about rules and regulations. We put it into your hands without thinking of any rules or regulations. Why didn't you remember rules and regulations then, son?'

It was difficult to counter Dattappa's irregular argument.

'All the people of the village gave it to me. So it was legal. Now only you have come to ask me for it. That's why I remembered the laws.'

'So are you saying that I should get all the people of the village to ask for it back?'

Gudsikara realized too late that such a feat wasn't at all impossible for Dattappa. If the villagers force me to do this, he thought, I'll have to back out. And I know that apart from my four members, there's no one else to back me.

He cursed this nuisance.

'Look, I know why your eyes are on the panchayat now. First, when the panchayat came, you didn't know what it was. You gave it to me. Now that we have been progressing a bit in this village, you're jealous. Don't think that we don't understand this!'

Confronted with such a deep delusion, Dattappa placed a finger on his mouth and sat quietly for a moment or two.

Then: 'Yes, boy! You have progressed. We have remained backward. Will you give us the panchayat now, so that we may progress?' he asked, savouring the irony of his own words.

Who knows what else he might have asked because just then, as if they'd had a huge fight, Gudsikara loudly cut through Dattappa's talk: 'How can I? Didn't I say we should wait till the elections?

Just because you want to rule this village, have you got some contract to do it? You ruled it all these days. Aren't you content? Now give a chance to new people.'

'Didn't we give you a chance, son? What good did you do?'

'You have shat and messed up things all these days. Don't we need sometime to clean it all up?' Hearing Gudsikara's raised voice, his mother came out, thinking they were fighting. Girija too stood a little away and listened. Passers-by paused outside the door and began to ask what was going on. Gudsikara grew brazen and said everything that came to his mind. He asked a boy, standing outside, to fetch the panchayat members. He declared that the old hawks were hindering him from doing whatever good he wished to do to the village. If not for them, this village would have become Belagavi by now. On and on he spoke, biding time until the members arrived. Gudsikara thought that if each member said a thing or two to Dattappa, the latter would be well and truly silenced.

Just as he had thought, the quartet arrived. By then there was a crowd in front of the house. Nobody knew what or why of the matter. They could only hear Gudsikara's voice. Dattappa sat playing with Gudsikara's petty eloquence. The quartet came, saluted Dattappa and moved to a corner. They smiled from time to time and wrung their hands. Gudsikara said to them, mockingly, 'Did you listen to what he said? It seems we've ruined this village. So he has come to ask us to give up the panchayat!' Then, turning to Dattappa, he said, 'Go now! Let the election come, let it all be decided there.' The crowds outside the door finally came to know what the matter was. The quartet stood there, their hands crossed like schoolboys who don't know the answer to a question.

Somebody in the crowd said, 'Yes, you must listen to the Elders.'

Gudsikara grew angrier and shouted, 'I didn't call you to play the elder. Now get away of my house!'

Dattappa got up and left. And everyone felt that Gudsikara had asked Dattappa to get out of his house. They got angry, and each saying something or other, slowly went away.

On the one hand the fact that the quartet hadn't talked, on the other that someone from the crowd intervened, and above all that Dattappa didn't sit back to hear more of his talk—everything made Gudsikara's blood boil. His mother was upset that her son hadn't behave respectfully with Dattappa. She couldn't figure out why he'd acted like this. Because Dattappa had talked calmly enough. Unable to confront the eyes of others, Gudsikara climbed up to the attic, and pacing up and down, started abusing everybody as if they were all, except himself, bad—just like Gowda or Dattappa.

To tell the truth, Gudsikara is not a villain. He may be a little presumptuous about his learning. This isn't so unexpected in a village where nobody else is educated. His is the arrogance of youth. Nothing to be surprised about, considering his age. There's the money his father had earned, but he was generous with it too. People never thought him their enemy. Nor did they think that there was any big enmity between the Gowda and him. Not even the quartet thought so.

Like all educated young men, he too wove the flames of idealism around himself. Then dreamed by that firelight. In its warmth, he found his energy. In Lugumavva's songs, she says that young men are 'like the sage Vishvamitra'. It's also true that he had the desire to correct the system here and there, the craving to re-create. Since he was the only educated man in the village, and someone who'd seen the worldly life of Belagavi, he believed that his responsibility was greater. Sure, I can't change the whole nation, but what did Gandhiji tell the educated? To go back to the villages. So, okay, if I focus on reforming my village, what is more worthwhile than this? Didn't join the movement but wore khadi. What else? Just a minor addiction to alcohol. It's not even a bad habit in the eyes of the villagers. If Gandhiji came and asked him something, he'd have answers for every question. But if Gandhiji asked, 'Why do you drink, Gudsikara?' he would have no answer. Sometimes, unable to give up the addiction that had seeped into his system, he would search for a pretext. This isn't a big thing. It's only a little thing, like the pimples on his face.

With Gandhiji's photo in his hands and disquiet in his head, he walked to the village. He didn't see any people—only the animals. Crooked roads, alleys without drains, stinking garbage everywhere, infants rolling in the dust, stray puppies and dogs roaming about, cattle, crowds—seeing all this, he'd felt a great pity. And he'd decided that his first task was to clean up this filth.

He'd finally had the chance to do so. There was the panchayat. He'd become the sarpanch. He'd called for meetings. We already know the fate of these meetings. And then there'd been Ningu's case—it had been such a shock to Gudsikara. In broad daylight, with eyes wide open, imagine, they all covered up the murder! Murder is murder. Nothing more, nothing less. It must be decided in the court of law. There are no different laws for villages and cities. If the village Gowda and the village accountant take the law into their hands, will law survive? Che che, it's impossible to even think of it.

True, so far he hadn't any respect for the Gowda or Dattappa. Nor had he been unduly upset with them. But now he was—now he was angry. He thought they were ruining the village in the name of protecting it. As if this wasn't enough, everyone in the village had teamed up with Gowda and Dattappa, and talked like they had done in front of the foujudara.

The more ignorant the people are, the more deified these two will be. No wonder, if anybody talks knowledgably, these two find it irksome. If I come forward and give some awareness to people, the Gowda and Dattu's greatness will begin to dim, right? That's why they are jealous of me.

Today, he'd got that same kind of shock. It's true that the Elders had handed him the panchayat without elections. But the reason for it was different—there was no other educated person in the village. No other person who knew what a panchayat was. Hence they'd handed it to him on a platter. And now they want it back? Why? Have any newly educated men come to the village? Say Dattappa called all the villagers and conducted a panchayati, an election. In fear of the Gowda, the people might even raise their hands. So? Does that become a panchayat? Everyone in the village has a right to choose. But these men don't want it.

Thus—

He thought of all this in a variety of ways. And whichever direction he looked at it from, he was convinced he was right. But he was sure of one thing—they will not hand him the panchayat easily as they did the last time. Elections will happen for sure. So he must prepare for them from now. The play that they were going to perform on Kara Moon day was going to bring them closer to victory.

## THE ABDUCTION OF SITA

The arrangements for the play were done in great style. As the Kara Moon day neared, the bustle of the boys knew no bounds. People's mouths and ears were full of the news of this play. When the village lasses went to fetch water, this was the story they told on the way. People flocked in herds just to see the rehearsals. The excitement of those practice sessions —that bustle, their style, che, the boys in the play seemed to walk on air those days!

Wasn't the Thief playing Ravana? He grew a big moustache and rubbed it with oil every day. Trying to learn his lines by heart, he would scream the words anywhere at all. If he happened to get hold of Ningu, he would call him Sita and sing till he grew hoarse— this is not a lie, okay? Now whenever he talked of anything to anybody, he did it in Ravana style. Even his gait changed—now he walked with long strides.

Similarly, Rumps Ramesa's excitement at playing Sita was beyond words. He grew his hair nine inches long. He oiled it till the grease ran down his neck. He began to comb his hair in the style of the city whores and put on feminine airs. The exaggerated gestures, the sexy eyebrow-raising and lip-biting—oh, no wonder it made Ningu as jealous as a rival wife. Even the village girls were green with envy.

Aayi Mereminda, who was to play monkey god Anjaneya, now leapt rather than walked.

All this bustle and excitement made the other village boys yearn for the luck of those who had a role in the play.

While the people got more and more excited about watching the play, Ningu grew more and more jealous—because he hadn't been given the role of Sita. If I were Sita, how would I have stood, danced and performed? How would I have felt when Thief Sidrama came before me? How I would give in when he pulled me towards him? How I would be so easy when he bore me away? He kept thinking such things and felt very jealous indeed. He felt that his being a eunuch was a waste. He thought: Let me see how they put up this play!

The news spread to all the neighbouring fourteen villages. If, early on, it was about a chimana coming from Belagavi and dancing, and getting electric lights for the play, later other bits of news sprouted like bird's feathers. News about how when the Thief shouted during one of the practise sessions, a pregnant woman in the neighbourhood had miscarried. About how God Anjaneya himself would possess the body of Aayi Mereminda. Ningu even said that Rumps Ramesa, playing Sita, had begun to menstruate every month, just like a real woman.

When bits of such news reached the ears of the performers, they felt thrilled, and acted as if all of it was indeed true.

Every creature there was waiting for the day of the play. Thank God, it finally came.

That day, around six in the evening, Gowda was sitting under the tree in front of his hut and fixing some farming tools. Shivaningu, making hay for the cattle, stood there, looking towards the village. Noticing the direction of his gaze, Gowda too turned to look. At a distance, Dattappa, Lagumavva and two more people from another village were all coming towards the hut. Dattappa was not the type to come at this odd hour. Gowda was a bit surprised, and wondered why he was coming. He stood watching.

The other two saluted the Gowda. The long hair of these unknown visitors, and the black caps they wore, confirmed Gowda's guess that they were performers. They all sat on the porch. They were from the neighbouring village. They had learnt the play *Krishna Parijata*. Dattappa said that they had come to perform. In a sense, Kara Full Moon Day was the feast of Gowda's family. But now they no longer have the racing bullocks. Years ago, their winning bullock had escaped to some other village. According to custom, that night, Karimayi and her children come to the Gowda's house with the invitation for the hunt, watch the games and fun and then go back to the temple in the morning. Gowda didn't think it proper to put up another play on the very day that Gudsikara's group was performing. But his visitors refused to listen to him. 'If you don't want to see it, what's the use of our learning it?' This is natural to artistes in those parts. And such was also Gowda's taste. Whether it was singing, dancing or speaking—he could always discern excellence. He knew the difference between it and mere showy art. The general mood among the artists was that anyone who hadn't got the Gowda's appreciation wasn't an artiste at all.

Gowda's obsession with art was well known. He had appreciated Koujalagi Ningavva, applauded Shivagureppa. Nobody could stop Gowda's generous hands when he was in the mood to give. Gowda felt this madness—he would become one with art. Once in the past, when Ningavva had played Satyabhama and called out 'Krishna' piteously, Gowda had cried like an old woman. The artistes were like that too. Once, Dattappa had held the hand of that same Ningavva and told her, 'Ask what you want.' Only to be reprimanded: 'This body is like the pot from which Krishna drank milk—why do you touch it?' Immediately, Dattappa touched her feet and saluted her. Those artistes, and their art, had thrilled these people like the deepest secrets of existence. They felt fulfilled by such artistic experiences.

But today, they didn't want that experience. Today was not the day when beautiful singing could thrill you. Not a day when the exchange of sparkling speech could light up your mind. Their eyes were in no state to enjoy dancing. Because of Gudsikara's play. But how can you expose the faults of the village to visitors? On the other hand, how can you disappoint those who have come from afar?

Finally, Shivaninga, who was standing at a distance, said, 'Let them perform if they want to. Why should we give up our custom?'

Perhaps Gowda would have appreciated these words in another context but now he just said, 'Do what you want' and left it to Dattappa.

Dattappa had wanted only that much. Happy, he took the artistes away.

In another part of the village, there was a strange liveliness. Putting up the stage and sets and props, people jostling, their excitement raised to a pitch beyond words. The play was only going to start at night, at the time when the village usually went to bed, but crowds of men and women were already waiting around the stage. Young men from neighbouring villages had come too, their dinners packed for the night. Every performer was acting like a bridegroom for whose marriage all the people had gathered. They looked at, and were being looked at, by people. They strutted up and down excitedly. For them, heaven was only three inches away. And, after all, the crowd should know they are performers, right? They walked among groups of people practising their lines. No one could stop talking about the electric lights and Chimana. Story after story flew through the air.

Chimana was in Gudsikara's house. So a group of boys had gathered outside his door. Each one was anxious to see Chimana then and there. They were hoping she would come out for a moment, at least to spit. All the voices inside sounded like female voices to those outside. Girija was overexcited and bustled about. Call the boys she knew, or summon the performers, and send them off on errands. She'd walk in and out of the house, full of importance, like a puffed-up calf.

Even the Bayalata players knew that there was another play in the village that same day. They also knew that there weren't going to be any people for their Bayalata. They were disappointed. But at least the Gowda and the Elders were going to watch their performance. They thought that was enough.

At last, the sun had set. The new players had lit the lights even before it was dark. Need you ask? People ate in a hurry, found a good place in front of the stage and then sat down, jostling to be as close to it as possible.

The one who stood out among the audience was Girija. She was so proud that she was Gudsikara's sister. And because Chimana was staying with them. She talked loudly, as if everybody was there to listen to her. Around her, a few girls her age, with unblinking eyes and open mouths, drank in everything she said with great respect, reverence and awe.

Girija's mouth, it seemed, would never tire of describing Chimana.

'What do you think of Chimana? She is like a doll in the shop. True, she wears a saree. But she doesn't cover her head with the serugu—she drapes it over her shoulder like the brahmins. It seems, she's very rich. She has a bungalow so high that if you look up at it, the turban on your head will fall off. She has six maids only to wash her sarees. And there is a woman each for doing the beds, cooking, serving food and giving her betel leaves and arecanuts after her meals. Do you think, like us, she eats a basketful of food and shits a tubful later? Haven't I seen her eating in our house? Just this much rice, this much of soup to mix with it, ghee made of milk! She eats about three morsels and washes her hands, that's it! You know what the bra inside her blouse is like? She changes bras three times a day. She scents even her bras . . .' and on and on.

One ignorant lass asked, 'Does she also fart like us?' Funnily enough, nobody laughed at the question. Girija answered with even more seriousness. And so she kept on, telling story after story until the play began. The rest listened. She didn't tire of telling, and they didn't tire of listening. Such 'holy' tales were also being exchanged among people here and there.

In front of the Gowda's house, the Bayalata had begun.

Finally, this play also began. First, Gudsikara came out onto the stage and gave a lecture on the art of drama. Nobody understood a word of it. But nobody made a sound. At the end of the speech, Poor Master came on the stage, put a garland round Gudsikara's neck and babbled a bit about 'In our village, Gudsikara is world famous.'

Gudsikara climbed down and went to sit in style among the audience, on a chair from the school that had all its four legs intact.

The curtain rose.

The play began. A scene in Shiva and Parvati's court. This couple, the divine father and mother of all creation, have forgotten about the welfare of the world and are indulging in frivolous love-games. When Narada comes in.

The villagers had goose pimples when Narada entered. Setting his foot inside a loose knot made at the end of a rope hanging from the top, sage Narada alias Aayi Mereminda swung halfway down mid-stage, singing of Lord Narayana. He was clutching the rope tightly with his left hand and balancing the tamboori in his right. The sentimental ones in the audience imagined him to be descending straight from the sky. Wonder-struck, they sat gaping, oblivious of the tiny insects flying in and out of their mouths.

Now Narada was to say, 'Yeh, divine God who controls the whole world,' and leap. But when he tried to do so, the knot suddenly became tight and his foot got stuck. So the sage lost his balance and fell. Luckily, the knot was tight, so he didn't hit the ground. But he hung there, upside down, unable to fall or rise! The audience roared with laughter. A few were silent at first for they thought it was a part of the play. But looking at Narada's evident agitation, they realized that this was not meant to be so.

Gudsikara got up and shouted, 'Get the curtain down.' Shiva ran back into the wings, alarmed. Gudsikara shouted again. Poor Parvathi, unable to deal with the laughing audience and hanging Narada, began to sing her song in a shrill voice and dance, her hands on her waist. The crowd went mad laughing. Whom should they look at now? Swinging Narada, dancing Parvati or shouting Gudsikara?

Finally, Gudsikara got up and went backstage. There he discovered that Ravana was completely stoned. Before Gudsikara could react, Ravana had run out on stage, thinking that Anjaneya was there already, screaming, 'Yeh, yeh, evil monkey!' Losing his balance at the same time as he swung his mace, he tried to avoid hitting Narada suspended from the rope and ended up smashing the fuse box instead. The power went off—with the lights gone, the people started shouting even louder. Women and children began to scream.

Now the people remembered the *Parijata*. After catching their breath from this commotion, they rushed off in that direction, this play forgotten.

Everybody was gone. The stage was still. Gudsikara switched on his flashlight, and went backstage, calling everyone by their name. Behind the curtain, Thief Sidrama had fallen unconscious, like a cloth spread out for drying, with either his hand or leg up. Gudsikara tried to wake him. It was clear that he was stoned. Next to him, Sita had fallen like a broken doll. The rest had run away.

As he searched, he saw Chimana blinking and shrinking in a corner. Gudsikara was already burning with rage, resentment and disappointment. Now the fire in his loins leapt up in flames. Unaware of what he was doing, he went to her and embraced her.

Ningu had taken his revenge nicely. He had branded them with fire and made them feel the hurt. He had folded betel leaves and arecanuts and coaxed Ravana alias Thief Sidrama, and Sita alias Rumps Ramesa, to eat them, telling them that it would redden their lips. They didn't know that he had filled the leaf pockets with intoxicating herbs. So by the time Gudsikara's speech was over, Ravana's head was swimming, and he had begun to see each person in front of him as two. Sita, leaning in a corner chewing the betel and running his tongue over his lips, never got up again. The Thief was incredibly drowsy. Suddenly he'd heard people shouting. What was happening? Who was swinging from the rope? 'Oh, Hanumanta has already entered!' He'd remembered his role and rushed off to hit him. And hit the fuse box instead. You know the rest of the story.

In the dark, people began to scream and shout, and the alarmed actors ran for their lives like scared sheep.

However, until the end, nobody knew who was responsible. If the Thief believed that someone had worked black magic on him, Sita believed that someone had cast an evil eye on him. The people believed it was because of Karimayi. And that was not an entirely unfounded belief.

While Gudsikara's play was going on here, there in front of the Gowda's house, the *Parijata* was also going on, right? Devaresi was sitting there and watching the play. And, more or less at the time that Narada was hanging in mid-air here, it seems

Devaresi sobbed a couple of times there. The moment the Mother sobbed there coincided with power going off here. Mother had, until now, stopped flowing water. Brought on rains from the white clouds. But no one knew that she could make electric lights go off.

The next day, according to the agreement, Gudsikara paid off the electricity man. But rumours spread about how this man went back weeping or how he lost his eyes. People believed them all. Even Gowda and Dattappa believed them.

The quartet became a bit frightened because of this. But Gudsikara felt no fear, not an iota of it, not a pin prick. In the pleasure of Chimana's company, the boy had loosened up inside. He didn't bother to find out why the play had gone wrong.

After the play, for three of four days, the village was very disturbed. From everybody's mouth what came out was only the talk of Karimayi. Or news of Chimana. Or news of the play. Now Gudsikara had become the Gowda's opponent. People remembered how it was the Gowda who had given the panchayat to Gudsikara. How, when Gudsikara passed his law exams, the Gowda had joyfully distributed sugar to everyone. But the imagination of girls and adulteresses sprouted wings and soared high now. The sky was no limit. If old hags dreamt of going to holy places like Kashi or Kailasa, these young women began to dream of Belagavi with the same intensity.

Chimana was in the village. Another man, who'd come with her, now steps into our story. This is Basavaraju.

Gudsikara recovered. He called the quartet. Each one of them was already trembling with guilt inside, thinking the play had gone wrong because of him. All these three days, they had spent their time trying to find excuses and ward off the blame. Afraid about why they had been sent for, they were surprised when Gudsikara didn't even mention the play.

'Why, have you forgotten about the tea shop? Go, go, don't we have that place at the edge of the outcaste neighbourhood? Put up a hut there. Tomorrow is a good day. We'll start. Get going.'

Need we ask? The next day, before midday, outside the outcaste neighbourhood, at a short distance from Lagumavva's hut, a new hut arose. Gudsikara stood there, supervising the process. Taking care of all the arrangements. He employed a couple of extra hands and oversaw everything. People didn't much notice any of this. Only Durgi would slip away from Lagumavva's watch, under some excuse or other, and come to drink in Gudsikara with hungry eyes. She walked up and down in front of him, hoping he would look at her at least once. She talked to the women passing by in a loud voice and kept laughing. Lagumavva noticed this cheap behaviour and scolded her. Until she had no choice but to go back indoors.

From the day they arrived, Chimana and Basavaraju had stayed in Gudsikara's fields. Now their place was ready, right? It was afternoon, the sun was scorching, there was no sign of rain or life. The cattle stood waiting for some shade or shelter. The children swimming in the lake refused to come out and stayed there, huddled and half-submerged like the cows. If any sentimental devotees went to the temple now, they might have seen the sweat running down Karimayi's face too. That is, it was very hot.

Under this scorching sun, Chimana and Basavaraju came to the hut made for them, led by the Thief.

When they entered it, some devotees of Chimana came and stood outside. Since nobody scared them away, they continued to stand there. Gudsikara carried on supervising. The quartet was moving about. Devotees, their hands on each other's shoulders, were talking and drooling over Chimana. Suddenly, they heard music from the hut. At once every ear pricked up. Those who had been working stopped at once and stood still, like dolls, as if some artist had etched the contours of their body. Even the quartet grew curious and still. They couldn't go in and see what it was when Gudsikara was right there. Of them all, only Gudsikara knew what it was.

At this moment, Chimana came out and stood at the door of the tea shop.

Let's salute Karimayi and welcome the new heroine who has stepped into our story. Let's hope for a new breeze to blow through the village, and wish that our children remain healthy and that the newly lit lamps never go off.

So Chimana came out. What rare beauty! Large eyes lined thickly with kohl. Delicate nose. Lips that look like she has just stopped laughing, or is about to laugh. Pointed chin, and curls of hair pasted to the brow by a thin film of sweat—one look fills your eyes, your heart too. For now we can finish describing her with only one simile—she's like

Karimayi's idol when the golden face is put on. If you gaze at her sentimentally, she looks like that.

But nobody in the village would have thought of this comparison.

Basavaraju, the one who had come with her, also came out, holding a small radio in his left hand. He wore a multicoloured long-sleeved shirt, tucked into trousers that ran the length of his legs, right down to his feet. And he wore shoes that covered those feet. The radio was in his left hand. And in his right a cigarette. As he puffed, faint swirls of smoke drifted out of his nose and mouth. And formed a chain of small and big smoke rings. He knew that everybody was watching him. He also knew that they would follow him wherever he went. So he didn't speak to Gudsikara who was standing in front of him. As if he was rapt in listening to the radio, he set out to see the village. A buzz ran through the crowd which immediately began to follow him, spellbound.

And, in truth, their imaginations had been dealt a blow. Such a small box, how can it sing so well? Children thought there were tiny creatures, the size of your little finger, inside the box. Some of the older ones said it was either magic or machine. Yes, there're people who can perform this kind of magic in Malenadu—it must be their doing. Some others argued that it was the sorcery of the British. And these were not the only versions. By the time they'd followed Basavaraju for about ten steps, tens of such theories had risen and sunk in their heads.

Everybody's imagination became overactive. Everybody became two things—ears to listen to the radio, and eyes to see Basavaraju.

It was the quartet which benefitted most from this situation. After all, wasn't Basavaraju someone they'd brought here? They felt a novel pride in him. Thief Sidrama tried to put his hands on Basavaraju's shoulder as he walked. When it wasn't possible, he laughed to himself, thought of him as 'our buddy'. The pity the quartet felt for people's ignorance was boundless. They took it upon themselves to enlighten anyone who talked nonsense or let their imagination run wild. They remembered Gudsikara telling them that the name of the box was something like *redave*. Now they proudly shared that knowledge—with everyone. In the group that trailed after Basavaraju, a new person joined in at every step. So at every step, the quartet would give the description afresh. Surprisingly enough, even Aayi Mereminda who wasn't known for his generosity, became very generous that day—he gave two people from the group some of his cigarette stubs, and even lent his box of matches to light them.

The news of Basavaraju's *redave* spread across the village with the same intensity as the news of a sudden death. Girls, boys, young ones, old ones—thus from ten or twenty of them in the beginning, the group now swelled to hundreds. Although Basavaraju was a bit scared at first, soon he began to get a strange pleasure out of it. He smoked more.

Blew more smoke rings. Like the rolling chain of smoke from some invisible machine, they emerged from his mouth. He roamed through the village and came back to the hut.

Well, this is how the new tea shop began.

Since this wasn't the usual week, it wasn't necessary for Karimayi to possess Devaresi. But that evening Karimayi possessed him. Immediately, there was a call to the Gowda and Elders. They all came. Mother was sobbing strangely. She was in distress. Gowda asked, 'Mother why are you crying? What is it? Can't you say it in front of your children?' But Mother didn't open her mouth. She was in sorrow. Sobbing. Shedding tears. They threw bhandara so she could speak. A couple of times she made noises like a weeping old woman. Then wept again. Sobbed. Didn't open her mouth at all. Gowda rolled on the ground and clutched at her feet. The Elders did too. They made vows.

But the description of the Mother as 'the one who always protects those who make a vow' turned into a lie that day.

# HUNTING SPREE

You saw the extravagant beginnings of the tea shop, didn't you? But business didn't grow. No one really bothered about it. On and off, Gudsikara went himself and drank some tea. The quartet, only if it was free, drank a sip or two. What they got was one cup for all the four. So how could they become addicted to it, sharing one cup of tea among all of them? It isn't a thing to intoxicate you after drinking. So, fine if they got it, fine if they didn't. Not happy when they got it, nor unhappy when they didn't. They remained so.

Chimana didn't worry about leaving because there was no business. Nor did Basavaraju. But the relationship between Chimana and Gudsikara stayed secret no longer. Even if Gudsikara wished it otherwise. People gossiped. Stopping only when they got tired of it. Gudsikara's mother, worried because of this, tried to talk to him about it a few times. But each time Gudsikara would explode in anger. A house without elders. She lamented that her son had turned into a shameless creature. She begged Gowda and Dattappa with folded hands to advise her son. When they told her he was beyond their control, she cursed her luck and fell silent.

Now the 'meeting' venue had changed. After meeting until midnight in the hut, the quartet would go home. Basavaraju would sleep alone in the old panchayat office. Then get up before sunrise and go to the hut. By then Gudsikara would have gone home.

Gudsikara was disappointed for the first three months. True, he had staged the play because he was upset with the Gowda. But there had also been the desire to win the hearts of the villagers before bringing in his reforms, to cultivate in them the taste for art. He believed starting a tea shop was the first step in turning the village into Belagavi. He knew also that Chimana was a Harijan, and her occupation that of a Harijan too. But why shouldn't people, who drank liquor when a Harijan like Lagumavva gave it, drink tea when Chimana gave it? But the people didn't. Although the reason for this wasn't what Gudsikara thought. People didn't get into this addiction, that's all!

This was yet another reason for Gudsikara's disappointment.

What was the use of bringing reforms that people didn't want? How much, he thought sometimes, could he struggle in the slush with these fools. Added to that—the quartet hadn't come up to his expectations either. But as time passed, a new ray of hope shone. He knew people gossiped about him and Chimana. But he decided to be proud of it. Moreover, when a couple of people had talked badly about it, it seems Gowda had exclaimed, 'He is a man. It's no big deal.' When he came to hear this, he felt as if two horns of pride had sprouted close to his ears. But, in the end, what lent strength to his shoulders was not Chimana. It was Basavaraju.

At all Gudsikara's vulnerable moments, Basavaraju was by him. He filled the empty spaces of the former's personality with his flattery. He turned defeats into victories. God knows how educated Basavaraju was but they grew as close as schoolmates. They had the same ideals and views about village reform. They got on so well that in a very short time they became as one. Especially when they were drunk! How they would hug, eat off each other's plate and vow to give their life for the other! Till then Gudsikara hadn't found a single friend like Basavaraju.

Because of Basavaraju, Gudsikara developed a new interest in the elections. Basavaraju was a great talker. He assured Gudsikara that the election meant the victory of their ideals through the use of clever logic. Can people like Gowda and Dattappa, even in their dreams, understand the ideals of a man such as Gandhiji? Okay, do they even know this name? Imagine someone has a serious sickness. Does it go away by smearing Karimayi's bhandara on him? If a woman has a problem at childbirth, can Karimayi save her? Can superstitions save lives? Che che, this isn't serious talk. Shouldn't every village have a hospital and a high school? Can the illiterate Gowda, who presses his thumb on paper, ever bring these to the village? Shouldn't we look at Belagavi? The Belagavi of today is different from Belagavi of tomorrow. It's developing like that. Where's Belagavi going—and where're these people going? What can you do about such people? They're superstitious. They may not understand the importance of 'develop' in the beginning. But as time passes, they will. We can't just leave it to them to understand. We must make them understand. We should say that if we win the elections this time, we will do this and that and show them—and so on and so forth.

What should Gudsikara feel when he heard talk like that? He whipped out all the ideals hidden in the recesses of his mind. Who should suffer defeat if not an idealist? How many times hasn't Gandhiji lost? He decided to win this election at any cost.

We don't know what Basavaraju was in his previous life. He had confessed that he had been 'in the movement'. But he seemed to adapt quickly and quite well to village life. He watched people's secrets through his dark glasses. He found out their weaknesses. He figured out how to talk to them and please them. Always using the respectful mode of address, irrespective of age. Above all, he came to know the one secret weakness of the village that Gudsikara did not!

That the center of these people's lives was Karimayi.

Basavaraju's *redave* had become very popular. And his clothes, and the way he walked and talked. A talkative man too. He'd describe Belagavi so deliciously that it made the listener's mouth water. Hotels, *tamasha* dances, cinema, college girls, Ingreji ma'ms—che che, the youngsters who were listening to it all just couldn't wait until their village became Belagavi. People who'd only heard stories of ghosts before now heard about a colourful Belagavi that rose up and shone before their eyes. What more? He became the model for young men. Even Ningu, of all people, fantasized about being with him.

Basavaraju even talked about the VD he'd contracted once. The quartet thought that it was a disease that only the big people got. Now they lamented, 'Ayyo, shouldn't we get this disease too.' They would pretend to cough, and if someone asked them why they were coughing, they would lie and say, 'Yes, you know, I have developed a little VD . . . ' Not only this, for weeks together they acted out the symptoms of all the diseases that Basavaraju may have mentioned.

Gudsikara believed in Basavaraju as firmly as one believes in money. Therefore, naturally, Basavaraju used to be in and out of the house. He would go to eat there at least three or four times a week. Seeing the influence Basavaraju had on her son, the old woman once told him, 'Please ask him to get married.' He told Gudsikara. Nothing happened. Finally, she said, 'Okay, at least tell him to get his grown-up sister married.'

That's true. It was Girija who was more in need of marriage than Gudsikara. Like crop ready for harvesting, irrespective of whether it found open spaces or narrow confines to grow, wherever, however, she had grown, and now her body, full and rounded, filled the eyes of those who saw her. Moreover, the girl had cat eyes. Small eyes. And with those half-open intoxicating eyes, she looked like she was always inebriated with youth. The moment a man's eyes rested on her, her body swayed like a stalk of corn on which a parrot had alighted. Who knows what kind of new longings were born in that body? If boys were passing at a distance, even before the eyes saw them, her body felt their presence. Prickly pressing desires broke out, flowed all over her and made her shiver and shiver with an ache. Of late, Basavaraju's comings and goings had increased, right? Naturally, the smell of his attar scent blew over her like a gentle breeze, thrilling her body. All this happened without her being aware of it—only her flesh knew.

As it is, this is the age when you are confused about whether you want to sing or fuck. She laughed a little more than she should. She swayed without reason. If he came to the fields, she would be there too. She looked at him as if she wanted to eat him up.

One day, she sent her maid to borrow his *redave* and listened to it. Like a hunter who knows the nature and movements of animals in every situation, he knew the very roots and ends of her mental and physical state.

A born hunter, he was waiting.

One afternoon, Basavaraju had lunch with Gudsikara and then fell asleep in his house. Suddenly, a ball of crushed paper landed on him. He got up immediately and looked at Gudsikara. The latter was snoring on the bed. Being on the bed, Gudsikara couldn't know what was going on below. Basavaraju looked around, like a cat come to steal. Girija stood on the steps so that only her face was visible. When she saw him wake up, she tittered and went downstairs. He decided that the hunt was over. He went down. Girija was standing at the door. Her mother wasn't there. 'Tell Gudsikara I am going to the fields,' he said, winked and left.

Girija's heart beat like a drum.

Nagarapanchami, the festival of snake worship, was over. It was green everywhere, as if each plant was unable to decide whether to sprout or put forth leaves. The Earth looked like the young whose bodies are heavy, and who see dreams out of the corners of their eyes. You don't feel like touching even a sprout now. For the blossoms fade as soon as you hold them. You grieve to tread on grass. And colourful flowers sprang up everywhere, butterflies flitted over them. Such a green abundance melts even a heart of stone. The mind is full of wonder. 'Che, Karimayi is great,' you think. As a folk poet has sung: if death is true, then let it come here and now—that's how you feel.

Like a deer separated from the herd, frightened by her own footsteps, wide-eyed, Girija walked towards the fields among this lush green that came up to her waist. It was late in the day. The dust rose from the earth as the cattle came home. The hazy sunlight looked as if someone had thrown Karimayi's bhandara into the air. Groups of sparrows, coming back to their nests after feeding, surrounded each plant and tree. They were screeching madly, perhaps because another bird had occupied their nest or simply because they were excited with all this greenness.

Their field was not far away. Nobody could have felt anything suspicious about her being there. She reached the well in the field, heaving with a blend of fear and excitement, and her mind full of airy fancies. But there was nobody there. Then the corn in the neighbouring field shook. She saw Basavaraju standing there, smiling, waving at her, and beckoning her to join him. She was a little frightened. She thought, 'Shall I run away?' Basavaraju picked up a marigold and threw it at her. The floral arrow struck the girl's heart. She took a step forward and stopped.

He threw another flower. It hit her waist, her thighs shook and she took another step forward, walking to him, one step at a time.

Until the tiger pounced and ravaged the fawn.

The thrashing and flailing of their bodies made the tender corn shake violently.

At this time, there's nothing but crop and Earth on the villager's mind. Nature, of course, had given of her plenty. Rains, crops and weeds too. They must separate the crop and weed. Manage the plenty and give the strong and healthy things a chance to grow. If you work hard now, fine. If not, nothing. If you delay, then the crop is as good as gone. Irrespective of age and sex, everybody was in the fields. From morning to night they bent down to work, until their limbs gave way with fatigue. Where's the time for gossip? Nobody had the time to even scratch an itch. And after working like this, when they came home, all they wanted was some hot or cold food to eat. Then scramble for space on the floor and lie down anywhere, anyhow, and snore.

The only people not working now were Basavaraju, Gudsikara and Chimana—only these three.

The work in Gudsikara's fields was done by servants. Basavaraju had nothing to do except smoke cigarettes, listen to the *redave* and wander about Gudsikara's fields. He couldn't find a single person to listen to his Belagavi exploits. While everyone slept, only these three were awake, like ghosts, muttering to themselves.

Chimana's past is hazy. We come to know something of her life through her private conversations with Basavaraju. Her name is Sundari. She trained in her profession with Altagi Sitavva. But she hadn't come to a neighbouring village for the Bayalata. She hadn't made a name for herself. All she had was her beautiful body. At the moment, it was her only chimana-like asset. At some vulnerable moment, when the intoxication of youth had gone to her head, she must have let Basavaraju take her. It seems she'd left Sitavva's house and joined a couple of drama companies. Seen films. Earned something. Then spent her earnings on food and clothes. Even at this young age, the sarees she so carelessly wore, slit with her big toe, and tore, numbered over a dozen!

Here, it wasn't possible to indulge in airy-fairy feelings like in Belagavi. Nowhere to go dressed up. Can't be merry and show off. The tea shop that Gudsikara put up wasn't working at all. She expressed her dissatisfaction to Basavaraju a few times. He kept saying: 'Wait, let this business get over.' This business, whatever it was, she thought had to do with collecting payment from Gudsikara for her stay here all these days.

She was more restless because they had confined her in that hut. She had always loafed about like a heifer let loose from its tether. She had eaten well, roamed about. It didn't suit her nature to be like a tied heifer, always sitting in front of the kitchen stove. Am I Gudsikara's wedded wife? Why should I be kept here, trying to be obedient to him for the food he gives? Gudsikara was always bragging. He only scratched himself for lack of ability to do anything big. Complaining and scheming like a woman. Imagine what any other man with his status, youth and money could do? He has generosity, but it flows uselessly. He has an illusion that honour and respect can be bought with money. Maybe it works for some people. Not for me. Generosity needs money. But to pour out money only to be called a generous man is such a low thing to do. It must be something in the blood that determines our behaviour. Anyway, why all these circumlocutions? Gudsikara is not the horse I want to mount. Basavaraju is a man, true. But he asks money for that too.

But there was a difference between her and a born professional—she never worried about money. It came and went. If a customer gave it, she took it. If not, she remained silent. She didn't feel happy when he gave. Didn't feel sad when he didn't. This nature of hers was very convenient for Basavaraju. He managed the business of give and take and only sent the hungry body to her. He saw the customer's pocket. She saw the body. He concluded that the loins that could satisfy her thighs weren't born on this Earth. And he used that to exploit her. For she was a discontented creature. Not knowing what she wanted, she was searching for it all the time.

Of late, Gudsikara's attraction for her had diminished. Earlier she'd called him 'sarpanch' and used the respectful suffix 're' with it. Now she just called him in the singular, just 'Gudsikara', no suffix. This was a huge blow to his ego. He wanted to tell her that he didn't like it, but she was a big-mouth. She didn't know how to rein in her tongue. No knowing when she'd blurt out something. So he told Basavaraju. But she came to know and began taunting him more. Once when Gudsikara was sitting with the quartet, Thief Sidrama kept staring at her. She too encouraged him. Finally, in front of everybody, she asked, 'Why, Thief, why do you stare like this? Do you want it? Come.'

Gudsikara's bile rose.

'Why, bitch? Do you think this is a whorehouse? Do what you are told to do and shut up'

'Why, pimp? Have you married me or what? Have you paid to get me here? You said it this once. If you say it again, I'll slaughter you like sheep.'

Need we ask? Unaware of what he was doing, Gudsikara took off his sandal and stood up. She said, 'Hit.' If Basavaraju hadn't turned up, who knows how it would have ended. Thankfully, he came as if he had been expressly sent for and calmed both of them.

That same day, Gudsikara took Basavaraju home, gave him 200 rupees and insisted that he send her away to Belagavi. Pocketing the 200, Basavaraju dug a trench in Gudsikara's mind. Then he filled it with words. If Gowda can show his generosity to wayside whores, why can't you show it to Chimana? It's no big deal. You'll see it for yourself. In a fit of anger she must have done this. If you send her back to Belagavi, then what Dattappa said—'How will he manage her?'—becomes true. Even if that doesn't matter, we need her to win the elections. So on and so forth.

One day, it was just noon. Chimana took a pot and went to get water from the lake. Who could be there at this odd hour? She slapped the water into the pot. Big pot, she couldn't lift it. She had come when there was no one there. She waited for someone to come. Nobody came. She washed her face, hands, and feet, scrubbed them thoroughly. God knows what came over her, she thought she'd swim, so she stepped into the water and went in a few steps. But she lost her foothold and began to sink. Alarmed, she began screaming, 'Ayyo, father, mother,' and sank deeper down. Gowda's son Shivaninga, who'd heard the screams, came running and jumped in to save her. Since Chimana hadn't gone into the mid-waters, it wasn't difficult to rescue her. Shivaninga pulled at her wet hair. She, on her part, was very frightened. Hugging him, she kept trying to pull him into the water. He used all his strength, escaped from her hold and managed to swim to the shore with her, then turned her over on her stomach and put pressure on her back. She began to vomit. Meanwhile, Basetti and Aayi Mereminda arrived. All of them ministered to her and brought her back to the hut.

If there had been a little miss, if Shivaninga hadn't come, or if he'd been delayed, Chimana's story would have ended that day. This thought never sank into Basavaraju's head. There was another worm burrowing into it. So he sent for Ningu. Indifferently, he went and covered Chimana, who lay unconscious, with some cloth. Then he heard Ningu call and came out.

It was already evening. Farmers were returning from the fields. But nobody noticed Ningu and Basavaraju sitting intimately on the katte of the hut. Until people stopped passing by, Basavaraju chatted about unimportant things. Of many things that Ningu was fond of. He objected to Ningu not having shaved his beard. He talked about the proper 'hairstyle' that Ningu should have. It was already night and there weren't many people passing by now. So he took Ningu inside and gave him a cup full of bhirandi. After drinking it, he didn't light the lamp but rubbed his hand over Ningu's cheek. But Basavaraju didn't know that he was playing with a tiger. The moment he rubbed

Ningu's cheek, the latter turned into an animal in heat. He held, pulled, mauled and felled Basavaraju to the ground till he choked and gasped. Basavaraju was on the verge of howling and beating on his mouth with his hands. Both were heavyweights, and soon it started getting noisy like a wrestling match. Chimana got up and asked, 'Who's it?'

Both became human again.

Basavaraju lit the lamp, and made them sit with him and swear that they wouldn't repeat to anyone what he was about to say.

Basavaraju had noticed that Durgi got excited whenever she saw Gudsikara. If she saw him come to the hut, she would go crazy, like a cat with a burnt mouth. Unable to sit or stand, she ran about her hut with all kinds of excuses, babbling to Lagumavva in a high voice or laughing for no reason. She was like a restless butterfly. Gudsikara hadn't noticed anything. One day, she had sent a child with folded betel leaves and arecanuts to give to the sarpanch. By mistake, that came into Basavaraju's hands. When he opened it, he saw that the )( shape had been etched on the leaf with lime.

On that day when Chimana went to the lake? Basavaraju was sleeping alone inside, with the door closed. Gudsikara, who had gone to the fields, thought he would drop in. But Chimana wasn't in, right? He sat for a bit and left. Durgi, who was in her hut, knew that the sarpanch had come. She knew Chimana wasn't there. She went in. Then she came out. She didn't notice Gudsikara leaving. Thinking he was still inside, she had etched a mandala with lime on a muttuga leaf, made a dot in the middle, kept three jasmine flowers in it, folded it, thrown it into the hut and run away. Naturally, it was Basavaraju who found this. Since he had grown up in the city, he couldn't figure out the meaning of these signs.

He didn't have anyone to share such private things with. The quartet was unfit. These days, Ningu had grown close to him. When he went to the fields, sometimes he also visited Ningu's hut. Which was why he had sent for him. Now he asked Ningu the meaning of Durgi's message.

'Why? Is any girl after you?' Ningu asked jealously.

'Not me—Gudsikara!'

'Who's she?'

Ningu pestered him to tell him the name, so he finally said it was Durgi. Then Ningu deciphered the message to Basavaraju: A day before the full moon, come to the back of the temple at dusk. Basavaraju asked, 'How do we show our acceptance?' 'If the sarpanch throws an arecanut at her, that's acceptance,' said Ningu. Then he got up and left, telling Basavaraju to 'come home some time.'

That night, only three people tossed on their beds, unable to sleep—Basavaraju, Chimana and Durgi. Chimana, because she was still in shock.

Basavaraju's calculative mind was full of friction, sparks of thought. He had squeezed and used Chimana as much as was possible. Now she had become so dry that no juice spurted, no matter how hard he tried to squeeze. He had to get rid of her. That too with a careful plan and at least some profit. What's turned dry must become firewood, or husk. Firewood lights the stove. It wasn't possible to light Gudsikara's stove with this firewood. But feed it some husk, and even a cow that doesn't give milk will start to do so.

Durgi was in a state of strange anxiety. Her body was taut with desire, but whether it was an anxiety of the mind or body, it was impossible to tell. An innocent girl, she was like fresh clay. Clay that was ready to take any shape according to how it was mixed and moulded. She wasn't Abai's daughter. The daughter of a jogati of Savadatti Ellamma.[9] When her mother died, Durgi had been only ten. Since then Durgi had been in Abai's house. Abai was scheming to make her a jogati in another year and a half. In the meanwhile, Durgi was on her toes to get Gudsikara.

In the middle of all this—Basavaraju was calculating his gains.

Now how're all these things connected?

## FIRE PIT

This is an unusual situation. Beginning from Mahanavami New Moon to Shige Full Moon, the farmers have no work to do.[10] They needn't do weeding, needn't be concerned about the crop. The grain comes out of the crop's throat. It is lovely to look at the Earth now—like a fully pregnant woman. To tell you the truth, there's nothing in the world as beautiful as a pregnant woman. It is when you see woman as maya.[11] So wonderful, suffused with an intoxicating, yet content, beauty in every limb of her body.

In the face of this divine beauty, man becomes a child. You want to praise God when you look at this silent Earth, rapt in the stirring treasure of her womb.

Now menstruating women shouldn't go anywhere near the fields. Men shouldn't be adulterous. You shouldn't go across the pepper fields, or over the creepers wearing your sandals .

The farmers know this. Therefore, as if they are fulfilling the cravings of a pregnant woman, they make a variety of dishes and strew them all over the fields. The sky is clear whether it's day or night. In the day, there's a wonderful smiling sun. At night, a sky full of stars like popcorn strewn everywhere—here's my light, there's your twinkling. Add to that, a cold which is pressing softly, surrounding you . . .

But the moment I say cold, don't go and listen to people's talk of how cold accentuates the longing of separated lovers, lovers' desire and desire for pleasure. All that might sound fancy in useless poetry, in poetic palaces or in cities where people have nothing to do. After all, there's a season for everything. This certainly isn't the season for any mischief.

It is so nice to see Devaresi's face now. With a braid that reaches down to his knees, his forehead smeared with bhandara, a cloak-like blanket on one shoulder and the bhandara bag hanging from the other—he sets off to work every day, to throw bhandara until he reaches the village limits. When he moves from field to field and sits there, saying: 'It's like this, son, like that, son,' the farmers feel as if Karimayi herself is visiting their fields. Whether it's the sight of this splendid green Earth, or the beauty of the Mother's face smeared with bhandara, the farmers are overwhelmingly grateful for both.

Day after day, the Full Moon was getting nearer. Mother herself had indicated long ago that this Full Moon was one of the three major days of worship. On this Full Moon, the more you please the Mother, the more she gives of her plenty. Mother, that is Devaresi, who goes to mark the village limits on the Mahanavami day, visits Gowda's house the day before the full moon. That day, Mother's food comes from Gowda's house. There are some rules to follow, though. A good wife, who has borne a son, should get up when the cock crows, bathe in cold water and then, wearing the same wet clothes, cook a meal for the Mother. This good wife, starting from when she gets up to when she goes to the fields to feed the Mother, shouldn't talk to anyone or look anyone in the eye. Since this is a custom followed through generations, the villagers know of it and leave her alone. They take care to not step anywhere close to where she may be passing by.

At dusk, Mother, that is, Devaresi, must be offered liquor. This is Lagumavva's responsibility. And this requires three new dishes. First, Mother's served a large dishful. She drinks it in one gulp. Then another, and yet another. Finishing all three, Mother, without a word, falls face down on the floor. That description of Mother drinking three gulps of liquor in Lagumavva's song? Those three gulps are of this sort! After all, she's the great Mother—everything about big people will be big.

The same day, in the afternoon, playing wind and percussion instruments, the farmers bear big logs of wood to the temple entrance, dig a pit, throw wood into it, light it and leave. Once they leave, they can only come back the next day, along with Mother. Until then even an insect shouldn't pass this way.

One must not forget that Mother's like fire. So devotees must keep pure and clean. The next day, they come with the Mother's golden idol in a procession, the oracle speaks and then the festivities are over.

Well, Karimayi finished marking the village limits. Then she came and camped in the Gowda's fields. The morning meal was over. It was noon. Instructing Durgi to sit in the hut, Lagumavva went to gather flowers, hay and corn stalks. Durgi was alone in the hut, wasn't she? Again and again, she hopped out to see if Gudsikara had come. Did he get my earlier message? Will he come to the temple in the evening? When there's Chimana, will he still desire me? If not, why did he send me money during the Holi festival? She was lost in all this strange and complicated logic. Only Basavaraju noticed her flit in and out. Gudsikara didn't know the head or tail of this.

Basavaraju was cautious. He made Gudsikara sit on the katte and talked causally for a while. Then, slowly, he brought up the matter, making sure Chimana couldn't hear. He described very colourfully how a girl was hungry and waiting for Gudsikara. This naturally kindled Gudsikara's interest—who is this girl? He kept asking. Basavaraju played with him for a while—'You tell me who she is.' Until, finally, he said, 'Close your eyes, I'll show you.' Then he gave Gudsikara an arecanut and told him that if he threw it in front of him, the girl would manifest herself. So Gudsikara closed his eyes and threw the nut. It fell in front of Durgi who stepped out of her hut at just that moment. Overcome with shyness, she took the nut and ran inside. Gudsikara thought, 'Yes!' He wasn't terribly excited, though. Basavaraju noticed this immediately.

But the fun that has to happen will happen anyway. Basavaraju assured Gudsikara that this too must be done for the sake of the coming elections.

'What's next?'

'That's my responsibility.'

Durgi panicked. Sun doesn't set. Evening doesn't come. She was walking on air. Her mind refused to be still. She came out and cursed the sun. Went in and sat. Couldn't sit and stood up. Couldn't stand and paced up and down. Couldn't pace up and down and sat down again. Stood. Glided. Sighed. Measured the heaving of her own bosom. Finally, it was evening. Lagumavva wasn't in the hut. She had known by the sound of the trumpet that the farmers had gone to the pit, thrown the logs in and then set them alight. It was evening. Her body was afire. Her mind was aroused. Who could stop her now?

She went near the trees at the back of the temple and looked around. No one. Hadn't he come yet? Did he throw the nut without meaning it? She thought of all sorts of things as she sat there hoping he would come. Tired, she went searching again. Finally, as she passed in front of the temple, she heard a soft call. She turned. He was standing in the darkness inside the temple and beckoning to her to join him. She knew that nobody would come to the temple today. For a moment, she stood wavering. Then, suddenly, as if swept up by a wind, she rushed into the temple without any thought of things such as taboo or purity or pollution. He lifted her and took her behind the idol of the goddess. The thrashing and flailing of their bodies shook the wooden idol of the Mother so violently that the dagger-holding right arm broke and fell off.

They didn't notice anything in the dark. They weren't in any state to notice anything either.

The flames in the pit raged on.

Thinking that Gudsikara might have come to the temple after what he had told Basavaraju, Ningu went to the grove at the back. No one. He decided it was all a lie and started walking back along the path beside the temple. Suddenly, from inside, he heard a woman moan. It was impossible for him to imagine that something vile could be going on in the inner sanctum. Tomorrow is the Full Moon, after all! And ghosts gather in the temple today, don't they? Alarmed, he ran off a bit, then stopped and looked back through the entrance door. The fire in the pit, which had been lit just then, was burning. Beyond the flames, he could see the sanctum shaking from side to side. Terrified now, he ran off, screaming, 'Ayyoyo, there's a female ghost in the temple—I heard her with my own ears!'

It was only after she returned to the hut that Durgi regained consciousness. She felt like someone who had just escaped from a flood. Her senses settled back into place and began to function again. She was trembling. Fresh blood trickled down her thighs. She cleaned them. What shouldn't have happened at the temple of Karimayi had happened. She remembered Mother's fierce face of wood and the hand that held the weapon. She remembered the face of Devaresi possessed by Mother. She trembled some more. Some other day, maybe it wouldn't have been quite so bad. But these were days when the taboos of purity and pollution mattered. Tomorrow, Mother will come to the temple. There has been pollution. I can't be saved. Tomorrow, Mother will pull me up and set fire to my head. Ayyo, this is disastrous. She was terrified. Fearing for her life, she clutched her heart and slumped on the bamboo mat. Her heart beat so loudly that the sound of it seemed to fill the room.

When Basavaraju came, Gudsikara was talking to Chimana. Basavaraju was in a jubilant mood. He called in a voice louder than usual, 'Hello, sarpanch!' and went in. There was fresh blood on his shorts. He changed and came out bearing a bottle. A deep satisfaction shone on his face. He forced Gudsikara to have a drink and poured some for himself. He poured some for Chimana. After every word, he called Gudsikara, 'old boy' and patted his shoulder. From time to time, he laughed loudly and victoriously. He was tired, right? Like a snake which has swallowed a frog, he went to sleep where he sat.

Before the cock crowed, Lagummava got up and bathed. She wore clothes that had been made ritually 'pure,' gathered all the things and went to wake up two good wives in the neighbourhood.

The cock crowed.

All three went to the temple. The wooden logs in the pit had turned into bright embers.

Today, Karimayi will be dressed in special clothes. Decorated with aavare flowers from neck to waist. This looks like Mother's yellow blouse. From waist down to the feet, they stick corn stalks in a row. This looks like the crisp folds of her saree. Then a marigold garland round her neck. When the procession arrives, they fix the golden face. These adornments fill the eyes of the onlookers. Those flowers, those stalks, that golden face—it looks like Mother has taken the avatar of the goddess of plenty. By the time they are done decorating her body, it will be sunrise.

In the morning light, Lagummava saw the broken wooden arm of Mother. Her heart leapt to her mouth. She crossed her hands over her chest and cried, 'Ayyo, Mother'. Everybody was alarmed at the sight. The broken arm with its dagger had fallen to the ground. Beside it were some drops of blood. They wondered if, in the excitement of decorating her, they had broken the arm. But they didn't remember anything like that happening. They said Mother was angry. It's bad luck, they said.

Lagumavva ran anxiously to the Gowda's house.

The Elders had already gathered there. The wives had come to do the aarti. The goddess' followers were playing the large drum, the dollu. Horn-player Singa turned in every direction and blew the horn. Dattappa hadn't come yet. Lagumavva ran up to the Gowda and whispered the news of Mother's broken arm in his ear. Gowda felt as if he had lost all the strength in his limbs. He asked everybody to wait, signalled to Dattappa, who was approaching, to follow him and then rushed to the temple.

Lagummava followed.

Gowda was stunned when he saw the Mother's broken arm. He looked at Lagumavva. She said it wasn't their fault. Dattappa suggested they attach the arm somehow, until the goddess arrived, and fix it properly later. 'Right,' they said, and with a thin cord, bound the arm to the idol. To cover it up, they also hung a couple of garlands on the break. Whatever they did, their hearts kept thumping with fear. They suspected that some pollution had occurred. Gowda called Lagumavva aside and asked if it had. She swore on Karimayi that it hadn't. Moreover, it isn't as if Lagumavva doesn't know all this—need we teach her the responsibilities of god's worship? But he only asked because he was so perturbed. He glared at the others, asked them to speak the truth. They ran to touch Mother's bhandara and swore their innocence. Anyway, there was no time to sit and think on this matter now. Dattappa and Gowda left, instructing Lagumavva to clean the floor, purify herself again and perform the worship of the altar before the goddess came.

Even though the Gowda and the others didn't say anything, their expressions were enough to tell the people who had gathered that some untoward thing had happened. They set the golden face—usually kept in Gowda's house—on the palanquin. Then the procession went to the Gowda's fields. By the time they brought the Mother, who was sitting in the fields, to the temple, four hours had passed.

When the procession reached the temple entrance, the rest of the village was waiting. Durgi hadn't come. But Sundari, Gudsikara and Basavaraju had. Basavaraju had come to watch the fun. Gudsikara had some faith. But he didn't want to show it in front of Basavaraju, so he acted as if he had been forced to come. Now the procession was drawing close to the enclosure. They had wrapped a blanket around the priest. He was carrying the palanquin in his left hand, and he looked as if he was floating in the air. At some distance from the enclosure gate, twenty or thirty devotees who had made vows—men, women and children—were prostrating themselves. Then screaming 'Chaangu, Bhale' everybody raced towards the temple. The drummers drummed, people with hairy chouri switches swished them and then all together they ran up to the gate with wild cries. This is Mother's miracle. That the people prostrating were unharmed—the procession which ran over them didn't even graze their legs. To tell the truth, there were infants down there who could have been squashed with a single tread of those feet. It's not impossible to tread like that in such a mad rush. But can people's faith be false? Or is Lagumavva's song that says of Mother, 'She's the one who makes a boulder float and a ball sink,' be false?

God knows why that day, but, mysteriously, the palanquin came to the enclosure gate and stopped dead. The palanquin bearers felt as if their feet were paralysed. Even when they tried to drag Devaresi by the arm, he wouldn't budge. Everyone was frightened and surprised. Gowda, Dattappa and Lagumavva had been dreading just such a thing. Instead of one coconut, they broke ten. They threw lemons in all ten directions. The usual custom was that when the palanquin came to the enclosure, Mother possessed Devaresi. And once possessed, he never stood like this but began to run round the pit.

But today Mother didn't budge even after they performed the coconut and lemon rituals to ward off the evil. Nothing like this had ever happened. The musicians fell silent. Mother, who had possessed Devaresi, was trembling in a strange manner. Gowda quickly clutched her feet and begged, 'Please forgive the sins of your children—just swallow them up.' People were stunned into silence. Gowda wouldn't let go of her feet. But Mother wouldn't open her mouth. Dattappa too clutched her feet and said, 'Mother, we don't know what's wrong. But we will pay any penalty for it. Come in.'

Suddenly, Mother let out a terrible scream, and, pushing aside the men holding her feet, ran into the temple.

According to custom, after going in, Mother runs around the pit thrice. Those who have made vows pour salt into the pit. Mother passes through the pit.

Then she identifies those whose devotion has flagged and makes them walk over the fire. She stabs at her tongue with her dagger. Slashes her stomach with her sword. Perhaps this is a way of making sure their faith doesn't diminish. But the devotees don't let this happen—by the time she has run the sword over her stomach a couple of times, they rush to seize both dagger and sword. You should know better than to test Mother!

But this time it didn't happen this way. Mother ran to Basavaraju, who stood with his arm flung round Gudsikara's shoulder, and dragged him outside. Even before the shocked people could open their mouths, she made him walk up and down over the fire on which salt hadn't yet been poured. Then she wrenched the unsheathed dagger from the man who stood at the edge of the pit holding it. Slashing her stomach and tongue, she began to move in a state of frenzy. Lagumavva's sentimental eyes saw the original avatar of the Mother now. God knows what would have happened if they hadn't interfered, but the wrestler boys jumped right into the pit, held the Mother tight and freed Basavaraju. The moment he was free, Basavaraju jumped out of the pit and collapsed. People who had made vows hurriedly poured salt into the pit. Immediately, Mother ran and stepped on the the mullavige, the ritual sandals with spikes.

Gowda came running and held her feet. Dattappa sat behind her. They put the coconut into Mother's hands for a blessing. Mother shrieked—and the sound seemed to burst people's eardrums. Everybody went quiet. Mother kept sobbing. The words that were stuck in her throat wouldn't come out. Mother seemed to be struggling with something—with saying something unpleasant or not saying it.

Finally, she seemed to have made up her mind. 'Gowda!' she called. No longer sobbing. She waited for a while and then continued to speak as the oracle: 'They might steal the golden baby. Be careful.' She dropped the coconut that had to be blessed. Luckily, it didn't fall to the ground. Dattappa, who was ready for it, caught it. Mother entered the inner sanctum.

Nobody was happy with the oracle. Today, people had seen a hell of a lot of things happen. Mother coming and stopping at the enclosure gate, entering the pit without going round it, dragging Basavaraju, who wasn't even a man from the village, all over the place. . . some said Basavaraju must have committed some sin, others thought he must have insulted the gods, yet others thought he's a city boy, he lacks faith, so this happened.

Despite all this talk, they weren't satisfied.

Basavaraju hadn't regained his courage. Not yet. If he had known, he could have prepared his mind to face this. Or he could have stayed back. True, he didn't have faith in the goddess. And despite all this turmoil, faith couldn't be born now. If everyone was standing there thinking of one thing, he was thinking of something else. True, he hadn't expected this punishment, this insult. Nor was he cultured enough to regret any misdeed he might have committed. Well, he had come to watch the fun. He stood there feeling merry, wearing his dark glasses, searching for Durgi in the crowd and joking. Like an enemy pouncing on an unarmed man, Devaresi had dragged him out. He didn't know what happened or why until he was freed later. He only regained consciousness after Devaresi let go of him. When he was free, there was no strength left in his limbs or tongue. He collapsed where he stood. Busy listening to Mother's oracle, nobody, not even Gudsikara, had attended to him then.

Tomorrow is the time to harvest the crop of the monsoon rains. Today, this terrible event has occurred. People's minds, never disturbed in this manner before, had turned restless. They stood in groups and talked about nothing else. They listened with interest to any naive or dumb explanation that was offered. Moreover, they hadn't quite understood the meaning of the oracle. What's the golden baby? Who takes it away? Nobody could figure any of it out. Gowda or Dattappa or Lagumavva should tell them. They still hadn't opened their mouths. Elders recalled old festivals and said nothing like this had ever happened. Today's event was outside the imagination of even Lagumavva's songs.

The news of Mother's broken arm had spread everywhere. Hadn't Ningu heard the moaning of the female ghost last night? That was also talked about. Women, in particular, remembered all the other women who had died that year and thought: Could she have become a ghost? Or was it that other one?—Basvi loved her children madly, Chaluvi was crazy about her husband . . . they kept guessing. According to the villagers, there are only two kinds of dying—dying contented and dying discontented. Even after dying, it isn't as if the dead went to fancy places like the heaven or Vaikunta or Kailasa. Those who die contented become honeybees and enter into the service of Mother. The discontented become the ghostly minions and suffer. Perhaps only Dattappa, that too because he was Brahmin, longed for Vaikunta!

They spoke about Basavaraju too. Nobody though that he had committed a sin. But yes, he didn't care for rituals or purity or gods. The more people tried, the less they could solve this mystery. Yet until they solved it, they couldn't stop thinking about it.

Who knows how the Mother's dark maya envelopes people's minds? They tried to interpret the oracle through the light of their understanding. They inquired of others. Lagumavva isn't just any other woman—she's someone who has seen, sat in front of and talked to Karimayi. Karimayi had sat on Lagumavva's tongue and made her tell her story! If even Lagumavva couldn't figure out the oracle? Wonder-struck, she took to sleeping with her right forefinger on her nose.

For once, Dattappa's epic intellect had failed. They couldn't find an answer in his *Chintamani* either. Gowda was intelligent, wise and experienced. But none of that helped him get anywhere near to explaining the oracle. Only this much was certain—Goddess' arm was broken. And then the oracle had turned out this way. Because of these things, some calamity was about to befall the village. But as the village Gowda, he had to find out the cause of Mother's broken arm. Perhaps then they would also come to know the meaning of the oracle.

As things were, the one whose mind was a little lighter now was Durgi's. She wasn't there when Mother went to the temple. She was afraid—because she had polluted the temple. She was sure that Mother would make her pass through the pit. So she had stayed away.

She had also thought that the Mother would certainly make the sarpanch pass through fire. She was sure that Mother's arm broke because of all their thrashing and flailing. But the one Mother dragged out was Basavaraju. What do you say to that? What the hell was that all about? Shall I call it Mother's compassion? Or shall I say that even Mother didn't know? The girl who chattered so much every day, now sealed her lips, as if the moment she opened them, her misdeed would come tumbling out.

There was an emergency meeting in Sundari's hut. The quartet had gathered there on the ruse of talking about the insult to Basavaraju. It was in any case clear to Gudsikara why Mother had dragged Basavaraju out. He is from Belagavi, he has no faith, he is someone who is yet to get used to the ways of this village, and so on. The quartet weren't unhappy about what happened. They weren't happy either. They just said the usual things one said on an occasion like this.

After everybody had finished, Basavaraju began to talk slowly. The sarpanch certainly needs his help in the coming elections. Gowda knows this. He's trying to make arrangements from now on so that whatever trick he pulls off later, people won't see through it. That's why he made the Goddess say all this—it's clearly a put-up job, done according to Gowda's orders.

Everybody agreed with this logic. Gudsikara more than others. What a trick they played without our knowing!

Inside the hut, Sundari chuckled.

Sundari wasn't interested in their conversation. She was contemplating something on the mattress. She too was surprised that, of all people, Devaresi had dragged out Basavaraju. She knew him inside out. She had overheard him mention the matter of Durgi to Ningu. Only last night, she had observed fresh blood on his shorts. She'd heard people talk about pollution and Mother's broken arm. Therefore, what happened to him was punishment. But how did Mother, who was outside the village, discover the thief?

While she was thinking about this, outside, Basavaraju was saying that it was Gowda who got all this done. Listening to him, she couldn't stop laughing. She came out, still laughing. Without speaking to anybody, she picked up the liquor bottle, added another layer to her laugh and went back inside.

Basavaraju lit a cigarette in triumph.

# UNSEASONAL RAINS

It wasn't just that Shivaninga was Gowda's son—he was an able young man himself. He never abused anybody, nor did anyone abuse him. He only concerned himself with his home. He was the kind who could never cross other people. Never stare at another's face. Not a talker. Fond of keeping a mongoose or a sparrow or a parrot for a pet. He could imitate the call of birds and wild animals, climb trees like a monkey and play. His mother Shivasani thought, 'When will he mix with people?' Especially when he saw women, the boy shrank into himself like a tortoise and felt shy. When he saved Sundari from drowning in the lake, some people, because of their anger against Gudsikara, told him that he shouldn't have done it. But Dattappa applauded his act. Lagumavva said, 'After all, he is the Gowda's seed.'

Sundari sometimes thought of the brave boy who saved her life. She would go to Gudsikara's fields. The next field was the boy's. But he was hardly there. When she wandered in the village, or went to get water, or whenever she went out, she searched for him. He was indeed a rare one to find, even for the village lasses. How could she get him? He's not one who is in the news. Never jumped the fence. Not someone at whom you can point a finger. 'Avva, how grave he is!' she thought. 'I want nothing more, if I see him once, I just want to tell him: Thank you, Appa.'

She found that opportunity at last.

Once, it wasn't late in the day, the dense clouds of untimely rains had gathered in the sky, masking the sun. And from behind the hill, with those flashes of lightning, they seemed to be arching their brows and mocking at the Earth. Plants ready for the harvest still stood in the fields. Another four or five days, on the day of the festival of lights, Deepavali, the crop should be in their hands. If it rains now, what is almost in their hands is gone. Farmers rarely go to their fields in groups now. Even if some do, it is only to get animal feed or vegetables, or perhaps graze their cattle. The moment the clouds gathered, the farmers raised their hands to their foreheads in desperation and looked pleadingly at the sky. A cool breeze was blowing. This wasn't the cold breeze out of the basket of Shige Full Moon, though. Certain it would rain, the farmers fretted and took their cattle back to the village. People who had built huts stayed back in them. Because of these untimely rains, they knew for sure that Karimayi was angry.

In the hut in his fields, Shivaninga sat alone, making a rope out of coir. It looked like Chimana was there in the next field. She seemed to be humming some film song. Or it might not even be Chimana singing, Basavaraju's radio also sang in the same way. Suddenly, the song stopped. Whether she is singing or not, what's it to him? He kept twisting the rope.

Suddenly, he sensed someone standing close by and observing him. He looked up. Chimana stood before him. He became terribly flustered. His throat went dry, his heart began to thump. Whoever the visitor was, since she had come to his hut, it was his duty to talk to her, right? He was still holding the rope in his hands as he tried to form the words, but they stuck in his throat and he just remained sitting in that stunned posture.

Chimana tittered seeing the boy's wonder.

'What're you doing alone?' Shivaninga didn't speak, merely stretched out his hand and showed her the rope. 'What? Let me see,' she said and drew closer, but he leapt back like someone who had seen a snake. Chimana chuckled again. 'How idiotic!' But that idiocy drew her like a magnet. The boy became more confused and stood away. Forget touching him, it's difficult even to make him talk. The more she stood there, the dumber he got. The more she saw of his dumbness, the more stimulated she became.

'Look, if there're some peanuts in the field, can't you roast them for me?'

Shivaninga set forth with great enthusiasm to get some peanuts from the edge of the field. Chimana followed. He began to run. If Chimana took a step, he took ten. For some part, they progressed in this manner—the pit near the fields, beyond the pit, into the corn fields, and finally, to the edge of the fields where the peanut crop was.

Shivaninga yanked out a handful of creepers, tore the nuts and then ran off to get twigs and sticks to light the fire. Gathering the peanuts, he poured them out. Then he looked around for fire. Far away, behind the hillock, he saw smoke spiralling up into the sky. Perhaps the boy had legs like a horse! Even as she watched, he ran across and then ran back as swift as lightning with a few cakes of dried cowdung and lit the fire. Chimana, who sat watching him from a distance, pointed to the hillock and asked 'Why's the fire there?' As if he'd hardly heard, he answered, 'Lagumavva brews liquor there.'

The moment he mentioned liquor, her mouth began to water. 'Let's go and drink some,' she said. Without so much as a 'why' or 'what,' Shivaninga ran off again. Chimana was taken aback. After he had run some distance, she realized he was going to get the drink and so she set off too. If she hadn't got there on time, he would, in all probability, have fetched the entire pot. A large earthen pot in a place secure from rain. A fire. A wide dish covering the pot. This is Lagumavva's brewery. Shivaninga thought he could tell Lagumavva later and tilted the pot into the dish. Then offered it reverentially to Sundari. It had brewed nicely. Her tongue loved the rare taste of the warm country liquor. She gulped it down. Then she held out the dish once more. He filled it again. He filled it yet again. After three long gulps, she belched hard like a man and gestured to him to have some.

He said, 'No.'

She walked back to where the peanuts were roasting. Oblivious of the clouds, not even thinking of the boy in front of her, she sat with splayed legs, that is, in the posture of Karimayi, and began to noisily chew the nuts. Then she remembered Shivaninga. Turned her drowsy eyes to him. He sat there, not eating but watching her eat. As she turned to him, he bent his face shyly. He would be a grown man today or tomorrow. Now in his tender years, he was growing up like a strong bull. A slender line of moustache which had just sprouted. His cheeks and face aglow. He reminded you of Gowda in his youth.

Looking at this handsome young man, with his big bright wonder-struck eyes, stealing glances at her, she laughed. Then, stretching her arms, she yawned loudly, 'H-a-a-a.' Then she got up.

There was a light drizzle.

She couldn't keep her balance. Couldn't walk, couldn't stand. She swayed and couldn't manage to take a step right. Although Shivaninga was walking ahead, he kept coming back, fearing she'd fall.

The drizzle had turned into heavy rain.

The boy would run, turn back and stop again.

Both were drenched.

It wasn't difficult to go past the peanut crop. But when they went into the corn field, unable to keep her balance, she kept falling all over and then getting up again. Suddenly, she slipped and screamed, 'Yavva . . . ' Shivaninga ran back and stood at a distance. Her saree was spattered with mud. She got up slowly. The rain poured on. The liquor in her stomach had risen to the brim and gone to her head. In this state, she put her hands on her head, stammered out the song 'Where, I can't see, where . . . ' and began staggering about, trying to dance. Set the crop around her waving because of her movements. The saree slipped from her bosom and was about to slip away from her waist too. Alarmed, Shivaninga took a couple of steps back, ready to run away to the hut if necessary. All of a sudden, Sundari went to him and kicked at his waist with all her might. Staggered by this unexpected kick, the boy fell face down. His mouth filled with mud. He turned over quickly, then saw Chimana and was shocked! The saree had slipped away fully. Plump rosy thighs and rounded buttocks strained against the titillating and tight red panties. A slender waist and an unruly bosom bursting out of the blouse. Smiling sweetly and stammering the song, she was still dancing with drunken drowsy eyes. Flames shot through him, a sudden tightness in the crotch—the frightened bull of a boy was bewildered by the new and rousing feelings flooding in him! He felt like a bull freed from its tether. Even as these irrepressible sensations surged through him a couple of times, she stubbed her muddy foot on his chest, lost her balance and fell on him. The boy wanted to get up. But she hugged him tight. Like a parrot hanging from a corn stalk and pecking at it, she pulled at his cheek and bit it repeatedly.

The force of their thrashing bodies broke the corn stalks again and again.

Thunder roared and tore at the clouds above. The rain came down harder. The whole sky seemed to split, and water cascaded in endless torrents. Flowed into every cranny of the leaves and roots. Unable to bear its force, the crop struggled and swayed. Uncaring, the sky poured until finally the clouds cleared. And the Earth shut its eyes, contented.

By the time she came to her senses, Sundari was like a faded tender banana leaf. Her waist muscles had loosened but there was also a slight pain. She was still panting. Her body was bruised as if she had just escaped from the tiger's mouth. She got up and wore the mud-spattered saree again. Shivaninga sat slumped some distance away, with a weepy face, looking very guilty. His lower lip was bleeding. There were teeth marks on his cheeks and neck. Satisfied that she had created a tough man out of a tender awestruck boy, she walked away without a word. He followed, stooping as he walked, afraid that someone might see him.

They passed the corn crop. The stream was full and flowing. Shivaninga crossed over. Water came up to the chest, and there was a strong current. She was left on the other bank. She got frightened. She was still hung-over. Her head felt heavy. She gestured to him and asked him to help her across. Shivaninga stood silently. 'I won't tell anybody,' she begged, 'Come.' He made sure that there was no one around and then crossed over to her. Held her hand. Acting as if she was terrified, she pulled him low and hoisted herself on his shoulders. He crossed the stream as quickly as he could. Sundari caressed the teeth marks on his cheek. Just as they were about to reach the other bank, someone suddenly called out, 'Yeh, Shivaninga.'

Exclaiming, 'Yappa, someone's come!' he dropped her there, leapt away and disappeared into the sugar-cane field.

# CLANDESTINE PREGNANCY

The next day onwards, there was strange activity in the field. Unable to bear the force of the rains, the corn and paddy had collapsed to the ground. People were raising the stalks and tying them up. If they left the peanuts the way they were, there was a chance of the fallen nuts sprouting. In some places, heaps and heaps of creepers had been washed away. In every field, half the crop stood in water. People were picking the shoots of sajje. Plucking the still-tender grain.

But the state of the corn was uncertain.

In the hut, Basavaraju sat with Sundari, feeling rather confused about what she had just told him— she was pregnant! If Gudsikara came to know, he would surely explode. What do you do when something like this happens just at election time? Enemies might use this against him. Gudsikara was not the type to brave this sort of a thing. Inside, he was a coward. As it is, had lost his enthusiasm for the elections. In fact, his followers had to constantly pump some into him, remind him of Gowda's misdeeds to whet his anger, then refer to the elections and point out how indispensable they were to him.

Moreover, he no longer felt the same attraction to Sundari's body.

Sundari had taken too long to tell him. This thorn had to be removed before the others came to know. But how! It wasn't as if she didn't know Gudsikara's nature. There's no doubt that if pregnancy is mentioned to a man like Gudsikara, who can only do easy things like 'somersaulting on a cotton sack,' he will leap a couple of yards away. It may be okay with the other whores. But she had decided that it wasn't for her. She was willing to do anything to get rid of this nuisance. She begged Basavaraju, 'Somehow, please get this sin out.' In desperation, Basavaraju finally turned to Ningu.

It's true that nobody could equal Ningu in the art of performing abortions. Which is why nobody in the village knew as many stories of clandestine pregnancies as he did. Ningu listened to everything that Basavaraju said. But how could he give the medicine without asking to whom, and by whom, this had happened? Basavaraju, pretended to be sad, said that the pregnant one was Durgi. Looking at his anxious face, Ningu felt some pity. He told Basavaraju to go to the forest, get some herbs, pound them into juice and make her drink. But because she might be in acute pain and start screaming, he advised Basavaraju to take her to the fields and make her drink it there. He didn't forget to mention that if Basavaraju had done it with him instead, he wouldn't have had to go through all this worry!

One afternoon, Gudsikara was sleeping at home. Sometimes, he walked in the fields in the evening. Sometimes he did, sometimes he didn't. Thinking that there was little possibility of it this evening, Basavaraju took the cup with the herbal concoction and went to Gudsikara's field with Sundari. There was nobody there. First, he made her go into the sugar-cane crop. When he was about to enter, he saw some-one in home-spun khadi clothes walking towards him from the barricade of Gowda's fields. He thought he'd seen the man somewhere, but couldn't remember. After the man was gone, he followed Sundari into the crop.

It must have been about a half hour later. Sundari began to scream, 'Yappa, I'm dead.' The moment the medicine got into her stomach, it felt like her bowels were burning and her insides were being torn to pieces. Unable to bear the pain, she started rolling on the ground. Squeezing her stomach with one hand and beating on her mouth with the other, she howled as if she was going to bring the sky down. Perhaps even the wooden idol of Karimayi in the temple faraway could hear her. Basavaraju didn't know what to do. Thrashing her feet and hands on the ground, she writhed in pain. Certain that she would die, and scared to go near her, Basavaraju jumped to his feet and ran away, not heeding the crops or stones or thorns he encountered on the way.

The Gowda, in the next field, heard the screams. He ran there, sickle in hand. Along with him came the khadi-clad Mudukappa Gowda. When they both reached the place where the crop was disturbed, they saw Sundari lying on the ground and bleeding profusely. She had lost her tongue and they could only hear a 'gor-gor' sound coming out of her mouth. She was like a dying animal. Then her limbs shook and she went still. Even before the Gowda could turn to him for help, Mudukappa Gowda had run off to get Dattappa. Gowda went over to her and squeezed her little finger. It wiggled. He squeezed again. It didn't wiggle. He started blowing air vigorously into her ear. Kept doing it. No signs of life. But Gowda wouldn't let go. He kept blowing, as if he wanted to bring back the life which was gone. After a long time, there were some signs of life. Warmth returned to the body. Squeezing the little finger, he called, 'Yeh, avoo, avoo.' She opened her eyes once and closed them again. He thought, 'Thank God—there's nothing to fear.'

Out there, Basavaraju was running like an animal that has escaped from the hunter, right?

Gudsikara walked from the edge of the field that same way. Saw the bewildered Basavaraju running. 'Yeh, Basavaraju,' he called out, and then thinking that there had been some accident, ran towards him. Then he gripped Basavaraju's arm, shook it and asked, 'Why? What happened?'

Basavaraju, oblivious of what he was doing, took Gudsikara with him and came to where Sundari had fallen.

Sundari's head was on Gowda's lap. With one hand, he was holding her little finger tight and with the other he was fanning her. Both their heads were dishevelled. Sundari's saree was rumpled. Sarpanch's whole body began to boil in anger. The moment he saw the scene, Basavaraju felt as though he got his life back. Sundari wasn't dead—she was on Gowda's lap! In an instant, he was back to his natural form. His mind regained its balance. An 'idea' flashed across his mind. He tapped Gudsikara a couple times on the shoulder. Gudsikara was standing there with flaming eyes, biting his lips and torturing himself. Basavaraju struggled to get his attention. Gowda hadn't seen them yet. Gudsikara thundered, 'Gowda, aren't you ashamed of doing this sort of a thing in your old age?' and left without waiting for an answer.

At these words, Gowda looked up. Who knows what the Gowda would have said or done, if the one who uttered such words had stood there a moment longer? Or if he really understood what the other had said? Even as he saw the two men, and opened his mouth to speak, they'd disappeared. Gowda felt bad—no need to thank me for saving her life but Gudsikara could at least have taken care of his girl instead of running away like that. Gowda had only heard Gudsikara's voice but hadn't understood what he had really said. He thought of calling him back. Sundari moaned. He didn't want to leave her and get up.

By then Dattappa, Lagumavva and Mudukappa Gowda arrived.

Dattappa held her pulse and checked. He could barely feel it. Immediately, he whispered the name of an herb in Lagumavva's ears. Lagumavva ran off. It took an hour after drinking the medicine for Sundari to regain consciousness. It took some more time for her to recover. It was already evening. She didn't have the energy to walk. By the time Lagumavva helped her back to her hut, it was night.

When Sundari came back, Gudsikara wasn't there. Basavaraju didn't say a word. Lagumavva took her inside, put her to bed and went home. Sundari lay down for a while, then got up slowly, took out an old newspaper from her trunk and gave it to Basavaraju. She laughed meaningfully and asked him to come in. She whispered something conspiratorially in his ear.

Then Gudsikara came.

Hadn't Gudsikara turned back after seeing Sundari on Gowda's lap? He went home. Basavaraju came to the hut. Neither of them talked. Gudsikara felt as if the old Gowda had challenged his youthful masculinity. All the old revenge surfaced again in his mind. Sundari had cheated on the man who gave her food and shelter. If this news spreads, there's no doubt the whole village will clap their hands and mock me with their laughter. True, he had lost to the Gowda many times. But this defeat would stand above all others. It looks like this Gowda won't let him survive in the village. He was also angry with the quartet. They were such wastrels. If not, he could have made them bear the Gowda's corpse now. What's worse, the wrestler boys were on Gowda's side. How can he show his blackened face to the people? He thought: mild strategies aren't going to be of use any more. The main cause of all this is that bitch. He thought he should hammer her nicely in the hut and set fire to it. It isn't possible to counter the Gowda in all his foxiness. There's only one solution—one cut, two pieces!

Basavaraju, who was silent, waiting like a good blacksmith for the iron to be really hot, now struck. He talked and talked. 'How?' he asked. 'Thus,' he answered. 'Sundari isn't a wife bound by marriage. She's a whore.' Why should a whore be loyal? It's not a big deal. If Gowda grabs your whore, you grab his whore—Durgi. Then the account is settled with interest. But you'll never get another advantage like this. Gowda grabbed her because of his vengeance against you. Now she's pregnant.

Gudsikara got another shock. 'Pregnant?' Basavaraju again wove a web of words, coolly and smoothly. Gowda was again caught in his net. Things had gone beyond the Gowda's revenge scheme. That's why Gowda got scared and gave her medicine to abort.

'Gave medicine!'

'If we let Sundari go, he'll have her aborted for sure. She must be in our hands. On one side, the election frenzy, on the other an anonymous complaint. Unconsciously, Gowda has dug his own grave. People aren't crazy, or at least not always. Sundari might have become pregnant by anybody. But the name is Gowda's. And don't think people don't understand this. Let that be! Do you want to send the Gowda to jail right now?'

'To jail?'

Basavaraju got up, went in, brought out the newspaper that Sundari had given him, and held it before Gudsikara. He showed him the picture of an old man in it and laughed meaningfully. There was a notice declaring a Rs 5,000 prize for anyone who caught Kolavi Mudukappa Gowdappa, alive or dead. Gudsikara still didn't understand.

'Ha, ha, ha,' laughed Basavaraju, 'Old boy, Kolavi Mudukappa is part of the freedom movement. And Gowda has hidden him in his house.'

# PEOPLE TALKED AND SANG ABOUT IT

Soon after sending Sundari back, Dattappa went with Gowda to his house. Both had come to know the truth of the matter, and they talked about how that boy is the kind to 'fix a fence round his house and seal it up'. Gowda lamented that he couldn't advise him. Shouldn't that old woman at least have some sense? Is this the age to dance to her son's tunes?—he asked. It isn't as if Chintamani Dattappa doesn't know how to teach a lesson to someone.

'Look, there's a way to teach him some good sense, if you agree . . . '

'What's that?'

'If we send an anonymous letter that he has made Sundari pregnant, the boy will shut up and listen to us.'

'The plan is good. But don't we have to deal with the dirt? Police coming and beating Gudsikara, court-marshalling him, Panchayat decisions, witnesses—you and me—forget all that mess, but with Mudukappa Gowda hiding in my house, it isn't good for us to have the police here. We will start out doing one thing and end up doing another. No, forget it.'

Dattappa agreed. What if we try putting some sense into the old woman? Old woman might listen to them, but will the boy do?

They finally decided that it was each one's karma and kept quiet.

But did it end there?

This matter sprang to people's mouths. Each day, some nice gossip did the rounds. After the monsoon rains, the harvesting had come to a standstill. So the people had a lot of time for scandal-mongering. They talked and laughed and taunted the quartet. They wrote limericks and sang them. Gudsikara and Basavaraju never understood the meaning of those verses. The quartet did. But they didn't tell the two. So when the two laughed, charmed by the verses, people laughed back at their inability to understand them.

Sundari cursed her fate and resigned herself to her pregnancy. Her body was weak with medicine. She would lie in the hut and hear them talk. After that incident, there was a change in Gudsikara's manner. He wouldn't come to the hut. Even if he did, he wouldn't look at her even by mistake. Or if he did, there would only be anger in his eyes. Basavaraju talked to her as usual. He would get a couple of pots of water. Make rice. Eat, give her some too.

But Gudsikara's mother felt as if the main pillar of the house had come loose and fallen on her head. News came in a different form every day. It seems her son had married in secret. If one daughter of the village asked, 'Is it true, Avva?' another sister inquired, 'It seems he has made out his property to your grandson—is this true, sister?' And of course, one old woman told her that none of this would have happened if she'd got her son married at the right time. She wanted to discuss all this with her son but he was always frowning. Scolding her if she as much as opened her mouth. She also asked Gowda and Dattappa why they didn't advise her son—knowing fully well that the son wouldn't listen to them. She remembered her dead husband and cried. Unable to face the women in the neighbourhood, she sat alone in the kitchen, holding her head in her hands and muttering, 'Karimayi!'

Since Girija's brother Gudsikara usually only came home for his meals and spent most of his time in the fields, Basavaraju would only visit the house occasionally. Now he took every opportunity to come.

Girija took capital advantage of the situation, and with interest too.

# THEY TAUNTED A HORSE

Elections were unavoidable. In Gudsikara's case, to begin with, he had to be sure of his own status in the village before the others did. He had seen and enjoyed the sarpanchhood which the Elders had given him. Now these matters provided fuel for his anger. Or you could say that they were like bits of hay falling from time to time into the burning fire inside him. Mainly, it was the thought of Gowda having a relationship with Sundari that made a deep wound inside the boy. He fretted and struggled and drank more every day, smoked more, puffed with bravado and called the quartet and scolded them, 'Are you men?' The quartet had got to know the news. But they didn't believe it. They didn't talk about it either. Only once, unable to bear his pestering, when they found Gowda's old horse grazing in Gudsikara's field, all of them went with Gudsikara, beat the horse, cut him and heaped stones on him. Finally, they forced him into the slush of the lake. And if that wasn't enough, Gudsikara drove a big nail into the struggling animal's behind.

The same evening, Gowda heard the news. It hurt his pride and provoked him greatly. How can they torture a dumb animal like this? In the fourteen villages around, no one had ever had the guts to stand up against the Gowda. And now some stray boys have the audacity to do so? Day after day, this boy's misdemeanours are growing. He hasn't learnt anything at all. He hasn't learnt a lesson looking at my own patience, thought Gowda. Immediately, he sent for Dattappa.

The wrestler boys had already heard the news about the horse being trapped in the slush. They ran to free it. While some tried to lift it up with a bamboo pole, the rest began to look for Gudsikara and the quartet.

The sun had set just then, and it was dark. Gowda and Dattappa sat together, talking about this very thing. Then the boys walked the horse slowly over to them. His thighs were trembling. His body was full of wounds, and his behind was bleeding. Unable to stand, he collapsed on his knees. Gowda trembled with anger. And Dattappa's eyes were full of tears. He suddenly got up and asked, 'Where are those untouchables?'

Gowda got up too.

Gudsikara's mother had just then lit the lantern and was about to hang it on the nail. It was like thunder to her ears when she heard the words, 'Where are you, Gudsya?' She turned and saw the Gowda filling the door frame. Not knowing the head or tail of this, and unable to think of what to say, she invited them in, 'Come, Appa.' And then without waiting for his answer, she called out shrilly, 'Yeh, Girija,' and steadying her wobbly legs, moved inside.

'Where's he?' asked the Gowda. The old woman had never seen Gowda's anger until then. Even before she could understand what happened, Gowda drew closer. Dattappa was standing at his back. Realizing that her son had done something dreadful, and that if they found him now, they would break him to pieces, she pulled at the serugu on her head, held it on the ground in supplication, bent her head and begged, 'Yappa, think that he isn't my son—think that he is yours.'

At once Gowda became human again. He slumped on the fodder heap. Dattappa told her everything that had happened. The old woman too scolded her son. Begged them to give him some advice.

The words are still in her mouth, and the serugu still on the floor, when in a mad rush Gudsikara comes in, as if he is being chased. Comes in like hunted prey and runs into the kitchen. Shivaninga followed like an arrow. Before the rest of them could understand what was happening or why, they could hear Gudsikara screaming horribly. Girija and the old woman began to howl, beating their mouths with their hands, and tried to go to him. But the Gowda had already rushed in.

Gudsikara rushed out, still screaming.

Shivaninga pushed away Gowda, who was holding him tight, and pounced on Gudsikara as he tried to run away. He clasped Gudsikara, lifted him up and flung him to the ground. Then he wrenched out the nail from the wall, kicked Gudsikara who was writhing on the ground, turned him over on his stomach and reached for his pants.

All this happened before you could blink. The old woman came running and shouting 'Yappa,' and fell on her son's body.

Gowda shouted from inside, 'Yeh, Shivaninga.'

Dattappa ran and held him back.

More people came and held Shivaninga.

The whole village was there.

# THEY BECAME INVOLVED

As a result of all this, posse after posse of policemen stormed the village. Those who had come for one thing got involved in something else.

The very next day, Gudsikara went to Belagavi with his men. He didn't come back for two or three days. Until then the Elders hadn't thought that the quartet counted. Now the moment the miscreants returned, the Elders decided to tell them to stay away from Gudsikara. People talked, said that the quartet had left the village in fear of Shivaninga.

Gudsikara came back with the quartet. Surprisingly enough, there were no lines of worry under anyone's eyes. What's more, they were full of high spirits like those who had just won a victory. Torturing the horse had been a casual matter with them. Unable to stay silent, Ningu asked Thief Sidrama, 'Don't you know better than to beat a dumb animal like that? Wait, the Gowda will teach you a lesson.'

'You wait,' answered the Thief, 'you will see who teaches whom a lesson.'

The next day, the cock crowed and it was morning. Because these are cold days, people don't get up early. When they finally got up, rubbing their eyes and uttering Karimayi's name, in every nook and corner of the streets, they saw policemen with rifles. Their hearts full of fear, they said 'Karimayi,' went back into their houses and shut the doors. At this time of the day, there's usually the noise of children making fires to warm themselves, the clucking of hens, the excitement of girls fetching water, the lively boys watching them, much mischievous talk, arrogant answers—now everything was still, only whispers and sighs inside the houses. Nobody knows why the police had come. They guessed that Gudsikara had brought them to catch Gowda and Shivaninga.

On the other side, the police had surrounded Gowda's house and fields. The moment the door opened, they searched his house. They spilt the tender grain from the jars. They spilt the grain sacks stacked inside. Pushing Shivaninga aside, they scattered the husk all over the attic. Luckily, they didn't open the trunk which was right there. Inside it was Karimayi's golden face. They ransacked every corner, scattered everything, left it looking like a house that's been robbed and then came out to stand guard.

When Shivaninga went to the fields to inform his father, it was the same there. Outside the hut, the foujudara sat on the cot. Police had entered the sugarcane crop and were searching. Gowda stood there wringing his hands while the foujudara scolded him, 'I will get you a reward of 5,000 rupees—tell me Gowda, where have you hidden Kolavi Mudukappa?'

Gowda was saying, 'I don't know, Sahebara.'

Katti Foujudara was indeed a feared name in these parts. Within a few days of taking up this job, the great man had made a terrible name for himself. It seems he had plucked out the eyes of eitghteen boys in the movement, made them into thirty-six marbles and then played games with the Ingreji people. His form was eminently suited to support such stories. Dark body, thick moustache, a fat arrogance and the will to make everyone listen to him. His nose was fat, like a calf sleeping across his face. Therefore, it's only natural that when he looked down this nose, everybody looked small or vague. In the villages he stepped into, his fame was such that, if children didn't go to sleep, their mothers would scare them with 'I'll give you to Katti Foujudara!' Maybe this is true, because in that dark face only his mouth and eyes were stark red, as if they were painted. He had become the foujudara recently, right? He would dust off his cap again and again. Not only that, whenever he went out anywhere, he would take off his cap and make a policeman carry it as he walked, baring his bald head.

Suddenly, without any introduction or afterword to the matter, when Gudsikara arrived and announced that he would help him catch Mudukappa Gowda, he thought that his dear cap would have a new feather. The whole day, Mudukappa could not be found. Showing his picture, the police asked many people if they'd seen him. Tried to scare them. Also tried the bait of the reward. But everybody said, 'No I haven't seen, nobody has seen him.' Some also took the name of Karimayi and swore that anybody who did would go blind.

Gudsikara acted as if he had no connection with the foujudara's attack. But it wasn't possible to cover it up. That afternoon, if the police had their meal at the Gowda's house, the foujudara's meal was at Gudsikara's house. People cursed him. And sought refuge in Karimayi.

## CAT IN HEAT

To tell you the truth, nobody had seen Kolavi Mudukappa recently. People knew that he was related to the Gowda. In the last few years, Mudukappa Gowda hadn't even passed through Shivapura. That he had come, and was staying secretly in Gowda's house, was not known to anyone except four people —Gowda, Dattappa, Shivasani and Lagumavva. But they didn't know that Sundari had found out.

When they realized that this was Gudsikara's conspiracy, Gowda and Dattappa became inflamed. They said it had been a mistake to have stopped Shivaninga yesterday. If they could somehow escape this time, they would teach him a lesson he would never forget.

That day, it's said, Mother possessed Devaresi's body and sobbed. They couldn't even go and hold her feet, because the police were guarding both Gowda and Dattappa.

Whatever Mother wanted to say, they were kept away from her words.

On the other hand, Gudsikara's joy didn't last long. In the heat of revenge, he had given the rope to Basavaraju and ended up getting his own hands tied. Otherwise, what does it mean to be a great devotee of Gandhiji and give up a freedom fighter to the police? Is it a lie that he wanted to join the movement when he was in Belagavi? Is it a lie that he came to the village as Gandhiji advised? If there were boys of the movement in Shivapura, he would have been their leader. It was when the foujudara came to have a meal in his house that he realized that he had done a low thing indeed.

They were sitting there to eat, right? Foujudara pawed at Gudsikara's armpit, winked and pointed to Girija who was serving them, 'Isn't she a doll?' Gudsikara's bile rose. He controlled himself and said, 'She's my sister.' Foujudara didn't believe him. It seems like Gudsikara properly noticed his sister only now. She had grown taller and came up above his chest. She wore a bra under her blouse. She wore two braids with ribbons at the ends. Nobody who saw her could say that she was a village girl. Suddenly the sight of her filled him with rage. Foujudara opened his red eyes wide, and his dark sweaty cheeks wobbling, laughed loudly. And baring his white teeth on which were stuck some rice grains, he demanded 'Why do you lie?' he told Gudiskara, 'I'm someone who has plumbed the depths of such cases many times.' Now you should have seen Gudsikara's fury. Unable to bring his anger under control, with a face like a burning brass pot, he said, 'Sahebara, when you're visiting someone's house, this sort of behaviour is not proper.'

Foujudara got angry too. 'Are you teaching me proper behaviour? Do you think I don't know that you have brought Belagavi Chimana here, and you are keeping her?'

After the meal, quite unwillingly, he was forced to make arrangements for the foujudara to sleep upstairs. Then he unleashed his anger on Basavaraju. 'Listening to you has led me to bring shame on the whole village. Who're my people, and who're the outsiders?' He started prancing around in anger. Basavaraju let him talk first, and only after that, slowly exerted his natural cunning. Yes, the foujudara is a scoundrel. Does he have to be a nice man? Our work is important. Leave the responsibility of Mudukappa to me. Now read this, you will know who I am. He took out another letter from his pocket.

It was a petition addressed by Chimana Sundara Bai to the lotus feet of the kind foujudara-saheb. Chimana had accused Gowda and his son Shivaninga of raping and impregnating her. She requested him with folded hands that some provision be made for her living, and for the child in her womb. Underneath this plea was the signature of the petitioner. Since Shivaninga's name had also been included, Gudsikara's revenge was satisfied.

Basavaraju promised with his right hand that he would take care of the rest.

Basavaraju came back exactly when the foujudara got up. He smiled obsequiously ten times and handed over the petition. The red eyes of Katti Saheb, frustrated at not finding Mudukappa, now began to gleam. He loved cases related to women. And during his meal, he had also managed to lay eyes on someone who looked like this Chimana. He read the petition loudly so that Chimana, downstairs, could hear it too.

That night, Lord Katti-saheb held court. The Elders came. Swinging his stick, the foujudara ordered, 'Call Sundara Bai here.' Gowda didn't know who Sundara Bai was. There wasn't anyone of that name in the village. Hesitantly, he asked 'Which Sundara Bai?' Dattappa asnwered: 'That woman, the one whom Gudsya keeps. Chimana.' The watchman ran to fetch her. Both Gowda and Dattappa realized what the matter was. They were now certain that someone had sent an anonymous letter about Sundari being pregnant. Gowda got very scared. If something like this had come up earlier, we could have solved it ourselves. Which rascals have given the anonymous petition? If this was what Gowda was thinking, Dattappa was feeling happy. At least, Gudsya will now get it good, he felt.

At that moment, Gudsikara arrived with the quartet. Dattappa felt like laughing more when he saw Gudsikara's unclouded face. At a distance, a small crowd had gathered.

'Hasn't Chimana come?' the foujudara thundered. Sundari had come. But nobody had noticed her. The foujudara called Basavaraju, standing in the crowd, and gave him place to sit in the square. It was Gudsikara who told him that Sundari had arrived.

'Where is this man, Shivaninga?' the foujudara thundered again. The watchman ran off again.

The inquiry started without Shivaninga.

Everybody was shocked by the very first words of the foujudara: 'What Gowda? Being the Elder in the village, can you do such a cheap thing?'

'What? What happened?'

'Don't talk as if you don't know. How long do you want to hide the fact that you and your son have together impregnated Chimana?'

Everybody was stunned. The wrestler boys were boiling with anger. Before the Gowda opened his mouth, Dattappa spoke. 'What kind of talk is this? The one who brought her is Gudsya. Gowda doesn't even know her name. What do you mean he impregnated her?'

'Who are you to intervene?'

Everybody's anger rose. Foujudara's was worse. Mixing the arrogance of authority with his coarse voice, and using the disrespectful mode of address 'ley,' he began to shout. 'If the Gowda didn't do it, why didn't he send the petition himself?'

'Why should I send a petition about someone not of our village?' the Gowda countered.

'Just because she isn't from your village, will you let injustice happen to her?'

'It is the responsibility of those who brought her here.'

Now Dattappa spoke again. 'Who brought her here? Who had any business with her? The whole village knows. Why don't you inquire?'

All this talk darted back and forth like sparks from a flint. Foujudara hadn't expected this kind of disobedience from the Gowda and his accountant. He felt as insulted as if his moustache had been forcibly shaved and placed in his hands. He started hissing. 'What do you say?' he asked, turning to Gudsikara.

Gudsikara got up and came to the center of the square. 'Kind Foujudara-sahebare, village Elders, brothers and sisters—' he began.

Perhaps the foujudara wanted some rest. He didn't stop Gudsikara. Well, then who can stop Gudsikara now? You know, the same old thing, from 'India is a country of villages' to how the panchayat started and how he tried to bring progress to his village, to how the Elders stopped his steps and pulled him back and how they asked him to return the panchayat and how finally he had to tell them, 'Let the elections take place' . . . so on and so forth.

Finally, the foujudara lost his patience and shouted, 'Stop—'

Gudsikara now said that the Gowda was blaming him for this affair in order to defeat him in the elections. The people who had gathered talked among themselves, each one saying one thing or other. Gowda kept quiet thinking, let the foujudara control them if he wants to. Dattappa thought so too.

Suddenly, from the crowd, Ningu leapt up and stood before the foujudara. Even in that tense atmosphere, the foujudara was amused to see this rough-voiced man in woman's attire. In a frenzied voice, Ningu challenged: 'All right, sarpancha, you brought her here and kept her. Every day, you roll on the end of her saree. Now you come to say that Gowda has impregnated her. On top of it, you also bring up Shivaninga's name. Don't you know better? Is it something anyone can believe? Let's see, you make anyone from here say it. I'll call you a real man then.'

Seems like Gudsikara had already anticipated such words. 'Why should I make anyone say this? I have seen her sleeping with her head on Gowda's lap. If you want, ask Basavaraju.'

A reliable witness indeed! Like saying, 'The fence is the chameleon's witness.'

Now Gowda had to open his mouth. He got up, alternately facing the foujudara and the people, and folding his hands from time to time, began describing the incident as it had happened.

Gudsikara hadn't wanted Gowda to have this opportunity to speak. But the foujudara didn't bother to stop the Gowda. Every word he uttered had the sharpness and light of truth in it. Truth is like that. Thus Gudsikara was pulverized in front of everyone's eyes. From time to time, he tried to stop the Gowda but failed.

'Look, Sahebara,' finally Gowda said, 'this is how it happened. If these words are false, let Karimayi slit my tongue. If you want, ask Dattu. Ask Lagumavva. Why should we be angry with Gudsya? If we were angry, would we call him and give him the panchayat?'

At this, not only Lagumavva who sat at the edge of the crowd, but also many others, burst into tears.

Gudsikara felt that just as in all the earlier cases, here too he was failing. It looked like the foujudara himself was becoming a little vulnerable. Instantly, like people who become vehement when they are scared, he said shrilly: 'You do all this colourful talk in front of the kind foujudara, Gowda? He knows everything! Sahebara, if you want, Sundara-bai is here—you ask her. She will tell you what his real avatar is like.'

Ningu now understood why Basavaraju had taken the abortion medicine from him. In a frenzy again, he sat up abruptly in front of the foujudara and said, 'Sahebara, I know the real story.'

But the foujudara didn't have the patience to listen to his words.

'Will you shut up, or shall I kick you?'

'You kick me if you want to, but only after you hear me out. I gave the abortion medicine to this Basavaraju. He gave it the same day to Chimana. Everything that the Gowda said happened that day.'

All the people there were sure this was how it had happened.

Gudsikara's bile rose. 'Instead of asking the woman who is actually pregnant, why are you listening to all this kind of evidence?' he demanded, angry with the foujudara.

The foujudara also remembered his position.

'Why should I? Don't you know that giving medicine to abort is against the law? First, I will put you in jail. I'll take care of the others later. Where's that woman?'

He signalled for Sundari to be brought before him. Sundari, hiding in the corner until then, came out. And all the foujudara's curiosity drained away—this wasn't the one who'd served food that afternoon! The rest watched her with bated breath. There was no doubt that she would talk as Gudsikara had talked. She had his food and his body every day. What else could she say? Some were already grumbling about it. But this hadn't occurred to the foujudara. Meanwhile, Ningu had disappeared. Sundari came upfront and stood with a bent head.

'What? Tell us properly. Who made you pregnant?'

Everybody stood with pressed lips waiting to hear what she said. Sundari said softly, 'Gowda,' pointed to the Gowda and bent her head again. Only those who stood close to her heard this, not those who stood far away. Even as they kept confusedly asking each other, 'What did she say? What did she say?'

Snapping the joints of her fingers in anger, Lagumavva cursed, 'Thoo, bitch who can teach a cat in heat!' This inflamed everybody's dissatisfaction. They all started shouting, 'Che che, ha ho.'

The foujudara didn't try to stop them. Gudsikara became as lively as possible in the situation. The quartet stood like schoolchildren, arms crossed in front and lips sealed. The only one a little animated was Thief Sidrama. There was a reason for this. Just a moment ago, Ningu had talked with such courage, right? His courage, which nobody else there seemed to posses, his style like the city whores—looking at all this, the Thief thought, 'Bravo, bravo,' and drooled over Ningu. If this braveheart with a flat chest could be fitted with nice boobs, how would he look?

Anyway, why talk about his craven desires now?

People talked as they liked. The foujudara didn't bother silencing them. Amid the 'ha-ho' noise all around, he finally shouted out his judgement: Gowda should write two acres of his property to Sundari and her child.

Then he suddenly got up and left.

## HE DISAPPEARED

While this was going on in the square, here, the golden baby disappeared.

Shivaninga, who heard the news from Ningu, became desperate and lost the use of his limbs for a while. He thought, 'That bitch betrayed us. Let the foujudara go—I will hack her to pieces and skin her alive. That apart, how do I show my face to the village now? How to talk to Mother and Father, how to face them? Gudsya is not a man,' he said. 'You should break his leg and put it in his hand,' he said. He said harsh things about his father who had let Gudsya progress to this stage, he said harsh words about Dattappa who hadn't taught Gudsya a lesson. He called them old men hardened in their ways. Then beat his head with his hand in shame, thinking: Because of me, the Gowda's family has become something to point a finger at. Police all around the house, police in the fields, where should I hide, how shall I hide this wretched face? Sighing, he moved about the place like a caged tiger. He thought of the panchayat in front of the foujudara, of standing before the villagers, and fretted some more. After it got a little dark, he went to the fields, hiding from the eyes of the police and then, like magic, simply vanished.

God knows how late into the night it was. He jumped over the entrance wall at the back and entered Karimayi's temple. He went in, bending low. It was dark inside. When he was trying to make his way forward, to sit in front of Karimayi, he heard someone ask, 'Who is it?' He was taken aback. Then again: 'Appa, who are you?' He recognized the voice—it was Kolavi Mudukappa. He moved closer saying, 'Me, Grandpa. It's me—Shivaninga.'

'Why, brother? Has your father sent a message?'

'Nothing, Grandpa.'

'Then why come here like a thief, lad?' Shivaninga said nothing. Mudukappa too didn't speak any more. Darkness fell like soot from a chimney. The temple is away from the village, and is so silent in any case. Only the nocturnal insects made jarring sounds like sawing wood. Once he was sure the place was safe, his heartbeat slowed down a bit. Perhaps the police are searching for me now. Tomorrow morning, Father will skin me alive, that's for sure. The best thing is to leave the village. He thought it would have been proper if he had also finished Gudsya and Chimana before leaving. Suddenly, the old man's hand touched him. Saying 'brother,' he moved closer to Shivaninga and whispered, 'Brother, have you seen the Kundargi matha?'

'Yes.'

'How far from here?'

'Six or nine miles.'

'What can I do, boy? If I don't go there tomorrow, everything will go wrong. Ten people are sitting there waiting for me. Your father said he would send somebody. Will you go and remind your father at least?'

'My father has sent me, Grandpa.' So he tried a lie. I could do this job myself. Got a good pretext to leave the village, he thought.

'What? You! You didn't tell me when I asked earlier? Well, that's fine, come. You too can render a little service to this country. Will you go to Kundargi matha?'

'Who are the people sitting there? Neru and Gandhi?'

'You may think so.'

'I'll go. Tell me what to do.'

The old man pulled out something that had been tied into a bundle and hidden with great secrecy. He gave a note too and said, 'Go to the matha. There is a priest there, you'll see. Bearded man. Go to him, tell him Mudukappa has sent you. He will take you to meet Annu Guruji. You put this bundle and note into his hands. Tell them to stop thinking about me and not to come to Shivapura for another eight days.' Towards the end of this speech, the old man's voice shook. He became emotional, held Shivaninga's hand, clasped it to his chest and sat there silently for a while. He was crying too. A warm teardrop fell on Shivaninga's hand. He didn't know how to console the old man. The old man might be thinking I am reluctant to go, Shivaninga thought. He reassured him: 'Don't worry, Grandpa, I'll go.' The old man didn't say anything. Just embraced Shivaninga tightly. Like an old bull licking the calf, caressed the boy's back for a while. Seeing the old man's anxiety, Shivaninga thought that it must be a task of great significance. He just sat there until the old man became a little calmer.

'Yes, why didn't you tell me earlier.'

Shivaninga was silent.

'Were you doubtful whether it was me or not?' the old man asked.

'I'll go, Grandpa,' Shivaninga said, now anxious to be off.

'Yes, good if you go now. I too would have come. But these eyes—' he lamented over his helplessness. Shivaninga remembered now. The old man had night blindness. He got up and said, 'I'll go, Grandpa.' Whatever he was thinking of, the old man also got up, hugged Shivaninga and warned him: 'Be careful about the police. Give it there and come back immediately. Karimayi will take care of you.'

Shivaninga disappeared.

# LAST SALUTATIONS TO KARIMAYI

As Gowda looked pleadingly at Gudsikara here, there Kolavi Mudukappa Gowda offered his last salutations to Karimayi.

This was Gudsikara's first victory. That day, Sundari had performed services for the foujudara and come back home late. All seven celebrated their victory extravagantly, lavishly and wetly. They remembered Basavaraju and Sundari, responsible for this victory, at every gulp. Sundari became so high spirited that she hardly trod on the ground. She was thrilled about the success of her conspiracy and about Gudsikara's praise for her. In her inebriated state, she imitated Gowda's words again and again and made Gudsikara laugh.

The same day, the Elders met under Dattappa's leadership. Gowda hadn't come. Now they decided to excommunicate Sundari. And he'd talked about the elections, right? They decided to stand for it this time.

Next morning, they informed the Gowda of their decision. Gowda kept quiet.

After they left, he sent the watchman to bring Gudsikara.

When the watchman came, Gudsikara was in Sundari's hut. The moment the watchman informed him that the Gowda had sent for him, the boy sprang to life. He thumped Basavaraju's shoulder twice and pointed out, 'Did you see? How he's back on the right track?' He laughed loudly. He winked at Sundari and laughed again. That wretched quartet wasn't there. Otherwise, they could have, as a group, applauded and laughed. In their excitement, they had forgotten about the watchman. The moment Gudsikara remembered him, he said, 'I'm not free. If he wants me, ask him to come here.' The watchman hadn't expected this arrogance. He said, 'Okay,' and left.

Gudsikara's pride wouldn't come down. He thought: What a great war I've won. Perhaps he should have gone to the Gowda. If he had, he could have seen the Gowda's defeat with his own eyes, heard about it with his own ears. Why did the Gowda send for him? On the one hand losing his prestige in front of the villagers, on the other having to pay up those two acres of land. Perhaps to make a deal. Sonny has realized who I am at last. If he shuts his mouth from now on, okay. Otherwise, if I don't lead him through his nose—why should I call myself Gudsikara?

Thus, talking to himself, he set off towards the fields.

As he walked, there was a strange high-spiritedness in him. In the sugarcane fields, there were five or six servants gathering animal feed. He went over to them. None of them would approve of his view. Nevertheless, he began to blow his own trumpet. He reeled out the genealogy and names of some officers, saying that he was well acquainted with them. He narrated stories and incidents which showed his closeness with them. He talked loudly about the Gowda running about trying to come to a compromise. In his talk, he turned the Gowda into a worm, and himself as tall as an elephant.

Meanwhile, Gowda arrived. The sarpanch didn't speak to him. As if nothing had happened, he stood there saying inconsequential things to the servants. A couple of servants saluted the Gowda. Gowda came over to him and said, 'Brother, I need to talk to you. Will you come to the hut?'

Without turning around, the sarpanch said, 'What talk? Can't you do that right here?'

Gowda's heart shrank, he shrank into himself. But this behaviour of Gudsikara was not unexpected. Not that Gowda had no pride but he had a lot more wisdom. 'Okay, son. Let's sit here and talk,' he said and went to the ridge nearby.

The servants said they were going to the other end of the field and left.

'Look, brother,' Gowda said, 'our time's over. Until now we maintained a level of control in the village. Then we gave it to you. You are an educated man, someone who knows the world . . .' saying this, Gowda became quiet for a while. The sarpanch was already becoming wobbly inside and turning into mere Gudsikara. 'You are like my son,' the Gowda continued, 'It is because we thought so that we told you to do the panchayat and put the village in your hands. Tell me—what harm have I done to you? You act like I'm your enemy. Tell me if there's been any mistake. I'll put my head on your feet. Is it seemly for me to be fighting with you in my age? Here today, in the grave tomorrow. You're all still in your prime. Those that shall be the flowers and fruit in this village are not old people like us. The village needs you, people such as you. Well, we might tell you to do things in a particular way to satisfy the itch in our tongues. We Elders see the grave before us. It's this fear which makes us say things. If you don't like it, we'll stop that too. But because of your anger with me, why do you ruin the village, brother?'

Gudsikara melted completely. Poor thing, I too have misunderstood this old man, he thought. If I were to open my heart to him and ask, 'How do we do this?' the old man will feel flattered. What else? Other Elders also want this. All old men with drooping shoulders. How many days will they live? If I give them some respect while they are alive, what do I lose? This is a village panchayat. If I go and ask them, it's possible they will even give it to me without any elections.

The Gowda was still talking: 'Tell the truth, brother. Is it true that I made Chimana pregnant? You swear on your father's name and say "Yes." Now right here, and I'll give the two acres. Appa, at a time when I'm going to die, don't heap this scandal on me.'

Gowda folded his hands.

Neither could utter another word. Like pride melting into water, a couple of drops fell from Gudsikara's eyes. He was certain that the business of Sundari's pregnancy had to do with either him or Basavaraju. Ningu had spoken of Basavaraju's mischief yesterday. It looked like there was more of Basavaraju's part in this. Otherwise, they could have told him the news of pregnancy first, right? At least, told him about the abortion?

For a long time, neither of them spoke. Gudsikara hadn't said a word. He couldn't think of what to say. Once again, Gowda spoke: 'Look, brother! We are people who look at each other's face every morning. I must melt when you sigh. You should melt when I sigh. That Belagavi man is someone who is here today and gone tomorrow. Throw both of them out this moment. Rule the village the way you want. I'll tell you the truth—Appa, if you give her such lenience, she'll ruin the village,' and then became silent. Speech needs conclusion, right?

'Fine, don't worry. Let's go,' these words were still on Gudsikara's lips when, suddenly, they heard gun shots. Both were stunned. They looked at each other's faces. Then Gudsikara ran towards the noise.

Gowda's limbs gave way and he collapsed.

By the time Gudsikara came running, the police were already walking around the Karimayi temple. With the impact of the gunshot, one of the beehives had fallen. Honey spilt all around. Bees swarmed in the air, humming all over the place and chasing the police.

The foujudara, not caring about the bees, not even noticing Gudsikara, was ordering his men about with a sense of victory.

People came, one by one, and stood there, watching.

The body of Kolavi Sri Mudukappa Gowda lay face down in front of Karimayi, as if saluting her for the last time.

Under his stomach was a pool of blood.

## EXCOMMUNICATION

As if all this wasn't enough, Chimana went to Gowda's house to ask for her two acres of land.

Dattappa excommunicated her.

People mourned for Mudukappa Gowda. Not a thief. Not a liar. He was talking about something called serving the country and the movement. He mentioned Gandhi, Nehru. Just because of that, is it right to kill him like that? Some said Gudsikara had done it, greedy for the reward. That they saw the foujudara give him 5,000 rupees with their own eyes. People began to fear Gudsikara. The moment you say something, here's a devil that talks about police and foujudara. Messing with him is as foolish as insulting the foujudara by calling him, 'Ley, Foujudara!'

The quartet was regaled by all this. The day after Kolavi Mudukappa's body was taken away, they realized that the whole village was scared of them. People kept greeting and saluting them. So they plotted to make sure that the fear, which had emerged at this opportune time, wouldn't be a temporary phenomenon. They wove terrible tales about Gudsikara. They breathed into the village's ear all sorts of imaginary stories—that the police, foujudara, collector, subordinate revenue collector, all those Belgavi officers were known to Gudsikara. That if he so much as sent a note, the government would send in the military. The government sent a police party to burn this village for harbouring Mudukappa. But because of the sarpanch, Mudukappa was killed and the village saved. They added more details to these stories and made them sound as real as possible.

The Gowda never regained a sense of normalcy. On the one hand sorrow that he couldn't save a kin who came to him for help. On the other anger with Gudsikara for causing all this. He was wriggling in this dilemma like a worm caught in fire. He covered his face with his dhotra and cried like an old woman. As time passed, the sorrow of Mudukappa's death was pushed to the background and that of Shivaninga's disappearance came to the foreground. The servant who went to Kundargi matha came back with the news of the disappearance of everybody there. Gowda sent word to every village and to his in-laws. But Shivaninga didn't come. Shivaninga's news didn't come. He kept guessing that the boy had run away, or hanged himself, because his name had been in the anonymous petition. He sought refuge in Karimayi. Mother said: He will be back. But he couldn't believe it until he saw his son with his own eyes. Shivasani, always chanting the son's name, left off taking food or water and only kept lamenting, 'Shivaninga.' She receded to a corner of the house. In only a week, this fine woman became emaciated with grief and starvation. She became the walking stick in the corner.

On top of this, Chimana came and created a rumpus in front of the house. It happened thus:

One day, Gowda got up in the morning, bathed in the lake, prostrated before Karimayi and returned home. It was morning just then. Here and there, people were sweeping their yards. Letting the hens out. Letting out the cows to drink water. Those who were up saluted the Gowda. He crossed the street and turned towards his house.

There wasn't much activity on that street. In front of his house stood four or five women. He took longer strides. Seeing the Gowda come, the women moved aside. He saw Sundari sitting there leaning her left thigh on the threshold, her left arm stretched across its length and her right arm crossed over it. For a minute, Gowda didn't understand why or what. Inside stood the mother of his elder wife, Nijagunavva. Addressing all, he asked, 'What?' One woman said, 'She has come to ask for the two acres of land.' Gowda went in.

When Gowda finished his breakfast and came out, Dattappa was already present on the porch.

Balappa had come just then. People had gathered in front of the house. Chimana was sitting there, trying to ward off all the eyes on her. Crazy girl with a tender face. She dances to the tunes of those who make her dance. She doesn't know what all this dancing is worth. Her posture as she sat, the courage and stubbornness, all looked heavy on her frame, looked unnatural. It's in fact difficult to get angry with her. She seems to be a little child acting like an adult.

In such circumstances, the one who talks is of course Dattappa.

So when Dattappa asks her, 'What woman? Why did you come? To fight?' that shrew answers: 'I haven't come to fight. Let the Gowda write two acres of land in my name. I'll go quietly.'

Dattappa thought: What the hell! When he was pretending to be surprised and saying, 'Ad da da,' Balappa couldn't contain himself: 'What do you mean "ad da da"? Come, let's chop off this bitch's nose and throw her into the forest.'

Sundari couldn't contain herself either. 'Why? Did you think it's so easy in these parts? I too will go and bring the foujudara here.'

'Foujudara means government, right?' said Dattappa, 'Let it go to the court, and if the judgement comes from there, we'll give you the land. How's it that people like the police and foujudara have started giving judgements? You go to court if you want,'

But Sundari was not going to be stopped. 'Why didn't this talk happen in front of the foujudara? I'm a young girl. Do you want to do me injustice and live?'

'Okay, then go and get whichever foujudara you want!' Dattappa said equally harshly. Ningu, who was standing among the women, couldn't take it any more: 'My rival wife, what's this you've started, early in the morning too? Will you get out, or do you want me to pull you by the hair and throw you out?'

'What? Eunuch, pimp—come if you're a man,' she challenged and stood her ground.

Gowda is still not angry. If the Gowda says yes, the boys are ready to tear her to pieces then and there. The village is not used to such ugly incidents early in the morning, just when one gets up.

Meanwhile, Lagumavva came. Basetti came. Devaresi came. What more do you need? Balu said, 'We will excommunicate her right away!' Basetti said, 'Yes!' Until then Sundari had courage. She was thinking arrogantly: as long as the sarpanch is on my side, nobody can do anything to me. But this weapon of excommunication is new to her. She doesn't even know what it means. She realized that there was some danger and stood up, scared. 'I'm not some easy woman. Gowda's . . . fruit of . . . ' saying this to the crowd, not knowing what she was doing, she touched her tummy. Without her knowledge, tears started streaming from her eyes. She kept sobbing and finally collapsed.

Gowda couldn't bear it. 'Okay, I made you pregnant, right? Then come and live in my house. Why do you need the land?'

And then she realized that she was caught in the slush. I can't survive now. 'Why should I be in your house? I'll live where I want.'

There was nobody to show pity to Sundari. Dattappa thought that this was the right time, and without asking the Gowda (fearing that things would get more confused if he did), he went ahead and declared the excommunication. He broke a pumpkin which was there and asked Lagumavva to drain the water from it. Trying to do something but unable to do anything, Sundari ran like a hunted animal, crying and saying that she would tell the sarpanch. People said this was the right punishment for her. All this was over before you could count to ten or fifteen.

After everyone left, Gowda asked, 'Now, look. She's from a different village. How can we excommunicate her?'

'Does my *Chintamani* lie?' exploded Dattappa, 'Stop, stop, I still haven't had my bath,' he said and went back home.

# HE MELTED

Basavaraju had noticed that, of late, Gudsikara had mellowed. He didn't come to Basavaraju's hut. After waiting for him, Basavaraju himself came to the field. Gudsikara was working. Both didn't speak for a while. Later, Basavaraju used every guile, and some force, to get out of Gudsikara what he had talked with Gowda. It was difficult to get him away from Gowda's influence. So he pretended to be emotional and asked, 'Where's Gowda? Where's Mudukappa? Who's sacrificed for what?' For sometime, he set up a long wail. If Gowda really had this fondness for you, why did he remain silent until now? Now he is caught. He must give up two acres of land. As if that isn't enough, he has been shamed in front of the village. He has only one strategy now: getting you into his hands. You're a soft-hearted man . . . like Gandhiji, leader of men in the village. And so on and so forth, he went on. But no matter what he said, the sarpanch-side in Gudsikara didn't surface at all.

On the other hand, nobody was perturbed by Sundari's excommunication. What's it to Sundari even? Not of the clan. Doesn't need a bride or a bridegroom from the village to marry. If you ask, she isn't of the village. Doesn't have to work. Rather, the bitter effect of the excommunication fell on Gudsikara. Even when he sent for them, the quartet came up with all kinds of pretexts and tried to give him the slip. Couldn't get workers for his fields. Even if he came face to face with them, people wouldn't talk to him. If he had to experience such things being a man, the condition of his mother and sister was simply beyond words. The moment she saw his face, his mother would cover her face in her serugu and cry. In the end, Gudsikara talked to Basavaraju confidentially. He said unless they sent Sundari away, it was impossible to live in the village.

It took all their energy—almost like sacrificing lambs and bulls to appease gods—to make Sundari agree. Whatever the truth, on the outside, she acted as if it was Gudsikara who had made her pregnant. He doesn't have to treat me like a married wife. She had said this a couple of times before, adding, 'Let him marry another woman if he wants, it's enough if he keeps me like he is doing now.' She acted as if she was willing to give herself up wholly to him if he just talked to her a little warmly and openly. When Basavaraju told her to go and sit at the Gowda's door, it was only for this reason that she had agreed. To make Gudsikara sure of her love at least in this way.

Now when Basavaraju told her about leaving the village, she acted as if she was devastated. She clutched Gudsikara's feet. 'You come yourself and get this pregnancy terminated,' she said. 'I have nobody but you. Nobody to support me, knowing all, why do you make me feel like a corpse thrown in the forest?' They consoled her with things like 'It's only for a day or two—just a matter of being in Belagavi for a couple of days and getting the foetus out.'

When she was leaving, she held Gudsikara's feet again and again. She drenched his feet with her tears. She hugged his feet and cried. Finally, she had to go. And she did.

When they got to know that Sundari had left, the quartet slowly wandered back into the fields. People began to speak to Gudsikara. He found servants. Life went on as usual. But the boy became more and more lonely, day by day. Same house, same fields, same people—he uttered the expletive 'thoo', drank, smoked, slept, went there, came here. The quartet came sometimes. But he couldn't open his heart and speak to them. They'd wait and wait, and then leave.

Meanwhile, there was a letter asking people, who wanted to stand for the election, to register their names. He sent the letter through Thief Sidrama to Dattappa and sat quietly. In a day or two, he came to know that all the Elders had given their names as candidates under Gowda's leadership. He didn't feel bad. Not angry either. Only drank a little more that day.

There was one more day to give the names. At the end of it, rather dramatically, Gudsikara's hut in the fields caught fire. He was sleeping there. He got up and escaped. There wasn't much loss. People in the neighbourhood came and put out the fire. But Gudsikara was alarmed. He thought of his state and felt sad.

Exactly at this time, Basavaraju came back from Belagavi.

Then, at night, he went out and brought the quartet to the hut. Consoling Gudsikara, who was in a state of shock, he asked him to come too. And opened the foreign bhirandi he had brought from Belagavi. What doesn't he know about the happenings here? Because it was he who set Gudsikara's hut on fire. He had done it in such a way that nobody would know. If it's a matter of setting fire for the all the world to know, does it have to be Basavaraju? Talking about things casually, he started the meeting as usual. Forcing Gudsikara to drink some brandy, he drained the remaining stuff. He distributed the foreign god to everyone. Holding his glass up, he toasted those who had brought Gudsikara to this state and began crying copiously like an old woman.

The quartet didn't know whether to drink or not. They sat looking from face to face.

Then he scolded the quartet: 'When the people excommunicated Sundari, you too didn't come near the hut.' He called them useless fellows. Called them motherfuckers. British on the one side and Gandhiji on the other. Gowda's party is like the British, and Gudsikara is like Gandhiji. It was Gudsikara who did the sacred job of throwing the British out and bringing freedom to the village. But you don't have the capacity to work under his leadership. 'All of you are eunuchs. If you were men, would anybody have the courage to set fire to Gudsikara-saheb's hut?' And then he clasped Rumps Ramesa like a child and cried some more.

Already quite intoxicated, Gudsikara now became tearful. He said sending Sundari back was like accepting defeat. 'When we accepted our defeat for the whole village to know, what pride do we have to contest the elections?' 'Now we should have had Sundari here, Basavaraju,' he said in a weepy voice.

The quartet was feeling guilty. But they didn't know what to say. God knows how he got the idea that crying was the proper thing to do in the circumstance, but the Thief started crying and saying, 'Whatever happens, let there be unity.' Basavaraju wouldn't let him off: 'Why should there be unity? We need unity to stand for the elections and work together. What's the use of it otherwise?' Who knows what inspiration took Aayi Mereminda who had been sitting quiet until then. He went down on his knees and said, 'What's the problem now? There's still one more day to give the names for the elections. We'll all go and give it.' 'Thoo,' Basavaraju spat. 'Why should we believe you? You aren't men. Not even like

Ningu. At least he openly wears a saree and walks about. You don't even have the courage to do that!' Thus, in his talk, he began to bring down the quartet inch by inch and turn them into worms. Made them the dirt under his feet. In the end, less than dirt.

They sat on.

For a while, nobody spoke. Basavaraju and Gudsikara were the only ones drinking continuously. The atmosphere was terribly tense. Basavaraju hadn't expected this. Suddenly, he slapped Rumps Ramesa on the shoulder and said, 'What do you say?' Ramesa didn't say anything. Again, Basavaraju started talking. 'Will you stand for the elections making the villagers your enemies? If you have that level of manliness, drink,' he ordered.

Supressing their thirst, the rest sat still.

Finally, the Thief decided: 'Give, I'll be a man,' he said and reached for the glass. Basavaraju put his hand on his and said, 'Swear on Karimayi!' Thief felt like he was falling into slush. Until then he had been 'somersaulting on cotton sacks'. But swearing on Karimayi is no childish matter. Swearing on her and securing fire in the folds of your clothes amounts to the same thing. Basavaraju might say ten things. Gudsikara might nod assent to all those ten things. What's it to him? Gudsikara has nobody at his back, or in front of him. Beginning from the front door of his house to the back door, he has everything under his control. In my case, there're Elders to question me and tell me what to do. In the past, when there was some mention of Karimayi, true, he too had laughed. But when it came to swearing, he got frightened.

Basavaraju was satisfied now—as if he had caught the quartet out—found the roots of their weakness. But not Gudsikara. 'This talk doesn't lead to anything. Let go, Basavaraju,' he said. Basavaraju didn't let go. He gave another lecture. He gave the example of gods and demons. He said this was the righteous war to be fought in the name of Karimayi. He talked about how demons like Gowda and Dattappa were cheating people and robbing them, and in order to throw them out, Mother Karimayi herself had sent Gudsikara.

Listening to his description of Karimayi, the Thief had tears in his eyes. Unconscious of what he was doing, staring at Basavaraju and thumping on the floor, he suddenly said, 'I swear on Karimayi, I'll back the sarpanch—give it!' It was clear that he hadn't said this for the greed of bhirandi. Immediately, Basavaraju got up and embraced the Thief and made him drink from his own hands. The rest also swore.

After an hour and a half of this meeting, Basavaraju hurried the quartet out. The drunk quartet didn't think of asking why.

Gudsikara also got up.

'Take a look inside, lord. See what I've brought you!' said Basavaraju and went out with the others and then latched the door from outside.

Inside stood Chimana.

## THE VILLAGE BECAME STRANGE

Elections looked strange in this small village. The Elders scolded the quartet for standing against the Gowda and tried to talk some sense into them. Whether it was stubbornness or the alcohol inside them, they maintained they were doing nothing wrong. They will lose anyway, so let them stand—thought the Elders and fell silent. Despite all this, the life in the village was still calm. The election worm was only burrowing into the heads of Gudsikara's people.

A letter came from the government office certifying the candidature of those standing for the election. Sri Paragowda Shivagowda Nayaka, Sri Dattobha Dhondobha Kulkarni, Sri Balappa Basavantappa Muguli, Sri Basetti Paramasetti Pugasetti, Sri Ningappa Holera, Devaresi—these formed one party. And Sri B. M. Gudsikara BA LLB, Sri C. B. Rames, Sri M. Y. Mereminda, Sri D. B. Satira and Sri S. S. Kadli (Thief Sidrama) formed another.

It's not as if these people didn't know about the elections. In the past, one had taken place. Between the pictures of a yoked bullock and a hut. Since the Gowda had told them 'The yoked bullock is like our father, let's go and write our vote for it,' they had gone and written their vote for the yoked bullock. This time, Gudsikara's party had been given the symbol of a weighing scale.

Thanks to Gudsikara, the quartet didn't have to spend any money from their pockets. So all four became very generous. Handing out beedis to all who talked to them, they asked people to vote for them. Basavaraju sent for a painter from Belagavi. He came and drew a large weighing scale on the chalk wall of Gudsikara's house and under it wrote, 'Your hote for the scale.'

Drawn in colour, this picture was vivid and visible from afar. People stood in front of Gudsikara's house, walked up and down and kept looking at the picture. The moment they came to know that the painter had drawn it for free, they made him draw a similar picture on the wall of each house. Thus, a scale swung in front of every house. Children fought with each other: 'The scale on our house is bigger!' Some local artists added fruit and coconut and betel leaves to their scales. Another artist drew a bird on one scale and rupees on the other. Because they didn't get it drawn, the Gowda's symbol of the tree couldn't be seen anywhere. But the moment people came to know that Gowda's party symbol was a tree, they also began to draw pictures of a tree on their scales, a bird on the tree, cattle standing under its shade and Karimayi in the lake, holding a lotus in her hand.

Thus, the entire village became a strange exhibition of scales and trees.

The village looked colourful, right? The old people there, did they feel curious? Feel amused? They said: On this pretext, at least the village has become beautiful. But they never doubted their success—nobody did.

The quartet would meet at the hut to discuss the daily happenings. Basavaraju would describe the work to be done the next day. Now even in Gudsikara, a new confidence sprang up because of Basavaraju's strategies. Like the idea of drawing the scale. Now he talked and talked. The canvassing was by only one party. Until then they had been distributing beedis and asking people to 'hote for them'. Now they started distributing cigarettes. One day, Basavaraju went to Belagavi, brought about 100 or 200 bras, and through Girija, had them secretly distributed among the women. And made all those women swear upon Karimayi that they would vote for Gudsikara's party.

On their part, the quartet wasn't sitting quiet either. Every day, wearing garlands and leading processions of schoolchildren, they would distribute cigarettes to all and sundry and ask for their vote. Of course none of them wanted to miss this ample opportunity to give speeches. Whether people came to hear them or not, let there be one or many in the audience, they stood in the style Basavaraju had taught them and gave speeches. Even in gatherings where there were only one or two men, the quartet would still begin with, 'My dear brothers and sisters,' and end with 'Jai Hind!' When children set off on a procession, they shouted, 'The age of the oldies are over, times of youth have begun. Down, down! Old ways of old people. Victory to new ways! Whatever happens, let there be unity,' so on and so forth.

Among the quartet, the only two who had some originality were the Thief and Ramesa. Although the Thief started the speech like the others, he added juicy anecdotes in the middle. We give instances here, as much as possible, of the not-so-obscene parts:

'There was a woman, very lovely, a young girl. She became of marriageble age. Whom should she marry? If she marries a fellow her age, does he know how to do the night job properly? Therefore, if she marries an aged man, he will have experience, he'll do the job properly.

'My dear, dearest brothers and sisters of Shivapura, she thought so and married an old man. When she went to him all excited at night . . . ? He had experience, yes. But the tool? Therefore, my brothers and sisters, like this young woman, don't hote for the oldies, and later cry that they don't have the tool. Jai Hind!'

Rumps Ramesa's explanation for this would be:

'My dear brothers and sisters of Shivapura. Understand the words of the Thief properly. The story he told isn't false. In this, the young woman means you who hote. The old man means Gowda's party. Marrying means hoting. Night means after the elections. Like how the young woman married an oldie and cried at night that there was no tool, don't you hote for Gowda's party, brothers and sisters, and lament later. Marriage doesn't happen again and again in life. Now what should the young woman do? Old man without the tool on the one hand, on the other young woman with desire brimming in her. Think, what should she do?'

Someone in the gathering said helpfully, 'She should commit adultery.'

Rumps Ramesa continued: 'My dearest brothers and sisters, if she'd married a young man in the first place, why should she have to commit adultery? Therefore, hote for us. Jai Hind.'

After all this canvassing, if someone dared say, 'Che che, you are all little calves in front of the Gowda. The flesh on your head is still raw—and you will win the election, right?' If anyone said as much, the canvassing would become doubly intense.

The village, which hadn't seen any entertainment for a long time, found all this to be quite good fun. Nobody really bothered about winning or losing, unlike Gudsikara and his party. Gowda, who was going through the sorrow of losing his son, and the Elders who commiserated with him, didn't think of canvassing at all. They too found this childish canvassing of Gudsikara's party quite amusing. As the election day neared, the people of Gudsikara's party fretted more and more. In their fretting, sometimes they would even say nasty things. Made the children shout, 'Down down, Gowda who made Chimana pregnant!'

But since people spat, 'chi, thoo' and thrashed the kids, they went no further.

If the quartet canvassed during the day, at night, Basavaraju continued to plot. In the torchlight of the village, his machinations remained invisible.

The monsoon was over. But the late monsoon rains were still in the fields. Now Devaresi had a lot of work to do. He had to walk around and collect the aaya.[12] In the evening, after going from barn to barn, when he came back to the hut, all he could do was spread his blanket and go to sleep. But after all, he had a wanting and watering mouth. It wanted to drink to the hilt and kept drying up. But even Lagumavva had to collect the aaya. She didn't have the time to brew liquor. It was even rare for her to cook. She would be content with the rottis people gave her in the fields. All these days, there had been Durgi in the hut. If she wanted, Lagumavva could ask her to roast a rotti. Now Durgi wasn't there much.

It was neither the day nor the time for it, but Sundari's excitement was boundless. In the excitement of getting Gudsikara back, she went crazy. It was difficult to control her. Like a loafer heifer whose tether is loosened, she showed off the sassiness of her body everywhere she went. She showed off wearing a twenty-rupee-worth Shapoori sari with pleats that swept the ground. Inside the bra, she kept a couple of sharp daggers and pierced Gudsikara's eyes. Lit a fire in his loins. Haughty-nosed, she forgot to see the ground beneath her feet. Her clothes and all that luxury didn't fail to dazzle the eyes of people. But since everybody knew she was a whore, and of another village, they talked as much as they could and then kept quiet. But Sundari, whose eyes grew blind to anything beyond the range of her nose-ring, heard none of it. She was like a mad horse, lost in fun, sex and enjoyment. Right ho—whoever mounted her, she was ready for the race—unaware, unknowing, aimless, following any direction in front of her nose, whether it was pit or hill, and uncaring if she fell or rose. But she too didn't know. Who her real rider was.

On the other hand Basavaraju, like a born blacksmith, was heating many pieces of iron in his forge. He made the quartet stoke the fire. Fed fuel. The moment the iron was hot, he got Gudsikara to strike and make something out of it. But the others never knew to whom, or how, the thing that was made would be of use. There was an old rod which lay in his forge for a long time. He melted it and mixed some new and soft iron into it. Let's see what he makes out of this.

One day, Devaresi came back from the fields at dusk. Basavaraju stepped into Devaresi's hut. All of a sudden, he was there, shouting, 'Mother' and holding Devaresi's feet. Devaresi didn't have any anger towards him. Nor was he upset with him. But he never thought, even in his dreams, that Basavaraju would come to his hut. He came and held my feet! Devaresi felt happy about it. He'd always had a grouse that people who had learnt Engreji were contemptuous of him. Gudsikara had never touched his feet, hadn't called him, 'Mother'. Many said that this man was even more educated than Gudsikara. Now that Basavaraju came and touched his feet, Devaresi felt what people said must be true. But what should he do now? He didn't know what to say. He got up, opened the bhandara bag in the corner, put some on Basavaraju's forehead and sat down. Basavaraju sat too, folding his hands. 'Mother, please come to our hut and let us serve you,' he said. Devaresi got more scared. Like Basavaraju's coming here, he hadn't expected this talk either. Should I say yes? Or no? This odd day and odd time, how can I accept his service? Then he thought: I should go to his hut, right? Fine, I'll go and see what this service is. He said, 'Yes, I'll come.' Basavaraju got up, still folding his hands.

Seeing Basavaraju still standing there, Devaresi assumed that the other wanted him to go immediately. Basavaraju went in front. Devaresi followed.

The blanket was spread. Mother was seated on it.

Basavaraju kept walking in and out of the hut, made a lot of fuss. He poured whiskey into a dish and gave it to the Mother. Mother was overjoyed. He hadn't touched it for the past fifteen days, right? It seemed like he hadn't drunk in a year. And until now he had only drunk country liquor made by Lagumavva. But this came out of a bright shiny bottle which Basavaraju opened right there in front of him. The moment it was placed before her, Mother drank it in one gulp, left not even a drop at the bottom. It seemed like his insides were on fire, and warm air was gushing out of his nose and ears. Later Basavaraju went in and brought a dish full of mutton curry and seven or eight rottis. Mother's eyes widened, nose broadened, and, without looking hither and thither, she started gorging noisily.

When Devaresi drank a whole bottle of whiskey in one gulp, without even mixing water, Basavaraju's eyes opened wide in surprise. Chimana's eyes opened wide too. She bit her tongue, getting a huge kick out of it all. The sight of Devaresi making crude animal noises and eating made Basavaraju smile. Sundari, who was inside, suddenly laughed and exclaimed, 'Ishshi.'

Devaresi kept eating, oblivious. He was wearing nothing except the dhotra at the waist. All the meat and liquor he had consumed made the sweat stream over his body. As it is, it's a body dark like iron. It shone some more with sweat. This frame was over sixty years old. The muscles on his chest and arms were hard and taut. An arm-length braid at the back, beard in the front. Basavaraju felt amused by this shape, neither woman nor man. Sundari was amused too. She said she wanted to come out and ask him to read her palm. Basavaraju had told her not to come out, unless he told her to. She kept quiet. Perhaps the curry was too hot. Devaresi's nose ran, eyes ran, it all got mixed up. Wiping it away with his sweaty hand, he kept eating. Then he belched thunderously, almost making the hut shake and the children next door scream.

Sundari was disgusted.

After the meal, both Sundari and Basavaraju, laughing inwardly, prostrated before the Mother. Mother didn't smear the bhandara on their foreheads. Didn't prophecy. With drowsy eyes, she got up, saying, 'Mother'. And promptly lost her balance. Basavaraju went and steadied her. Then took her to her hut and left her there.

That night, Devaresi dreamt that someone was hammering on his head with an axe. He got up disturbed.

He couldn't interpret the meaning of the dream. But from the next day on, Mother's merciful eyes turned towards Basavaraju's hut.

Basavaraju didn't disappoint.

# VILLAGE IS ON THE STREET

Randi Full Moon or Widow's Full Moon was still four days away. That afternoon, the sun was like in the height of summer, and cattle slept in the lake in a cool stupor. People in the fields sought refuge in the place where they kept the fodder or under trees or in whatever patch of shade they could find. At the land's end, wherever you looked, you saw racing mirages. In the village, people sat in the cool shade of the katte or porch. The effect of the scorching sun was so bad that they weren't even in the mood to talk. Although it was day now, it was as silent as the night.

Suddenly, the villagers heard a terrible sound. Something they had never heard before. They could not imagine what it was. As if someone hammering a nail into your ear. As if the whole village had exploded or a hill had come tumbling over them. They were all was stunned for a few moments. Those who were sleeping got up with a jerk, as if they had seen a nightmare. The cows in the lake got scared and tore at their tethers. Many people's sarees and dhotras became wet. Children screamed in terror. If what Lagumavva says is true, hearing this voice, Karimayi's idol suddenly leapt and hopped and the broken arm fell off again. When Lagumavva put the arm back and looked at her, the idol seemed to be sweating slightly. The birds and other creatures in the trees and plants around the lake started screeching and flying around as if some calamity had come. To describe this without exaggeration, the whole village, old and young, male and female, like those whose stomachs turn and vomit, emptied out of their homes and came on the street! At first, they only heard the sound. Then when they heard the words 'For whom is your hote? For Gudsikara-saheb,' they became a little calmer and everyone sitting and standing rushed in the direction of the sound.

Gudsikara had got a loudspeaker, and the great man, let Karimayi keep him well, was having the election slogans shouted out in this burning afternoon.

On that day, it was the same talk in everybody's mouth. The village was in the fever of exciting stories and news and the scorching sun. Unfortunately, people couldn't hear one another. Screaming and mimicking, men who had gathered on the street, and women who came out of their houses—all talked. Even elders gossiped like women. They mimicked the 'oink-oink' sound of the loudspeaker. They estimated the expenses for all this. They said: Whatever his father had earned twisting people's necks, let the son spit it all up.

They all slept late that day.

The old panchayat people had to think now. Until then they had been confident of their success. Now they had no choice but to bend to the canvassing tactics of their opponents. The news of their opponents distributing bras among the women and making them swear, had already reached their ears. The only thing which gave them courage was that the election was on the day after the Full Moon. On that day, anyway, the golden idol will rise. God's oracle will take place. Karimayi will give some command to the village. That is, they believed the command would be in their favour. But thinking that they shouldn't sit quiet now, they too started telling whomever they met, 'Hote for the tree symbol.'

On the other hand it wasn't as if Gudsikara didn't fear the Full Moon. Because, among the five who stood for the elections, Devaresi was also one. But since Basavaraju had told him, 'That worry is mine, not yours,' he consoled himself.

Basavaraju didn't tell him a word of what he was planning on doing.

# THE LIGHT WENT OUT

The next day, Tuesday morning, Devaresi was performing the worship in the temple. He took off the jewels on the goddess and bathed her. He draped the saree round her. But then when he looked for the jewels to adorn the idol—thcy were gone! He searched here and there. He tried to remember, 'Were they here or not?' They had been there. Not only had they been there, but he also remembered taking them off and the spot he put them down on. But they weren't there any more. There's no one in the temple but him. Is it the Goddess' miracle? He got frightened for a moment. Then he thought: Maybe not. He took off her saree, shook it and searched again. Still didn't find them. He wondered if they were in his dhotra and shook that too. There're usually some clever spirits around the Goddess and sometimes they do all sorts of things.

As he loosened the folds of his dhotra and searched, he thought he heard a lilting laugh. When he turned to see—it was Sundari! He thought a spirit must have appeared in her form, and so he took out Mother's hair switch to ward it off. But this spirit didn't vanish. She was still laughing. Thank god, she opened her mouth and spoke: 'How does this chain look on me?' What do you see? The chain of large cowrie-shells, meant for the Goddess' neck, was now hanging round Chimana's! If you count, you see that there're twenty-one large shells. This chain is not just some adornment. If the Goddess had wanted it, the villagers would have made a golden chain for her. For people who had a golden face of that weight made for her, having a chain made isn't a big thing. But the story goes that Mother would let her children play until the evening, and then fearing the gods would kill them, turn them into shells after sunset, make a chain of the shells and wear it around her neck! The chain is of those shells! Like bathing Mother during worship, there's also the procedure of dipping this chain into water and then putting it round Mother's neck.

Why would Sundari care about all this stuff? Devaresi hurried behind the Goddess to drape the wet dhotra round himself. Meanwhile, he saw Dattappa coming. Devaresi didn't know what to do. As it is, Dattappa has a sharp mind. When he is saluting the Goddess, if he sees that there's no chain on the neck and asks where it is, what should I say? Without being seen by Dattappa, who was nearing the temple now, he went to Sundari. Pleaded with his hands for the chain. Even as she was gesturing her refusal, Dattappa came in. Devaresi closed her mouth, held her like a lamb, bent and hid under the Goddess' idol. Dattappa didn't know any of this. He threw the flowers he had brought on the goddess, prostrated before her and left.

After making certain that he had gone quite far away, Devaresi got up and said, 'Che, how you scared me! Now give, give the chain.' Not only Devaresi, nobody in the village would tolerate this kind of mischief. Devaresi was angry. As he was saying, 'Will you give it, or not . . . ,' suddenly Basavaraju appeared. Laughing playfully, Sundari answered, 'I won't!' and lifting the braid on his back, she slapped it back against his chest and ran away.

Basavaraju disappeared just as swiftly as he had appeared.

Devaresi felt as though the sky had fallen on his head. What's this? Playing mischief with a goddess who is like burning cinders and fire? He thought it wasn't proper to run after her and snatch the chain back. He quickly performed his worship. Draped the saree around Mother so as to cover her neck. Prostrated before her and cried, 'Yavva . . . ' Tears rolled down his eyes. He beat his chin with his hands asking forgiveness. He put pebbles in his ears. Made vows and oaths that he would never see their faces after getting the chain back. He prostrated again and again. Because of his breath, or the breeze, the lamp suddenly went out. His heart leapt to his mouth and he slumped to the ground, crying, 'Ayyo, yavva . . . ' His mouth dried up. He lost the strength in his limbs. Slowly, he groped around, got up, lit the lamp again and went back to his hut.

Spreading the blanket on the floor, he fell on it. Crying, 'Yavva . . . ,' he tossed and rolled and wept. A few hours later, he was running a fever and his dark body burned like a heated pan. His eyes were red from crying.

In this state, he went to Basavaraju's hut. Basavaraju was there, but he said Sundari wasn't. She'd gone to Gudsikara's fields and would be back at night. There was no way to go there and ask for her. It would be difficult if people came to know. Devaresi was also afraid about who might go to the temple and find the chain gone. His head was splitting from fever. The lamp in front of the Goddess was extinguished. He thought he was surely going to die that day. Indeed, it's good. Then the scandal won't descend on me. Maybe I did wrong. I should have got hold of Sundari, slapped her twice and snatched the chain. Devouring meat and liquor at their place was like consuming shit and piss, he thought with regret.

Thinking that she might be back, he went there again in the afternoon. But Basavaraju said no, she was still out.

Without uttering a word, Devaresi returned. By the time he took ten steps, he felt as if his head was reeling. He hadn't eaten. Scorching sun. Mental torment. He reached his hut, slumped in front it and vomited. In the end, there was also some blood. He thought Mother was making him spit blood. He went in, and, as if he was prostrating before the Mother, fell face down.

## RANDI FULL MOON, OR WIDOW'S FULL MOON

That night Devaresi's chain was returned. But he was separated from the Mother.

When Devaresi came, although Sundari was at home, Basavaraju had said she wasn't. Seeing the look on Devaresi's face, he laughed and slapped his thigh. At night, it was time to eat and sleep. Basavaraju and Sundari sat listening to the radio, their feet up, their legs crossed. As they had expected, Devaresi came again. His face looked like something that was sucked dry and thrown away. His eyes were red like corals. When he came, neither of them got up. Basavaraju said, 'Come in, Mother.' Sundari was amused by how the tone of his talk changed and how his hand gestures changed with his talk. Without saying anything, she went inside. Basavaraju crossed his legs the other way and said, 'Is it such a valuable chain? Why are you so anxious?'

Devaresi was angry. 'What are you saying, boy? Do you make fun of a goddess who is like burning cinders and fire? Mad man.'

Until now a trifle of a chain, Basavaraju realized its value when he saw how Devaresi was pleading for it. 'All right,' he said, 'we'll give it. Are we running away anywhere? What do we do, the girl's full of mischief. She brought it here, I'll make her give it back. Come sit.'

Sundari brought a dishful of arrack and put it in front of Devaresi. Sure that Basavaraju would get the chain back for him, Devaresi sat. Since morning, he hadn't eaten a morsel or drunk a drop of water. Suddenly, he realized he was hungry. He drank. Then he said, 'Now give me the chain.' Sundari filled the dish. He drank again. The mutton came—he ate. And he kept sitting there. Basavaraju said, 'You say that she is a goddess like burning cinders and fire—make that chain come and fall here from where it is.' Devaresi kept quiet. 'If Mother's power is so great,' added Sundari, 'let her make me die spitting blood,' and began to mingle her 'heh, heh' with Basavaraju's laughter. Devaresi belched loudly once and then started sobbing.

Immediately, Basavaraju told Sundari, 'Mother has come, run and hold her feet.' Sundari ran and held the feet. Holding the feet, she started rubbing it. Devaresi, blurry-eyed, swayed back and forth and kept sobbing. This is the sign of being possessed by the Goddess. Basavaraju, who was laughing, winked silently at Sundari. She kept rubbing Devaresi's feet and then slowly moved beyond the knees to the thighs. Mother's sobbing stopped and she pushed away the hand on her thigh. Sundari laughed aloud. In mock anger, Basavaraju said, 'There's fire in Mother's thigh. Don't play with her like that.' Sundari laughed some more. Unable to stop laughing, she went inside. She filled the dish again. Devaresi didn't drink. Crying loudly, he said, 'Mother will kill me. Give me the chain, yavva,' and folded his hands before Sundari. Basavaraju became alarmed. He told Sundari to hand over the chain immediately and then came out to see if anyone was watching any of this. Mercifully, there was no one.

Sundari brought the chain to Devaresi and said, 'Take it.' When Devaresi reached for it, she moved back with a laugh. Like a big tree felled at the root, Devaresi lost his balance and toppled over. She held it up again. He got up again, and swaying, went to her and stretched out his hand. She moved back some more. After she'd done this four or five times, he held her tight. Tried to snatch the chain. He had been hungry since morning and was weak. He had spat blood. He fell on her heavily, and Sundari pushed him away with some force. He lost his balance and collapsed. When he tried to get up, Sundari ran and sat heavily on his paunch. Devaresi was fighting like a pained beast, unable to get up or fall. As if he had been sent for, Basavaraju came back into the room. God knows what got into Sundari—laughing loudly, sitting in the posture of Karimayi on the tiger, she gave a blessing. Perhaps Basavaraju was frightened, because he folded his hands!

Anyway, the Full Moon came. Mother became a widow.

Perhaps because Mother became a widow, the moon blanched like a consumptive patient.

On that day, at dawn, Gowda had a dream—the central pillar of Karimayi's temple shook and then collapsed. He got up with a start. His heart trembled. Couldn't sit and think. Tried to see if the catastrophe could be averted. Couldn't find a way. Deciding to narrate the dream to Dattappa and Devaresi, he immediately set off towards the lake for a bath.

The morning hadn't yet dawned. He went to the temple. It was dark inside. The Mother's idol wasn't visible. He went round the temple, prostrated, came out and sat on the katte of the lamp post at the entrance. They hadn't been able to find out who broke Mother's arm during Shige Full Moon. He thought of his elders who had built the temple. He felt that Mother was taking revenge on them and felt scared. The memory of his son came back, and there was a catch in his throat. God knows how long he sat there—when he regained consciousness of his body, it was fully morning. He went round the temple again. He filled his eyes with the Mother's idol. He prostrated, saying, 'Mother who gave me birth, save the light of my house.' They had just bound and secured that broken arm during Shige Full Moon, right? It had fallen again. He bound it up, saying, 'Using the sword isn't befitting your stature, Mother! Again, sustain and save the life of the village.' That nightmare. This bad omen. He thought it all very inauspicious and started walking towards Dattu's house.

There, without even bathing, Dattappa sat looking at his *Chintamani*. He was holding his head in his hands in desperation. Even as Gowda opened his mouth to narrate his dream, Dattappa said—'Gowda, last night I dreamt that my *Chintamani* was lost!'

Gowda said nothing.

Perhaps she said this after she heard about their dreams, or remembered hers only then—being a poet, Lagumavva could weave all parallel events into her own stories, simply thinking on her feet. It seems, she too had a dream—that her tongue fell off.

Like it came to the whole village, morning came even in Devaresi's hut. Since he hadn't closed his eyes all night, they were as red as Karimayi's. His body was burning with fever. He was sure that he wouldn't live that day. What was it like, and what has it turned into!

Forget looking the villagers in the face, how can I look at the Mother with these eyes? How do I worship her with these hands? Shall I just shout out everything that's happened to the Gowda? Why? Instead, let me shout it out to Mother. But what can escape Mother's eyes? The village might have closed its eyes, but can Mother's eyes be closed? And it's not possible to back out today. This is Mother's most important Full Moon day—the full moon when Mother becomes a widow. Let whatever happen, if Mother wants it, let her kill me making me spit blood and choose another Devaresi, he thought. For someone who has been Devaresi until now, this is a respectable kind of death. Or Mother, after all she has the heart of a mother who gave birth to us—why shouldn't she swallow my sins and forgive me? We are mere mortals who eat salt and sour and peppers. People who sin. If not the Mother, who else should protect us? A child shits. Won't the mother clean it and draw the child close? Unaware of what it's doing, a child even hits the mother. When it's hungry again, it calls out Avva. She bears it when the child hits her. She gives her breast when the child is hungry. Or okay: Let's say, she spat on us. Is she some outsider? Isn't she the mother? She has the right to spit on us. Even if she spits me out of the temple, it's only proper. She gave birth to me. Let her kill, so he thought and picked up his dhotra.

There wasn't the usual energy in his body. No liveliness. No courage to look at people's faces.

Burning fever too. Slowly, avoiding as many people as possible, he went to the lake and bathed. Wearing the same wet cloth, he came to the temple. Had an attack of vertigo. Everything went dark, and he collapsed on the threshold. Got up again and went inside. He lit the lamp. While taking off Mother's saree and bathing her body, he felt his body freeze and shivered. With trembling hands, he draped the sanctified saree round her. Adorned her with the shell necklace he had brought with him. Put the flowers. Rang the bell. Finally, went round the temple and prostrated. He didn't have the heart to get up. The fever and chill were rising to his head.

Finally, he struggled to his feet and looked at Mother's face. Unable to bear the surging sorrow, he started crying, 'Yavva . . . ' Beating his chest, he cried out, 'Mother, don't make your heart into a stone. I'm still your son, Mother, you gave birth to me,' and slammed his head against the stone and Mother's altar. God knows what miracle of Karimayi it was—the flower on the right shoulder fell. Devaresi felt like the life he had lost had come back to him. He felt consoled as if Mother had hugged him, and caressing his body, had said 'Don't worry, son, I am here.' His body healed, the fever left him and he began to sweat. He became extremely respectful towards the Mother—gratitude filled his eyes as did tears. 'Mother has swallowed my sins, I have her blessing,' he said and set off towards the hut.

The whole day, Gudsikara's party was busy canvassing. They brought the band from Belagavi and the dancing whores. They made them dance all over the village. Gudsikara himself went from house to house with the quartet and requested the young and the old to vote for him. Gowda and Dattappa didn't go. Their minds were devastated by nightmares. Only Ningu took the wrestler boys and told everyone, men and women, to hote for the Gowda. Lagumavva said the same thing in a feminine way. Balu and Basetti also walked about, distributing the Goddess' bhandara to whomever they saw.

In the midst of this hullabaloo, they didn't realize it was already evening.

The sun was setting in the west. The dust which rose with the cattle coming home, the dust which rose because of people who were canvassing and walking all over the place, the dust that spread because of whores dancing and boys forming groups around them and going everywhere—in this strange adulterated dust-wave that spread like factory smoke, the details of the village got blurred. The noise of the loudspeaker, the band and the ugly voices of people—everything got mixed up until it seemed like the whole village was giving out a shattering scream. Now even if scared children forgot their mother's breast and screamed, nobody would hear.

The west sky was red like the eyes of Karimayi.

In the east, the full moon rose.

This was not like all other full-moon days. The rising dust hadn't stuck to the earth. The noise hadn't stopped. As the mad moonlight spread everywhere, everything that had shape had shadows. The shadow became denser and denser and turned into the child of darkness.

Among all these sounds was also the sound of the tabor and dollu drums. Some had finished their dinner, some not. Already, the Panchas, Elders, servants and good wives of the village had gathered in front of the Gowda's house. Placed the golden face in the palanquin. On the one side Dattappa, and on the other Gowda, fanned the Mother with hairy chouri switches. In the clamour of the drums, their voices couldn't be heard. When the Gowda was certain that all those who had to be there were there, he ordered the procession to start.

Saying 'Changu, bhale,' the procession set off.

It passed through the main streets of the village and came to Devaresi's hut. Devaresi was ready, wearing a green saree. Seeing that Devaresi's body was burning, Lagumavva said, 'Why, Mother's body is like burnt foil!' Even the other wives noticed this. Devaresi didn't reply. The wives sang and put bangles of five colours on both his arms, right up to the elbows. They smeared vermilion and bhandara all over his forehead. They decked the braid with flowers and put bhandara on it. They put the anklets on his feet. After holding the peacock-feather switch, the procession went towards the temple with more cries of 'Changu, bhale.'

When they came to the entrance, the trumpet began to play. Gowda hid the Mother's golden face in his lap and clasped it to his chest like a child. Dattappa fanned and showed the way. They took Mother's golden idol to the inner sanctum. Devaresi was so weak that he could barely walk. Lagumavva held his arm and took him inside. Only these people went in and then the door closed.

Then they fixed the golden face to the idol. They fit the red shining strips of eyes. They took out the shell chain and kept it before the Mother. They made crisp pleats and draped a green saree on her. They decorated her with a variety of gold ornaments. They put bangles of five colours on her arm too. You do not get to see this beautified idol of the Mother until another month. Therefore Gowda, Lagumavva and Dattappa, perhaps because they were frightened by the nightmares they'd seen, became very emotional and filled their eyes with the sight of the Mother. The sinner, who made the Mother's arm break, hadn't been found yet. This is how it is about Mother. Everything is known through its effects. If you know things before they happen, you can prevent these calamities from happening. But is Mother a mortal like us to make us know such things? How can we intervene in her business? When we think of all this, we know how weak we are. We can only fold our hands and witness whatever is going to happen.

They had to help Devaresi to his feet. Gowda also realized then that Devaresi's body was burning and became anxious. When Devaresi got up and took the incense aarti, the dhoopaarti, in his hands, they re-opened the door of the inner sanctum. All the devotees gathered outside crowded at the door and filled their eyes with the sight of the Mother's adorned golden idol. Devaresi came out bearing the dhoopaarti and went round the temple. When he went to the lamp-post and held up the dhoopaarti to the Goddess' minions there, shouted 'Changu, bhale' and threw it on the ground, the crowd of devotees started ringing or playing all the temple bells and drums and cymbals until the noise burst the ears of people, and they too screamed 'Changu, bhale!'

Devaresi ran into the inner sanctum. This meant: now Jademuni, in the forest for his penance, had been killed. Devaresi comes running and informs the Mother of this. Since Mother has now become a randi, or widow, they have to break her bangles. Gowda was holding Devaresi, who was in a passion, very tight. Lagumavva hurriedly broke the bangles. Wiped off his vermilion. Dattappa broke Karimayi's bangles. Wiped off her vermilion. Immediately, the devotees threw arecanuts at the idol. This meant: hitting her with bows and arrows like the gods and demons who had hunted her.

The moment the womb was gone, Devaresi screamed terribly. Gowda and Dattappa quickly secured a variety of fruits at Mother's waist. Instantly, Mother became angry. She possessed Devaresi and stepped on the mullavige. They gave her a sword. Put a torch in her left hand. She rushed out of the temple, went to the entrance. The entrance was full of men. This meant: Mother was going to kill the gods and demons. Even in her rush, she calls the privileged Elders, delivers three oracles about the well-being of the village and only then crosses its boundary. The moment she stood near the palanquin, Mother raised the hand with the torch and shouted, 'Yeh . . . ' Everybody stood still. Gowda bent and clutched the Mother's feet, which were on the mullavige, very firmly. Inside the temple, some of the women were chattering. Dattappa scolded them, and they fell silent. Still, there were some whispers.

But Mother didn't open her mouth soon enough —she just kept sobbing.

People were all ears. Surprisingly enough, even Gudsikara had come with Basavaraju to hear the oracle. Inwardly, he believed that the Goddess would give an oracle favouring his side in the election. Basavaraju stood next to him, darting glances at the women. He started to say something in Gudsikara's ear but then shut up in order to hear to the oracle. Girija didn't seem to be bothered about the oracle —she was busy throwing piercing glances at Basavaraju.

Even now Mother hadn't found her voice. She simply sobbed.

Gowda's heart beat fast. What might Mother's words be? She couldn't even find her voice. Ningu was watching Basavaraju's hunting glances. He felt jealous. Sundari, who was standing behind him, started sobbing slowly. Immediately, the women began to scold her. She stopped, but after a few moments, started again. Lagumavva scolded her loud enough for the other women to hear: 'What's ailing this bitch?' And then lent her ears to the oracle. When Ningu turned to see what was going on, Sundari was sobbing and had collapsed where she stood. She got up, fell again and again, and sobbed.

Meanwhile, Mother began, 'Yeh . . . '

People became still. Gowda held Mother's feet more tightly. He felt disturbed when Mother's warm tears fell on his ear. Mother found her voice:

The roots of the sheltering banyan tree
Have dried up without water
Don't forget to water it

Nobody doubted that the oracle was clearly about the elections. They all interpreted it as follows: watering the roots of the sheltering banyan tree means giving the vote to Gowda's party. They also said that this talk had some substance. A wrestler boy taunted, 'Well, go on Gudsikara, now.' Gudsikara was disappointed. He turned to look at Basavaraju. But he wasn't there.

On Randi Full Moon, three things happen. After the first words about village affairs, the second word relates to the Gowda's family. So he was anxious about what she was going to say about his lost son. The second word was still in the throat, just about to come out, when Sundari screamed in a frenzy, 'Yeh . . . ' exactly like Devaresi.

People were stunned.

Before they understood the what or why or how of it all—by the time they turned back and looked at the women, Sundari leapt from their midst, entered the men's crowd and hurled the bhandara she had been holding in her hands. Devaresi was astounded and began to tremble. Looking at the style in which she was swaying, on the one hand he felt sad that the Goddess had possessed her instead of him, on the other he was scared that she would make his secret public.

Sundari ran and stood next to Devaresi, and concentrating all her strength, screamed again. People's minds became distracted. Since the way she was swaying was exactly like that of Devaresi, some thought that the Goddess might have possessed her too. Some said this crazy bitch was leading them into some calamity. If she wasn't possessed, would she have the courage to scream like this in the gathering of the devotees? Would she have the courage to stand near the palanquin? If she was leading us to some calamity, would the Goddess have kept quiet? She would have made her spit blood right where she stood. Forget that, there's also a strangeness in her voice. Yes, she is a cheap woman. But if this is what comes to Mother's mind, what can you do? Devaresi must have committed something polluting. If not, discarding him, why would Mother choose another?

Gowda became afraid. The wisdom of Dattappa's *Chintamani* lost its lustre. Nobody could think of what to do now. Sundari screamed again and started sobbing. This was just like Devaresi's sobbing. Some sentimental ones, fully willing to believe, didn't have any more doubts. This just isn't the time to get into a debate.

Sundari raised her hand and screamed, 'Water the sprouts.' The torch in Devaresi's hand fell, just like that. People who were close by heard her. Those at a distance couldn't. They asked 'What? What?' They found out from the others. Immediately, Dattappa raised his hand and said, 'This is Gudsya's god.' People said, 'Goddess.' Some said, 'Shrew.' They shouted, 'Ha.' They shouted, 'Ho.'

'The Goddess has forsaken me . . . ' Devaresi screamed, and like a child that has seen a ghost, shoved people aside and ran out. While the people were screaming in alarm, 'Ho . . . ' Gowda shouted, 'He might die or something. Come, Dattu—' and ran after Devaresi. Dattappa ran too. Behind them ran some wrestler boys and a few others.

Basavaraju had, by now, managed to get into the inner sanctum. Without anyone's knowledge, he hit the three big bee hives with a long stick. With each hit, a hive loosened and fell to the ground. With the fallen hives, like raw blood—honey, bee and worm—sprang up and spilt everywhere. The insects, reeling under the attack, burst out like sudden smoke and stung whomever they found and wherever they could.

Screaming, shouting, yelling, 'Ayyo, appa, avva, Mother, Karimayi,' and 'Ho,' people ran for cover. Whether they fell or got up, stomped or got stomped —they tore away their clothes, took off their sarees and howled. But the bees didn't stop. They chased the people everywhere, thousands and thousands of bees attacking each person. When they killed one bee, a hundred sprang up from its blood. The insects didn't care for their lives, didn't stop to see if it was woman or child, didn't bother who fell or rose, didn't let go from where they entered, didn't let go when people fell. They stung on and on, buzzing and buzzing in the air. In a moment or two, the temple suddenly became empty. Only at a distance, the sounds of women and children crying, or the village dogs whining horribly, could be heard.

The devotees lay slumped under the blankets, thinking: Let them sting as much as they want to. Gudsikara, also hiding under someone's blanket, fortunately remembered the golden face of the Mother. The insects hadn't abated yet. There were no signs of them doing so either. Gowda, Dattappa—there was nobody there. Even as he lay there, he addressed the devotees and told them about the golden face. Then they too remembered. Saying, 'Get up,' he hauled some people to their feet, and, not even noticing the bees which stung him, ran into the inner sanctum and seized Mother's golden face. Because of the force with which he pulled at it, Mother's entire idol, without the head and only the torso, fell on its stomach and its limbs collapsed on the floor. The fruit in the temple scattered. For the people there, it seemed as though their life had flown away. They decided that they would fix everything the next day. Hiding the Mother's idol in his dhotra, Gudsikara picked up Mother's jewels and ran home with the devotees.

Back home he found Basavaraju.

All their faces were swollen and unrecognizable. Basavaraju's face and eyes and ears were so swollen that whenever he opened his mouth, he looked like the demon in Lagumavva's song. There was no use talking now. Each was busy scratching his body. Inside, Girija was crying softly. Faraway, the people's moaning could still be heard. Dogs were whining. Gudsikara sat, scratching himself and hoping that Gowda and Dattappa might turn up now, here, soon. But even after a long time, there was no sign of anybody. If all of us are here, how do we tell Gowda and Dattappa that the golden face is here? So he sent the devotees to Gowda's and Dattappa's houses. Looking at their crying faces, his heart rose to his mouth, there was a catch in his throat. Perhaps he would have cried if Basavaraju wasn't there! Basavaraju kept looking at Gudsikara. He too had had an unexpected shock.

Gudsikara waited for them for an hour. But there was still no sign of anyone coming to his house. He looked at his watch. It was already three. Basavaraju was snoring. Goddess's face was still sitting on the bed, its eyes open. He took it to their worship room and locked it in the cabinet there. Still nobody came.

Many thoughts and cares pressed down on him, made him cry. Tears streamed down his face. He was sure that what Sundari had done was a part of Basavaraju's scheming. Perhaps all that was for his own sake. But what they'd done wasn't right. He didn't want to destroy the mythology of his village for the sake of his hunger for power. But all this had happened unexpectedly. He felt that the Gowda was a much bigger man than himself. He thought he would give the Goddess's face back to the Gowda tomorrow morning and apologize. He thought of how the Gowda had distributed sugar when he had passed his LLB, how he handed him the election and this panchayat, and recently, meeting him in the fields, how he had pleaded. Gudsikara thought again about the commotion in the temple today. He remembered the crying faces of the Goddess' devotees. He felt that people wouldn't forgive him. He burnt with regret. Perhaps owing to this feeling of regret, his heart became a little lighter. Without his knowledge, he fell asleep.

In the morning, he heard someone scream. He woke up and opened his eyes. Downstairs, his mother was screaming. Confused, he ran to her. The old woman was pointing to the worship room, beating her chest with her fists and crying.

The cabinet in the worship room was open. And it was empty.

Basavaraju, with the golden face, jewels, money, and also Girija, had run away.

After all this, exactly a month has passed. Today is Wife's Full Moon. Today is when Mother Karimayi killed the seven-headed and five-shouldered gods and demons, regained the lives of her children and husband and then returned as a wife and mother.

But today, Mother didn't return at all.

Karimayi, who is the greatest on Earth, was like a cradle for children. For wives, she became the winnow holding the auspicious baagina.[13] The walking stick for ripe old men. The support of orphans. If you remembered her, even when you held burning cinders in your hands, they'd turn into red lotuses. Mud turned into gold. Daily millet turned into sweet jaggery. Gruel turned into the payasa. Huts became palaces.

But today this Mother, who is bigger than all the three worlds, didn't return at all.

Although they searched everywhere, Basavaraju couldn't be found. They had informed the police. But there was no news from them. That day, when Gudsikara yanked the golden face, the headless idol of the Mother fell on its stomach and its limbs collapsed on the ground. They should have lifted it up and at least fixed a wooden face to the torso. That could not be done without purification, though. And if Mother herself didn't come, what's the use of purifying? Frightened, Lagumavva hadn't passed anywhere near the temple of late. If she had seen Mother in this state, she probably would have sung a lament about the demons who had beheaded the Mother and played with her head like a ball!

At night, Lagumavva sat alone in the hut and sang verses like this—

Don't ask where she went
Say that Karimayi is in your mind!
Don't ask whither she went
Say Karimayi is a part of your psyche

—to console herself, perhaps. But her voice sounded terrible, and to those who heard it from a distance, it sounded like the howling of a pained beast.

Devaresi, that day, gave this all a miss and disappeared into the forest. After three days, they found his body hanging there. Mother might choose another Devaresi and give some sign of where the golden face is. Or people believed she might make Basavaraju spit blood, come back in fear and return the face. They waited thinking that such news would arrive, now, later, today or tomorrow. Only in Belagavi papers, the news was published under the head: 'Big Dacoity in Shivapura. Golden Idol Missing.' Seeing this, people cried loudly as if someone dear to them had died.

The entire village was silent like a house of mourning.

Now they are scared of uttering the name of Karimayi. Nobody raises their voice to speak. If anyone visits the village, they ask the news of Mother. Nobody's face has any life in it. It looks as if, next to everybody's navel, there is a huge gash. And that they are crying again and again with that pain. Perhaps they stopped just now, or bore the pain biting their lips.

In the corner of their eyes, there shone a sliver of hope that Mother might be found.

As days passed, even that began to fade.

In a month, Gowda, his skin sagging and his shoulder gone sloppy, had become like an old bull who can't even ward off the fly on his body with his tail. Gowda sat when he sat. Stood when he stood. Shaved his beard sometimes, and sometimes not. Mother, who left giving her word that she'd return, hadn't returned. Son Shivaninga hadn't returned. Nor was there any news of him. Gowda took to spending his days, thinking, 'If not Karimayi, at least can't Death have pity on me?'

But does Death have a heart? Gowda's only companion, Shivasani, also died, crying, 'Shivaninga.' Now it's my turn, Gowda said, and sat ready to die with 'Karimayi' on his lips. The only belief left shining in his eyes was that Mother, who would show his son, was going to manifest herself on Wife's Full Moon. His life was concentrated in his eyes. Always, he sat with his arms round his knees on the lamp-post katte in front of the temple, staring before him. Only when necessary, he said a word or two. Every time he spoke, he shed tears.

Whenever they saw him, people remembered the lost Mother and felt a surge of sorrow.

Dattappa's problem was how to get some food down the Gowda's gullet.

In that one month, many other things happened.

Chimana, now fully pregnant, came back. It was difficult to recognize her with her dishevelled hair, emaciated body, torn and patched clothes and her protruding tummy. The moment they realized it was her, all the villagers surrounded her. She was of no use. She had lost her tongue. As if that wasn't enough, she was mad too. Basavaraju had also cheated her. What's the use of picking on her? They thought

Mother had already given her the proper punishment and kept quiet. She would sit in front of her hut, howling like a dog. If some good soul gave her a morsel of food, she ate. If not, she just lay there.

These days, people didn't have the sort of inward peace to show her compassion. Who showed them any?

Today, Gowda was a little lively. It's Wife's Full Moon, when Mother comes back and ascends the altar. Mother will definitely come today. Or she will possess someone and tell us where she is now. He strongly believed that she would bring back Shivaninga too. Since early this morning, he's been sitting on the lamp-post katte of the temple, Dattappa beside him.

The moment someone passed by the temple, they looked up thinking that the passer-by was possessed by the Mother, or, at least, had brought news of somebody being possessed. Forgetting gruel and water, they looked in every direction and at every door. Their eyes lit up with hope, they kept looking.

It was evening, the cattle came home. As the sun set, the light in their eyes also dimmed. The moon rose in the east. It was past the time of the Mother's arrival. As the moonlight spread, the village turned ashy, like a consumptive patient.

Dattappa let out a big sigh.

'Get up, Gowda,' he said and put his hand on the Gowda's shoulder. Gowda got up quietly. Mother, who said she would come from wherever she was on the Wife's Full Moon day, hadn't kept her word!

On the way back, Dattappa, as if roused by some thought, asked, 'By the way, Gowda, Lagumavva hasn't come, right?'

Immediately Gowda's eyes shone. He thought, Yes. Who knows? Mother may incarnate in her neighbourhood.

'Come, let's see,' they said, and rushed to the untouchable neighbourhood.

The women had crowded into Chimana's hut. Unable to stop themselves, the two men ran inside. Women were bustling about. Lagumavva was talking loudly. Women were chattering. When they asked what had happened, one of them said that Chimana had given birth to a girl child.

The crowd didn't even know that Gowda and Dattappa had come.

One woman said of the baby, 'Yeh, yeh, see, its nose is exactly like that of Gudasya.'

But Lagumavva said, 'No, stop it. Its nose, mouth, looks—everything is exactly like the Gowda's. Looks like it has been dipped in the Gowda's mould and taken out.'

Gowda walked towards his house, disappointed.

Despite this disappointment, a soft smile played on Dattappa's lips:

Here, Hara Hara
Here, Shiva Shiva
Here, our story ends
Here, Hara, Hara, here, Shiva Shiva

Here, our story ends.

# *Notes*

I find the tendency to add excessive footnotes, which I see in some translators from non-English cultures, to be problematic in many ways. Apart from how this makes the translator turn into some kind of an ethnographer, I find that it also mars the readability of the translated text. So as far as possible, I choose to suggest, or provide briefly, what I think is essential information in the text (as a part of the sentence, paragraph or perhaps in parenthesis). The readers can find further information, and thus participate in the process of constructing the text and teasing out its multiple possibilities. [Trans.]

1 Full-moon day celebrated in North Karnataka after the Dasara festival, usually around October or November.

2 Panchayat is an older form of local government that has survived in India even today, although in a somewhat altered form. While traditionally it consisted of the five elders or respected members of the community, now the Panchas or Panchayat members are elected by people of the village.

3 Lingavanta, or Lingayata is a member of the Lingayata community, a religion that rose against the traditional Brahminical religion in twelfth-century Karnataka. Founded by Basavanna, it is well known for its protest

against the caste system and ritualism in traditional religion.

4 A jangama is a wandering Lingayat saint or mendicant. The term is associated with 'movement' or 'that which is moving'. This concept of the jangama is valorized in opposition to the sthavara or the static.

5 The expressions 'ri,' 're' or 'ra' are Kannada suffixes added to names to indicate respect in North Karnataka. The plural forms are used to denote respect even in the case of addressing, or referring to, one person. For instance, saheb (master) will be 'sahebara', with the respectful suffix 'ra'.

6 Karibete is the hunting event that is a part of Kara Hunnime (Kara Full Moon) festivities, a festival or custom in Karnataka celebrated in June. Mother Earth, agricultural implements and bullocks are worshipped during this time. In the evening, there is the Karihariyodu or bullock races, where pairs of bullocks are pitted against each other.

7 A katte is a bench-like structure of cement, stone or wood erected around buildings, monuments or trees. People sit on these, and they often become places for socializing.

8 Udyogaparva is the fifth of the eighteen parvas or chapters of the epic Mahabharata. This parva narrates the episode of Lord Krishna going as an ambassador to the court of the Kauravas in order to avert the war and bring about an understanding between the Pandavas and Kauravas. But the mission is unsuccessful, and war is inevitable. Similarly, Dattu's mission to Gudsikara ends in failure.

9 A jogati of Ellemma is a woman dedicated to the temple of Ellemma in Savadatti, Karnataka. Alhough these women, also called devadasis, were in the service of God, they were known to perform sexual services for the wealthy patrons. The colonial government, as well as the native reformers, saw this as a form of prostitution and tried to fight against it as a part of the anti-nautch campaign (1882). The practice was prohibited in post-Independence India.

10 Mahanavami is the ninth day of the Navaratri festival celebrated during October.

11 Maya or illusion in Sanskrit is explained in a variety of ways in Indian philosophy. Controversies range around the use of this word—as 'lack of knowledge', or 'illusion' or 'desire that keeps one away from salvation'. On the other hand, Maya is also the potent female form that binds one to Earth. It is the Mother's mystery.

12 Aaya is the annual share of grains collected by hereditary workers of the village for the work they do for the community.

13 Baagina refers to a series of household items related to women, such as grains, piece of cloth, bangles, vermilion and so on, exchanged on auspicious occasions. A small quantity of such things are symbolically placed within a winnow basket and exchanged among women or offered to the female deity.